Scent of a Shadow

Scent of a Shadow

Jennifer Johnson

Digital ISBN: 978-1-946608-10-9
Digital Release: May, 2017
Print ISBN: 978-1-946608-11-6
Print Release: May, 2017

Editor, Deelylah Mullin

DEDICATION

To Calvin who wanted an action book. Sorry, buddy. The characters refused to maim and kill each other. Maybe next time.

To my mom whose sleuthing skills for her job inspired the bloodhound.

And to every person who has felt the pain of not being a cherished child. May the child within find healing and wholeness.

SCENT OF A SHADOW

Ninjas don't exist, do they?

Bonnie Moore earned the name *the Bloodhound* because of her ability to track down beneficiaries for the retirement systems of the Commonwealth. As a divorced mother of three, she has her hands full with her daughter's relationship with a juvenile delinquent, her five-year-old son who sleeps on the floor next to her bed because he's afraid of the dark, and her middle child who is—well—caught in the middle. Bonnie has more important things to worry about than her present case—a delusional man who claims to be a ninja.

Brandt Sherrod makes his living slipping in and out of places undetected. So, when the Bloodhound finds him, he's intrigued by her no-nonsense attitude, observant blue eyes, and her fierce, protective loyalty for her family. As a man who's never had a family of his own, Brandt decides to give the Bloodhound a new trail to track.

Can Brandt be trusted, or has he drawn Bonnie into a fantasy world of his making?

Prologue

Billy sat on the cement divider at the parking garage and watched the guy across from him suck on a cigarette. "That'll kill you," he commented.

"Gotta die of something," his companion replied.

"There's better ways to die." Billy stared at the cars pulling out of the exit. He raised his hand and waved at a navy blue SUV.

"Who's that?"

"Bonnie Moore. She's a state worker. They call her *the Bloodhound.*"

"Why?"

"'Cause she's good at finding people. Mr. Brewer moved her to death benefits because she can find a needle in a haystack; even gave her an office because of the cases that come her way from all over the state. Last year she went out to this woman's house because she couldn't get her on the phone, and she was dead."

"Murdered?" the younger man blew out smoke, which dissipated in the warm breeze.

"Naw. Heart attack they decided, but her son was cashing her retirement checks. When Bonnie couldn't make contact with the woman, she called the police. They investigated and found the woman buried in the backyard."

"Get out."

Billy held up his right hand. "Truth. If there's a missing person, Bonnie's your gal."

"Bonnie's my gal. I'll remember that if I ever need somebody found." Stubbing the cigarette in the sand on top of the receptacle, he walked toward the entrance. "You coming?"

"We ought to wait until the offices close before we start cleaning. People don't like it if you empty their trash when they're still there."

"They don't notice me. I'm the invisible man."

He shook his head at the younger guy. "Invisible man. If I get complaints, you're going to wish you *was* the invisible man, especially if you go in people's offices smelling like cigarettes."

"Maybe I'll switch to a pipe. Pipe tobacco has a nice aroma."

"Nobody wants to smell tobacco at all. The only aroma you need to bring with you is the cleaner we use," Billy said.

"That stuff's worse than the cigarette smoke."

"You aren't going to be around very long with that kind of attitude," Billy predicted.

Chapter One

Ninja

Bonnie laughed at the occupation. Who would put that on their income tax form? Obviously, Brandt Sherrod thought it was okay to do. And the form had not been rejected.

Amazing.

She shook her head in derision.

Ah, well, if the commonwealth gets its money, that's all they care about. She scrolled to the W-2 form. Her eyes widened at the salary amount. Apparently, being a ninja was quite lucrative.

The job paid a lot better than her own state job.

So, who would employ a ninja? Bonnie looked at the employer name.

Benjamin and Associates in Bellini, Kentucky. Bonnie wrinkled her nose. She'd never heard of Bellini or Benjamin and Associates Consulting. She Googled the company but the link took her to ESPN. Well, that was weird. The zip code was also odd. It had a letter for the last digit.

Next Bonnie checked the Employer Identification Number. When she did a search on it, all she came up with was classification 47.

47? What's that mean?

Marla Standridge came back from lunch and crooked her head when she saw Bonnie sitting at her desk.

"What are you doing here?"

Here was Marla's own desk in the state income tax department. Bonnie had ventured there from her own office in the retirement systems looking for more information on the ninja. Bonnie adopted an innocent stare. "I'm trying to locate somebody."

"You're going to get me in big trouble, Bonnie."

"Look. The retirement system of Kentucky owes this guy money, and I can't find him."

"Turn it over to unclaimed then. I don't want to lose my job because you're playing detective again." Marla pulled her chair back and motioned for Bonnie to move.

Bonnie vacated the chair. "I can't link the employer to the EIN. I can't even find the location of the employer. Could this guy have filed false information?"

Marla took her seat and peered at the screen. "Let me see here." Bonnie stood next to her friend's chair and leaned down so she, too, could see the monitor. Marla typed on the keyboard. When the classification appeared, she closed the screen.

"What did you do that for?" Bonnie complained. "I want—"

All the color had drained from Marla's face. She craned her head around the office as if making sure no one was watching them. Turning her head to Bonnie's ear, she whispered. "EIN 47 means classified. My supervisor said it's a hornet's nest, and I'm not allowed to deal with those *ever.*"

"Why?"

"I don't know, and I don't want to know."

"Huh." Bonnie straightened. "Well, okay then." No sense in telling Marla that Bonnie had printed the form out. She walked out of the office to the printer in the copy room to snag the document before someone else did. Luckily, no one else was there when she picked up the sheets and walked back by Marla's cubicle. "Sorry, Marla. If you get in trouble, you can blame me."

"If I get in trouble, they may be dredging the river for my body."

Bonnie sniggered but stopped when she saw Marla's serious expression. "You're kidding, right?"

"Please don't do this again, Bonnie. I appreciate that you're committed to helping the beneficiaries of

Commonwealth employees, but you've got to go through proper channels to do it."

"I go through proper channels first. I'd only hack into the KRS if I—"

"Don't say *hack*," Marla interrupted. "Bonnie, stay on your floor, please, and out of my computer."

Bonnie slinked to the elevator feeling properly chastened. Marla had never minded her looking into the state income files before. Bonnie hoped Marla got over it because she was the only person Bonnie knew in revenue who didn't mind bending the rules. She didn't use Marla's computer often, but she'd sure hate to lose that avenue when she needed it. What was so horrible about Employer Identification 47? Could it be the Mafia or something? Surely Kentucky didn't have a Mafia...

Drugs? Sure, but the state wouldn't tolerate illegal drug dealers, would it?

Bonnie stepped into the empty elevator when the doors opened and studied the papers in her hand. If those drug dealers paid their income taxes, it would be tempting to let them continue in their business. Just assign them an Employer Identification Number and warn away the lackeys.

Bonnie sighed as she read his name. "Who are you, Brandt Sherrod, and who do you work for?"

****

Bonnie leafed through the file she kept on Delores Park, retired teacher, until she found the woman's obituary. The list didn't include Brandt Sherrod, so why would she make him her beneficiary? Mrs. Park had been a widow when she died. She had two sisters still living, one right here in town. Maybe she knew who Brandt was and how Bonnie could reach him. Bonnie reached for the telephone book but after calling the Tacketts listed there, she still hadn't reached the one she wanted. Dead ends every way she turned.

Studying the newspaper column again, Bonnie noted Mrs. Park had belonged to Eastern Star, a fraternal organization affiliated with the Masons. Bonnie recalled a funeral she had attended for one of her aunts who belonged to Eastern Star. Several women from the chapter had come to the funeral to perform a simple ceremony of farewell. Perhaps one of them knew Delores well enough to know who Brandt was, or maybe they had met him at the funeral. Bonnie did an Internet search for non-profits and clapped her hands in triumph. The secretary of the local organization was Louise Tackett. It had to be Mrs. Park's sister, and there was even a telephone number. *I love you, Eastern Star!*

Within half an hour, Bonnie stepped into a modest home in Westwood, an older neighborhood in the city. Louise Tackett ushered her inside and invited her to the parlor.

"Mrs. Tackett, I understand your sister Delores Park died earlier this year. I want to offer my condolences. On behalf of the Commonwealth of Kentucky, I'm trying to find Brandt Sherrod, her beneficiary. Did you know him?"

"Brand? Well, my yes. He was one of Delores's foster children."

Bonnie noted the variation of the name. Maybe that was why she hadn't been able to find him on the Internet. She leaned forward. "Mrs. Park had foster children?"

"Yes. Several of them. Brand, though, he was the last one and stayed with her the longest. Even after he was grown, he'd come back and visit her." The older woman stood with some effort and walked to a door, which she opened to reveal a closet. She indicated a box on the top shelf. "If you'll get that box for me. I may just have a picture."

Eagerly, Bonnie retrieved the box, and they sat on the couch while Mrs. Tackett leafed through neatly sorted photographs. She picked one up and peered at it. "Ah, yes. Here he is." She handed it to Bonnie.

Bonnie held the photo in her hand. A boy, perhaps twelve, gazed back at her with intense dark eyes under a thatch of black hair. A woman stood next to him with her arm on his shoulders. "Is this Delores with him?"

"Yes. Here's another one of Brand on his sixteenth birthday. Delores took him to get his driver's license."

"So, he went by Brand?"

"Brandt. Brand. I call him both. Delores called him Brand. It was a private joke between them. She called him her Brand New Child. He'd been passed around to several other families and told her the day he came that she wouldn't want him for long because he was 'used', not a baby. It made her more determined to love him." The woman held out the picture to Bonnie who took it.

Bonnie's eyebrows rose at the handsome teen behind the wheel of car with his hand at the window waving a greeting. "He was a cutie."

Mrs. Tackett smiled. "Indeed. Delores had to practically beat the girls off of him. He was a good boy though. Always home by curfew. Some of the other children she took in were hellions. Not Brand though, which was good because Delores was nearly retired when he came to live with her."

"How old is he now?"

"Goodness. I'd say he's around forty."

"What does Brand do now?"

"I don't really know. He never talked about his work to Delores, and after a while she quit asking."

Further evidence whatever Brandt did was illegal. Or maybe he knew his foster mother wouldn't buy the story he was a fourteenth-century Japanese spy.

"Where does he live?"

"He…he travels a lot. Sort of a rolling stone, I guess you could say."

"A rolling stone gathers no moss." Bonnie quoted the proverb.

"No, it doesn't. Probably has a lot to do with his childhood before he came to live with Delores."

"Do you know how I could get in touch with him?" Bonnie had already sent two letters to him at the address Delores had listed but had heard nothing. The tax form listed an LPO address, which she never heard of before—though she had sent a letter there anyway.

The woman studied Bonnie. "Brand is a very private person."

"I'm sure he wouldn't mind you giving me his number so I could contact him about the money the state owes him."

"Brandt doesn't need the money."

"It was your sister's wish for Brandt to have it."

Mrs. Tackett sighed. "Perhaps I could contact him for you."

"That would be very helpful." Bonnie slipped her business card out of her skirt pocket and placed it on the coffee table. "Here is my card."

The older woman's gaze fell to the card, but she didn't reach for it. Oh, darn it. Bonnie wondered if she'd do anything with the card but throw it in the trash the minute Bonnie left.

Her cell phone text ring sounded. "Excuse me, that's my cell phone. Do you mind if I see who it is?"

"Not at all."

Bonnie fished it out of her purse and looked at the screen.

Mall?

Kayla, Bonnie's daughter, was asking permission to go to the mall.

What about band practice?

Cancelled.

It had been thundering that afternoon. Bonnie knew sometimes the director cancelled practice if the gym wasn't available to march in.

Mall w/ who?

Hannah B.

Hannah Bradley. Sweet girl, and Bonnie could trust the two of them not to get into too much trouble. Bonnie's own daughter was fifteen and had been out of hand lately. Bonnie blamed Kayla's new boyfriend Rex, who was a very disrespectful seventeen. Why couldn't he corrupt someone his own age?

will call H's mom & get bck 2 u

Forget it.

Bonnie pursed her lips. Hmm.

She tucked her phone back in her purse. "Thank you, Mrs. Tackett."

When Bonnie arrived home later that afternoon with her two younger children, Andrew and Curtis, in tow she found Kayla already home and the obnoxious aroma of Rex's cologne in the air. Kayla sat on the couch in front of the TV with an open textbook in her lap.

Right.

"How long have you been home?" she asked her daughter.

"Since four. They cancelled practice because of the rain."

"You know the rules about no company in the house if I'm not here, right?"

Innocent eyes gazed at her. "Sure."

"So no one else was here with you today?" *Please tell me the truth.*

Kayla turned back to her book. "Just me, Mom. That's the rule."

Bonnie hid her anger. *The little liar.* "Thank you, honey. I really appreciate being able to trust you. You're such a good daughter." She tucked her purse in its cubby next to the back door, walked over to Kayla, and kissed the top of her head. "Let me get supper going." She headed toward the kitchen. After she got everybody fed, she was going to Radio Shack to fix her daughter's little red wagon.

****

Bonnie continued in her search for Brandt Sherrod. Nothing on any of the social networks many people usually wasted their time on. She drummed her fingers on the keyboard. If Brandt had grown up here, then he would have gone to school here. Louise Tackett had said he was popular with the girls. *Maybe I can talk to someone in his class.*

She went to a social media site specializing in reuniting

classmates from schools around the country and typed in both high schools in town. Of course, neither list included Brandt Sherrod's name when she searched. Going to the library, she went to their local history room. Unfortunately, only one of the high schools had books here. She made a mental note to check the electronic files for the other school and selected a yearbook for the year Brandt would have been either a junior or a senior, if Mrs. Tackett were correct in her estimation of his age. No luck. Going back to the shelf, she pulled several more books for the years before and after. She found him on page twenty-four—soulful dark eyes and black hair nearly to his shoulders. A senior, which would make him forty-one.

The same age as me.

His class was too big for her to write down every name, so she decided to search later for the year he graduated and contact any of his classmates online.

She showed up on Mrs. Tackett's doorstep hoping for an invitation inside. She'd set her cell phone alarm to ten minutes hoping to get a little more information on the elusive Brandt Sherrod.

At Bonnie's knock, a surprised Mrs. Tackett opened the door. By the look in the woman's eyes, Bonnie knew she remembered who she was and was hoping she wouldn't ever come back. Southern decorum dictated she should invite Bonnie in, which she did. They sat down, and Bonnie began.

"I haven't heard from Mr. Sherrod. Were you able to get a hold of him?"

"I tried. Sometimes he's…err…unavailable."

"Because of his job?"

"Yes."

"What did you tell me he did?"

"I don't know what he does."

Either she was a good liar, or she really didn't know.

"What did he do after he graduated high school? Did he go on to college?"

The older woman raised a shaky hand to her hair and

smoothed it around her ear. "It was a long time ago. He was doing really well in high school and then…" She sighed.

"And then?" Bonnie prompted seeing a spark of something in the woman's eyes. Whatever she had remembered, it hadn't been pleasant. Mrs. Tackett's gaze dropped, and Bonnie leaned forward. "I think that Brand was a good boy. But even good people make mistakes sometimes. If he got into trouble, obviously Delores didn't hold it against—"

"Don't." Shock and pain played along her face. For a moment she stared at Bonnie, and Bonnie had her answer. So he had gotten into trouble. But what kind? Had he been arrested?

"Your sister loved Brandt. She named him as her beneficiary. She wanted to do that one last thing for him when she died."

A look of resolve finally settled on her. "I can't help you. This is for Brandt to resolve. Give him time."

"We'd really like to close out Mrs. Park's case. I don't want to be heartless, Mrs. Tackett, but the inability to reach Mr. Sherrod about your sister's death benefits costs the Commonwealth of Kentucky revenue in employee time."

"Your time."

"Yes, ma'am. Perhaps Mr. Sherrod would sign an affidavit making you the beneficiary?"

Mrs. Tackett shook her head. "No, dear."

Bonnie raised her hands in a helpless gesture.

"I'm sorry this inconveniences you, but I think Brandt will take the money. You have to give him time."

"It's been eight months."

"With Brandt you have to be patient."

"The letters sent to the address we have on file have been returned to us unopened. I don't think Brandt even knows he is the beneficiary."

The older woman shrugged one shoulder. "I don't know what to tell you. It's difficult to get in touch with him, I know. I wasn't even sure he knew about Delores's death until he showed up at the visitation. He's just…" She sighed. "He's not one who is easily located."

Bonnie's alarm sounded. She pulled her cell phone out of her purse and looked at the screen, a look of concern on her face. Pushing a button, she shook her head. "I can't get a signal here. Mrs. Tackett, do you mind? I'd like to use your phone."

She pointed to one on the wall.

"Is there another one which is private? I'm sorry, but I'm having some family issues right now." It wasn't a lie. Not in the least. She was about ready to choke Kayla and Rex. The little jerk boyfriend wouldn't stay away from her daughter, and the more rules Bonnie imposed, the more Kayla found ways to be with him. The misrepresentation was that the alarm was about Kayla rather than a ruse to invade Mrs. Tackett's privacy.

Mrs. Tackett hesitated then showed Bonnie to a small room that obviously served as an office. With a desk and its requisite computer, Bonnie refrained from rubbing her hands together in glee. Oh, yeah. This was perfect!

When the other woman left, Bonnie wasted no time checking the recent activity on the device. Hmmm. Skype. Bonnie looked through the contacts. No Brandt or Brand. Next, Bonnie opened Mrs. Tackett's email. Quickly she went through the contacts.

sengoku@flymail.com

Hmmm.

Since finding the word *ninja* on Brandt's w-2, Bonnie had done a little research on the Japanese spies. Sengoku had been the warring period when ninjas had been prominent.

Could he be that obvious?

It wouldn't hurt to send an email to the address just in case it was Brandt Sherrod.

Bonnie copied the email address on a piece of paper and tucked it in her purse. *You are going to take your foster mom's money, you jerk, so I can put this case to bed.*

Chapter Two

Bonnie sat behind her desk and drummed her fingers against the keyboard and stared at the monitor in front of her while she tucked the telephone receiver to her shoulder. Patrice Simmons, who was a fifteen-year teacher for the state, had filled out her Category A form wrong. *Geez, you had to get a Bachelor's Degree to teach in this state. How hard is it to fill out a form listing two of your closest relatives to get the remainder of your retirement money you didn't spend in the nursing home?*

"I understand that, Ms. Simmons, but I have to have the Social Security numbers of the beneficiaries before the form is complete."

"Why do you have to have their social security numbers? I've given you their addresses and phone numbers."

"Lord willing, Ms. Simmons, you'll live many more years. It is likely that their information will change before your death."

"I'll give you their new addresses if they move."

Grrrr. "In case you can't, having those numbers would really help the Commonwealth help you take care of your loved ones when you're no longer alive."

Movement from the doorway caught her attention. A man in coveralls entered the door with an empty trash bag. Bonnie glanced at the clock on the computer screen. What was housekeeping doing here this early? They usually didn't start their rounds until after four. And where was Billy, the usual man who came in to empty the garbage? This guy presently bending over her desk and picking up her wastebasket was younger, his head bald though his skin tone and the shadow on his scalp hinted that his hair would be jet black if he hadn't shaved it. Bonnie's gaze roved over him, attempting to judge his age, not as easy to do without the hair. The tan coveralls stretched over wide shoulders and nicely formed biceps.

"Ms. Simmons, I'm going to send you the incomplete form so that you can gather that information and send it back to us."

Bonnie ended the call as the man walked to the door with her bagged garbage in his hand.

"Hi," she called. "I haven't seen you before. Is Billy okay?"

Though he paused, he kept his back to her. "Yeah."

"I'm Bonnie Moore." Bonnie came around the desk to greet the man. She made a point to know who worked in the building with her and made a concerted effort to treat the housekeeping staff no differently than Mr. Brewer, head of the retirement systems.

He grunted and shook the bag striding from her office before she could talk to him face-to-face. Bonnie rested her hands on her hips.

Huh. Well, the new guy must be in a hurry to get his work done. Obviously, he hasn't been a state employee for very long.

Turning to her computer, Bonnie checked her email. She'd sent a message to the address she'd pulled off of Mrs. Tackett's computer along with her contact information.

Bonnie used her carrot dangle email, a standard message she sent to beneficiaries when she wasn't sure they were who she was looking for:

Greetings:

I am looking for Brandt Sherrod who has been named beneficiary by an employee of the Commonwealth of Kentucky. If you are he, please contact me as soon as possible to claim your money.

It had been nearly a week, and she hadn't gotten a response back.

Her telephone rang and she answered it.

"Is this Bonnie Moore?" a woman's voice asked.

"Yes."

"This is Sheri Stillthorpe of the office of David

Bentley, Vice President of Security of the Commonwealth Retirement Systems. Mr. Bentley would like to meet with you at your earliest convenience.

David Bentley? She'd never heard of him.

Bonnie tucked the phone receiver in between her head and shoulder and searched David Bentley's name in the staff directory.

His name popped up on the screen.

Wow. Executive offices.

Anxiety filled her chest. "Concerning what, may I ask?"

"Your job. Can you come today?"

My job? That revved up her heart rate. "Today?"

"Sure."

"I can come right now."

"Very good. We'll be expecting you. The fourteenth floor, suite 20."

****

Bonnie ignored the butterflies in her stomach as she waited in the outer room of David Bentley's office. A frumpy woman sat behind a desk typing on a computer. She'd picked up her phone and announced Bonnie's arrival, but so far, the door had stayed closed.

So, what? The secretary had said they'd be expecting her. Bonnie crossed her legs on the loveseat and sighed.

I guess they expect me to wait.

The telephone dinged, and the woman picked it up. "Yes, Mr. Bentley?" She paused. "Yes, Mr. Bentley." She placed the receiver back in its cradle and stood. Looking at Bonnie, she spoke. "Mr. Bentley will see you now."

Walking around her desk, she went to the door, knocked twice, and then opened it gesturing for Bonnie to go inside. Bonnie walked into the office toward a man in a suit and tie who stood in front of a plate glass window looking over the city. His keen gaze assessed her as she approached him.

"Mrs. Moore?"

She'd rather go by *Ms.*, but Bonnie didn't bother to

23

correct him. She held her hand out to shake his. "Hello, Mr. Bentley, I presume?"

He nodded. His shake was firm, but brief. Stepping back, Bonnie held eye contact. "What can I do for you?"

He gestured toward a leather couch and chair on the far side of the room. "Won't you sit down?"

More butterflies, but Bonnie didn't show them. She hadn't done anything wrong. Well, except for hacking into the state's revenue files, but she had a good reason. Was that what this was about? She chose to sit on the chair, figuring it was the power seat in this set-up. Crossing her legs at the ankles, she waited. Mr. Bentley sat on the middle of the couch and gifted her with a smile.

Yep. He knew why she'd chosen the chair.

"How is work going?"

"I'm sorry, Mr. Bentley. Have we met before? I don't work on this floor. My supervisor is Charles Brewer."

One of his eyebrows quirked. "Yes. Charlie. Perhaps I should invite him to sit in with us. Would you prefer that he be here?"

"I suppose it depends on what your business is with me."

"You work in death benefits."

"Yes."

"How many cases are you pursuing presently?"

Bonnie shrugged. "Perhaps twenty. I'd have to look at my spreadsheet to give you an exact number. I'm constantly closing files, and obtaining new ones."

"What methods do you use to find beneficiaries?"

Oh, darn it. This was about breaking into the revenue files. Bonnie wasn't going to admit anything though. "Initially, I send a letter to the beneficiary informing that person he—or she—has been named beneficiary."

Mr. Bentley waited for her to continue. When she didn't, he crossed his ankle over his knee. "And if you get no response from the letter?"

"I send another one and wait."

"And what then?"

"I assume the address is inaccurate and try to find the correct address."

"With Internet Search engines?"

"Sometimes."

"And what at other times?"

"I try to find next of kin, but often they are not helpful because they are not the beneficiaries."

He didn't speak—just watched her. Bonnie returned his look. She had a teenager. She knew all about interrogation.

"Have you ever used unethical methods to obtain information?"

"Such as what?"

"Looked at unauthorized computer files?"

"What do you mean by unauthorized? Every case I handle is information-sensitive. I am very careful."

"Do you attempt to access files which you are not authorized to view?"

Bonnie lifted her chin. "Nothing specific comes to mind. Can you give me an example of what files you may be referring to or a certain case this pertains to?"

"I thought you might share that information with me. Surely there are one or two beneficiaries who have been more difficult to locate. And in your efforts to find them, maybe you justified…going the extra mile?"

"I believe having Mr. Brewer here is appropriate since you seem to have concerns about my performance. Would you like to contact him, or shall I?"

He bent his head in acknowledgement and stood. Going over his desk, he picked up the phone and dialed a number. "Sheri, get me Charlie Brewer please." He put the receiver down, and leaned back on his desk regarding Bonnie from across the room.

The silence bothered her. She broke eye contact and looked out the window. Ticking off the Vice President of Security of the Retirement Systems was probably not a good method of keeping job security. Still. Even if he was VP, Bonnie wasn't sure he should know the specifics of the cases she worked.

His phone rang, and he picked it up. "Hi, Charlie, this is David Bentley. How are you?" He laughed. "Do you have a few minutes to come to my office? ...Sure. Very good... Yes. Goodbye."

The click of him hanging up carried across the space. He came over to the couch and sat down again. Leaning forward, he now struck a *we're buddies* pose—yet another tactic Bonnie herself had used with Kayla.

"Do you have children, Mr. Bentley?" she asked.

His earnest expression fell a bit. He hesitated before answering. "Yes."

Bonnie watched him steadily. The nervous butterflies in her stomach had morphed into hornets. "Have you found that your method of intimidation first, then playing the nice guy second works? Because in my experience, I have found if I'm nice first, then resort to intimidation later if necessary, I am much more successful."

He sat back, his mouth turning up on one side. "Is there anything else you'd like to tell me before your supervisor gets here? Once he becomes involved, we will have to follow proper procedure for censure, probation, or termination if necessary. But if you would like to share anything with me now, we could deal with it..." He glanced down at her legs then back to her face. "*Mono a mono.* How's that for a method?"

Anger bubbled in Bonnie's chest, but she didn't show it. "If I admit to looking at unauthorized files, then you will deal with it in what way? Censure me yourself? Slap me on the wrist or the butt? Or did you have something else in mind?" She blinked at him. "I believe harassment practices—sexual or otherwise—are not tolerated here. As Vice President, I'm sure you know that."

He stood, his expression turning angry. "Did you access files you did not have clearance to?"

Bonnie arched her neck to look at him. *Calm. Keep calm.* "Feel free to look at all the activity on my computer if you suspect me of wrongdoing. But I'll tell you this. I'm a model employee, and I'm good at what I do. I've never had anything but glowing reviews on job performance." Bonnie stood up too. "I'm sorry, but I think I need to go. If you would like to schedule an appointment with Mr. Brewer and me, I will be happy to accommodate you."

She walked to the door without looking back at him. Opening it, she walked through the office and to the elevator. Once inside, she let out a pent-up breath and gripped the wall in case her shaky legs gave way under her.

****

Bonnie waited for Mr. Brewer to call her into his office and rake her across the coals for looking at unauthorized files, but the day passed without a summons. Other tasks demanded her attention, and by the end of the week, her tightly wound nerves had relaxed. When Mr. Brewer walked by her office and gave a friendly wave, Bonnie realized maybe the vice president hadn't viewed her firm response as insubordination.

And then she started to get mad.

What had the visit in David Bentley's office been about? If he were truly concerned about her behavior, he would have followed up with her supervisor. Was it his practice to intimidate women as a power high? Sexual misconduct? Had he treated other employees the way he had treated her? Had they cowered and given in to his thinly veiled threats?

For what purpose?

Bonnie stood and walked to Mr. Brewer's office. Since he'd passed by only a few minutes before, she knew he hadn't settled down to work yet. His door was open, and he sat at his desk sipping from a coffee cup. Bonnie knocked on the frame.

His eyes met hers over the ceramic rim, and he sat the cup down. He waved her into the room. "Good morning, Bonnie. What can I do for you?"

Bonnie entered. "Hi, Mr. Brewer." She stood behind the chair in front of his desk. "I met David Bentley earlier this week. He called me up to his office."

The man shook his head. "Who?"

"David Bentley. Vice President of Security."

He drew his head back, his quizzical expression appeared genuine. "There's not a Vice President of Security." He turned to his computer and moved the keyboard close to the edge of the desk, his fingers moving over the keys. "David Bentley. David Bentley. I'm not finding him."

That can't be. Bonnie had found him immediately in the staff search. Bonnie walked around to the corner of his desk so she could see his screen. "But you know him." The screen showed no such person was in their database. How could that be? Did Mr. Brewer's computer have a filter her computer didn't have?

He shrugged his shoulders. "If I've met him, I don't remember it."

"He called you during our meeting. He called you 'Charlie'."

"Well, there's a clue right there he doesn't know me. Nobody calls me Charlie and gets away with it."

"Not even the VP?"

He arched an eyebrow at her. "Of Security? Uh-uh. We have a Vice President of Investments, a Vice President of Services, and a General Vice President. The Vice President you met is of Practical Jokes. You surprise me. I wouldn't think you'd be gullible enough to be taken by anyone around here."

"I'm not usually. Who would do such a thing?"

"Jason in the mail room? He thinks everything is so funny." The older man huffed. "He ever comes within fifty feet of my office with another whoopee cushion, I'm having him escorted off the premises permanently after I wipe the floor with him."

Bonnie grimaced. She'd never been a big fan of bathroom humor.

Mr. Brewer sat back in his chair. "You don't think it was a scam, do you? Did they ask for information on anyone?"

Bonnie shifted in her chair. "Not any personal information, no." She didn't want to volunteer that the imposter VP had questioned her about looking at unauthorized files.

"Odd. Well, let me know if it's something we need to follow up on."

Bonnie nodded. The mystery churned in her mind. "Thanks. I will. See you later." She walked out of his office and headed toward her own workspace. Sitting down, she typed David Bentley's name in the database. Nothing. How could that be? If the staff listing no longer indicated him as a Vice President, then did he still have his office? Only one way to find out. She closed her screen, logged off, and marched toward the elevator. Pushing the up button, she crossed her arms over her chest, and her anger returned billowing into a mushroom cloud. If this was some practical joke, it sure wasn't funny. When the doors opened, she stepped inside and pressed the top floor.

Executive offices.

When the doors opened again, she stepped into the carpeted hallway and down to the office she'd been to previously. The door was locked, and the holder—which had held a sign identifying the office as belonging to David Bentley—was missing. Bonnie walked down the corridor and found three more closed doors, all with vacant holders. At the end of the hallway was the Vice President in charge of investments. Bonnie looked inside the open doorway. A man sat at the desk typing on a computer keyboard. He stopped and looked at her. "Hi. May I help you?"

Bonnie stepped into the room. "Hello. I'm looking for Mr. Bentley's office. I thought it was on this hallway, first door on the right?"

His eyebrows went down quizzically. "I don't know Mr. Bentley, and those offices are empty. The only people on this side of the floor are my boss, Felicia Stover and Becky Ross and Louis Fitzpatrick who are the chief investment officers. It's pretty quiet up here otherwise."

"I was up here Monday morning in a meeting with a

man who told me he was the Vice President of Security."

"On this floor?"

"Yes. Just down the hall."

"Monday we were at a stock holding workshop in Pittsburgh. There shouldn't have been anyone up here."

"May I use your phone? I'd like to call security."

Chapter Three

He nodded, and Bonnie placed the call. Twenty minutes later, Steven Preston, one of the security guards, stood next to her in the office where she had sparred with Mr. Bentley. The room was completely bare. No furniture. No computer, even the curtains were missing. If this were a prank, it sure had been an elaborate one.

"I know this is the office where I was," Bonnie insisted. Just to be sure, Steven had unlocked the two offices next to this one. They all appeared the same. Vacant.

Steven cast her a look of pity. He obviously thought she was crazy.

"I don't understand it. Why would someone do something like this?"

"No one could have gotten access to these offices without security knowing about it," Steven said. "Especially to move furniture. Are you sure you have the right floor?"

"Yes, I'm sure." Bonnie placed her hands on her hips in frustration. *Grrr.* The officer flicked his eyes at her stance. She huffed and crossed her arms.

"See, the thing about it is there isn't a Vice President of Security. I mean, we have Sergeant Beam, but he's—"

"This man implied he was in charge of protecting the security of information. Like, computer files and such."

"Oh." Steven reached into his pocket and pulled out a notepad. "I can take a description of him, and we can be on the lookout."

Bonnie sighed. "I suppose." She was pretty sure he was just placating her. Humoring the crazy woman in retirement systems.

A few minutes later, she rode down the elevator to her floor. Anger whirled with confusion inside her head. Someone had lied to her, but why? If it had been a joke, the culprit hadn't come forward. Was it to get information from one of her cases? That was the whole reason Marla had warned her….

Marla!

Was she trying to scare me into not hacking into any more files on her computer? Marla didn't seem the type.

But….

Bonnie entered her office and stopped short. A man sat on the chair in front of her desk. Jet-black hair, cut close to his head and broad shoulders under a charcoal suit jacket.

"Hello?" she asked as she walked around him and toward her desk. "I'm Bonnie Moore. May I help you?"

He'd had one ankle crossed over the other, his long legs stretched out in front of him. He was attractive; his prominent nose had a slight bump, giving him an edgy appearance that didn't quite fit with the suit. And his dark eyes pierced her as if he had X-ray vision. He uncrossed his legs and stood up. Holding his hand out to her, he bowed his head, and his perfectly shaped lips crooked in a flirty smile. Something familiar stirred in her. Had she met him before? No. She'd remember it. Him.

"Mrs. Moore. I'm Brandt Sherrod. I believe you've been trying to get in touch with me."

Bonnie reached forward and shook his hand. His clasp was warm and firm. She stepped back and walked toward the door to close it. The gesture gave her time to recover her shock. He was here. He was really here.

With the door shut, she turned around to face him. He watched her. That familiar feeling nibbled at her. It was more than just seeing his photograph at sixteen years old. "Have we met?"

"Not formally, no."

Bonnie studied him, ignoring the pull of attraction. Oh, my gosh, he was good looking, but it was in a bad boy kind of way. That suit didn't fool her.

"What does that mean? Not formally." Bonnie walked to her desk and sat down.

Brandt followed suit. "You sent me an email." He crooked his head; a sparkle of humor lit his gaze. "I admire your tactics though I should admonish you. Duping on old woman so you can troll the contacts on her computer seems unethical."

Bonnie's heart raced. "Excuse me?"

"My Aunt Louise. You visited her and found my email in her contacts on her computer."

"Is that what she told you? What must she think of me."

He sat back, his dark gaze assessing her. Bonnie kept eye contact as long as she could stand it, knowing he was attempting to…what? Intimidate her? No. It was more like he was working out a solution to a math problem written on a white board. She focused on her garbage can at the side of her desk and gasped.

That's it! She had seen Brandt before right here in this office. He'd worn a custodian uniform and had a bald head. Now his hair was short but not that short. How had he managed growing it back in less than a month? And why had he been dressed as a custodian? Had he been checking to see if she were legitimate?

Or was he actually a custodian impersonating Brandt Sherrod so he could receive a big fat check from the Commonwealth of Kentucky?

"Is there something wrong, Mrs. Moore?"

Play it cool. The best way to do that was to give her hands something to do so he didn't notice how bad they were shaking. She opened a drawer in her desk and withdrew Delores Park's file. Another drawer for a pen. Picking up her glasses, she slipped them on and opened the file folder. She glanced down at the acquisition form she'd placed there and then over the frames at the man sitting in front of her. "We didn't have an appointment. How did you get up here?"

"I'm a ninja. But I suppose you already know that."

The pen she had been holding clattered to the desk, and she picked it up. "You don't look like a ninja."

"Met a lot of us, have you?" His voice was soft as if he were sharing a secret. Bonnie ignored the tingle, which skittered down her spine. "I'll have to see some identification."

He blinked at her. "Why?"

"I will need proof of your identity as well as a valid social security number before"—Bonnie carefully worded her statement in case he wasn't Brandt Sherrod—"we can proceed with our business."

"Well, that could be a problem since I don't have any such identification."

"Driver's license."

He shook his head, a smile curving those lips.

"You don't drive," she said in disbelief.

"Sure, I drive. I just don't have a driver's license, per se."

"Driving without a license is against the law, Mr. Sherrod."

"I didn't realize you were with the Department of Transportation."

She tilted her face more so she could glare at him. "Fine. Social Security card then."

"I don't have one."

She looked down and placed her finger on the form she'd copied from Marla's file. "Everyone has one, and the one on your tax form is not valid."

"The thing about SSNs is they're a lot harder to manufacture than they used to be."

She couldn't believe he'd said what she'd just heard. Was he crazy? "What?"

"The information age makes my job a real pain in the butt. It used to be, you could make up a name and that was good enough. Now you have to write a whole biography of a fictitious person to make it believable."

"You're not Brandt Sherrod who was a foster child of

34

Delores Clarkston Park?"

"Her name was Delores Cyndale Park, but good try."

"Mr. Sherrod, you realize you are talking to an agent of the Commonwealth of Kentucky. I have the authority to begin proceedings to put you in prison for defrauding the government."

"For what? You're with the Teachers Retirement Systems. You can't arrest me for not claiming a benefits check."

"I'm talking about your tax form." Bonnie didn't really have the authority to do anything about him giving false information about his taxes, but Marla did.

"I've paid all my taxes."

"According to you. I cannot substantiate anything you've claimed on your form."

"If the Commonwealth had a ninja form, it'd make things a lot easier for me." His eyes twinkled in merriment though his expression gave nothing away.

"This isn't a joke."

"Really? I guess I need to work on my timing."

Bonnie glimpsed his smile before he contained it. She tutted and shook her head as she pushed the paper across the desk to him. "There is no Bellini, Kentucky, nor could I find a Benjamin and Associates Consulting."

Brandt returned her stare but said nothing.

"Well?"

"You're mistaken. Benjamin and Associates exists, and it is in Bellini." His tone was convincing. Confident.

"Where is Bellini? This zip code has a letter in it. It's fabricated."

"It's manufactured, not fabricated. There's a difference."

Bonnie watched him looking for a chink in his confident armor. "Who manufactured the zip code? You?"

"No." He shrugged as if unconcerned. "I assume some government agency assigns the zip codes. I'm a ninja. I only do secretive operations."

"You're delusional. Bellini, Kentucky, doesn't exist."

"Sure it does. You go up sixty-four and take a left at Winchester."

"This is ridiculous. I just want some type of identification so I can give you your check. If you're Brandt Sherrod, you ought to be able to prove it."

He didn't respond.

Bonnie took off her glasses. "Well? What do you have to say to that?"

"I don't want the check. I only came here today because you seem so determined for me to have it."

"Your foster mother named you as her beneficiary…if you are indeed Brandt Sherrod."

"You doubt me. I wonder why." He stood and walked over to the wastebasket, peered down in it then turned to her. He crossed her arms over his chest. "Ah, I see."

"What do you see?"

An expression of approval on Brandt's face warmed Bonnie's insides. "You figured out where you'd seen me before."

Bonnie didn't answer. No telling what information he had combed through, including information about Mrs. Park. Brandt laughed, a low chuckle, which made her toes curl in her pumps. Oh, he was slick.

"You impress me. If I didn't know better, I'd say you had experience in espionage."

His arrogance curdled her stomach.

"I live in the real world. I don't play games, and I don't go through other people's trash." She picked up the telephone and dialed. "Hello, security? This is Bonnie Moore. I think you need to come up here. We have a…" Bonnie glared at him wondering how she should I identify him. He smiled at her as if he were enjoying her loss for a word. "Trespasser."

She hung up the telephone and steepled her hands attempting to show a calm she didn't feel. Who was he really?

He sat down and leaned back in the chair, a pleasant expression on his face. Was he, too, presenting a façade he didn't feel? She'd just called security for goodness' sake.

"I just called security."

"I heard."

"They're on their way up here."

He nodded, his dark gaze caressed her. Not a creepy kind of look. One more of appreciation.

"It seems like you'd want to get out of here quickly. Don't you realize you're in trouble?"

"Only a guilty man flees, and I'd hate to deprive myself of your company, Ms. Moore."

He'd switched from a married title to Ms, reserved for women's libbers and divorcees. He must have noticed she wasn't wearing a ring. Instead of focusing on that, she decided to focus the other part of his statement. "I don't like insincerity."

"May I take you out for coffee?"

Bonnie sputtered. "What? No."

"You don't drink coffee?"

Bonnie stood and marched across the office. She opened the door and stood at the threshold. She studied the back of his dark head. He hadn't turned around to see what she was doing.

"Diet Coke? Even though it seems a shame to have a fountain drink without a meal. Perhaps lunch."

Bonnie bristled. Was he suggesting she was overweight? "Why do you assume I drink diet cola?"

"There's a case in the corner there, partially hidden by the plant."

She turned to see if indeed he could spot her case of cola from his vantage point, or had he been snooping another time while impersonating the custodian?

No. There was the case next to her potted plant.

"If you'd agree to a glass of wine, we could have dinner."

He knew.

Somehow he knew she was divorced. He probably thought she was lonely and hard up. "You want me to have dinner with you." Disbelief colored her tone so that the question sounded more like an accusation. "You're unbelievable. Any business I may have with Brandt Sherrod will appropriately occur in this building."

He moved the chair a bit, angling it toward her. "I accept." His eyes flicked beyond her, and Bonnie looked and saw Steven and Luke, the security guards, approaching.

She stepped out of the doorway and motioned them inside. "This man claims to be a beneficiary, but he refuses to show me any identification, and I have reason to believe he has been pretending to be a custodian so he can go through the trash and look for government information."

"Gentlemen." The man claiming to be Brandt Sherrod smiled at the two of them without a hint of unease. He stood and placed the chair back in its original position. "Where shall we go for the interrogation?"

They blinked at him. Obviously, they hadn't expected to have to interrogate anyone. Or to have that someone so willing to be interrogated. They didn't move, and their indecision irritated Bonnie. Geez, did she have to do everything?

"Why don't you take him down to your office and call the police?" Bonnie snapped. "Let them deal with him."

Steven sucked his tongue over his teeth in thought. "Are you pressing charges, Bonnie?"

"He's not who he claims to be, and he's trying to acquire benefits that don't belong to him. I think the Commonwealth will want to pursue this, yes. I'll talk to Mr. Brewer, and we will meet you down at the security offices. All right?"

"Okay." Steven cleared his throat and motioned to the ninja. "We'll need you to accompany us."

"Certainly." He nodded and walked toward Bonnie.

She resisted the urge to step out of his way. Just before reaching her, he pivoted to the door but not before he winked. At her! "Ms. Moore."

His address to her was more like a...a...caress.

"It's been a pleasure. See you later."

Bonnie huffed. She hated arrogant men. Hated them.

The three of them walked across the open space of the department, passing the desks of several people who stopped their work to watch the security guards and the well-dressed man between them. Bonnie stalked to Mr. Brewer's office.

She explained the situation to him. He nodded his agreement to having the police involved unless Mr. Sherrod could prove he was, indeed, Mr. Sherrod. Mr. Brewer alerted Karen Silver in their legal department, and when he hung up the telephone with Karen, he and Bonnie walked to the elevator to go down to the first floor where the security guards' offices were.

When they arrived, they found the door locked.

"That's odd," Bonnie said. "I know they said they were bringing him down here."

"Maybe they went on to the police station," Mr. Brewer supplied.

"Surely not both of them." Bonnie walked to the receptionist's desk in the main lobby. "Would you call security? We were supposed to meet Steven and Luke at their office."

The receptionist did as Bonnie asked. In a few minutes, Steve entered the lobby. The expression on his face caused Bonnie alarm.

"What's wrong?" she asked even as he walked toward them.

"He's gone."

"What?"

Steve shook his head. "I can't explain it. First he was there, then he wasn't. We rode down in the elevator, we got off, he was there. We walked right across here, and then Luke said, 'Where is he?' And I turned around, and he was gone."

"But how could you let him leave?"

Steve sighed. "Luke and I did a search. Tammy"—he indicated the receptionist sitting in front of them—"says no one was with us when we came into the lobby, but he was. He had to be. He was with us on the elevator because he made some comment about UK basketball."

"UK basketball?"

"Yeah, so Luke said something about the game, and then I started talking about the last quarter, and then Luke noticed he was gone."

Great.

The man who claimed to be Brandt Sherrod, ninja, had disappeared.

Chapter Four

Bonnie parked in her driveway and walked across the street to pick up Andy and Curtis from Veda's house. Veda, a retired schoolteacher, kept the boys after school each day until Bonnie arrived home from work. The arrangement had worked out well for Bonnie when Curtis started kindergarten in the fall, and Veda enjoyed the boys' energy and appreciation for her homemade cookies. A win/win situation.

Bonnie opened the door and walked into the foyer. Veda had admonished her long ago about knocking. "Knocking is for strangers," she said. "You come right in."

"Shouldn't you lock your door?" Bonnie had asked.

"Now why would I do that? Matilda is my security guard. Anyone comes inside who isn't supposed to be here is going to have a hunk of meat taken out of his hide." She had patted her German shepherd's head affectionately.

Matilda greeted her at the door now, her big tail thumping against the wall. "Hey, girl," she scratched her fur behind her ears. "How have the boys been today?"

Woof.

Bonnie walked through the house toward the living room Matilda accompanying her.

Veda sat in her favorite chair working Sudoku. Andy was at the computer in the corner playing a video game, and Curtis was watching television.

Veda looked up and smiled.

"Hi, everyone."

No response from the boys. "Hello, Bonnie," Veda said. "How was work today?"

"Interesting. Hellooo, Curtis and Andy. No one wants

to say hi to their mom?"

Andy turned his head and grinned. "Hey, Mom."

Curtis raised his hand in greeting but otherwise didn't move.

"Come on, boys. Let's go home so I can get supper started."

"Aww, Mom." Curtis finally granted her a glance. "Can't you let us stay until you get supper on the table? It's just getting to the good part."

"What? You can't watch this at home?"

"It's public TV. I'll miss something while we walk across the street, and there ain't no commercials."

"There aren't any commercials, young man," Veda admonished.

"That's what I said."

Bonnie laughed.

"I'm sure you can miss the couple of minutes it takes you to walk across two yards and a paved road, son."

The boys gathered their things, and they walked to the house. Curtis headed to the television as soon as they were inside, but Andy walked into the kitchen ahead of Bonnie. She took off her jacket and hung it on the back of her chair at the table.

"So, what should we have for supper?"

Andy's soulful gaze met hers. "Miss Veda says if you haven't decided what's for supper by ten in the morning, then you've already failed."

Bonnie opened the refrigerator and pulled out a pound of meat. "Hamburger Helper says differently." Opening the cabinet, she retrieved the box with triumph. With two cans of green beans, she could have the meal on the table by a quarter after six.

And speaking of time… She glanced at the clock. Kayla ought to be home by now. Bonnie fished her cell phone out of her purse and texted her daughter.

Where r u?

She set the phone down on the counter and started to brown the meat. If that child didn't text back in five minutes, she had better have a good reason and it better not have anything to do with Rex.

At four minutes, the text came.

Band running L8. Home @ 7.

Bonnie pursed her lips at the message. Practice ended around five, and Kayla rode home with Carrie who lived the next street over.

Andy pushed a chair over to the counter and climbed on it. He took plates out of the cabinet and crouched to set them on the surface top before jumping down and moving the chair back to its place. He then set the table.

He was such a thoughtful child.

Bonnie moved the hamburger meat around in the skillet with a spatula.

She hated for all of them not to be together for supper, but the boys were used to eating sooner than seven. Sighing, she continued with the meal preparation. Kayla would just miss eating with the rest of the family.

Andy stood back from the table and placed his hands on his hips. He looked at the table, and Bonnie wondered if he was trying to decide what else to do. "It looks great, son. Thanks."

He nodded. "You're welcome. You think I should put drinks on the table too?"

"Let's wait a bit. But good thinking. How did school go today? Who got in trouble?"

"Kerwin. He bit the bark off of a tree on the playground."

"Yeah? Did he get sick?"

"Not at school. But the teacher sent him to the nurse, then to the principal. He's already been in trouble in the past for eating stuff. Something's wrong with that kid."

Bonnie laughed. "Maybe he's trying to get more fiber in his diet."

She and the boys ate. The front door opened, and Bonnie glanced at the clock from where she stood in the kitchen wiping down the counter. Two minutes to seven.

Her daughter's footsteps sounded on the stairs.

"Kayla? Come in here and eat, honey."

She paused then continued upstairs. "Not that hungry."

Not that hungry?

Bonnie wiped her hands and followed her daughter. She found her in her room, her backpack already open, and Kayla rifling through it.

"Hi."

Kayla barely glanced up. "Hey, Mom. I have a ton of homework tonight."

"How come you had to stay two hours longer at band practice?"

She shrugged. "Guess we weren't getting the music right. We've got state competition coming up." She pulled out a notebook and opened it.

"You need to eat."

She sighed finally gracing her mother with a hard stare. "I'm fine. Quit trying to force feed me."

"I'm not trying to force feed you. I just think it would be good to eat something for supper unless you and Carrie grabbed something on the way home?"

"We didn't. I'll get something later, but right now I've got three chapters to read in biology. Okay?"

Hurt ached in Bonnie's chest, but she hid it. Her little girl didn't want to give her the time of day. "Okay, honey. I'll be downstairs if you need me."

Just before she shut the door, she heard Kayla's soft response. "I won't."

The next evening was the same—Kayla coming home late and holing herself up in her room. That night when Bonnie went to bed, she found Curtis asleep on the floor on the other side of her bed. She knelt beside him, straightened the blanket he used as a pallet, and leaned down to kiss his cheek. At five, he didn't remember when his father had lived with them, since Guy had moved out when he was still a baby. Curtis had been unplanned, conceived at a time when her and Guy's relationship was already falling apart, or at least when Bonnie had finally realized things weren't going to get any better. Within a month of returning to work from maternity leave, Bonnie received divorce papers. Instead of betrayal, she'd felt relief. The house was more peaceful with Guy gone.

But even though he couldn't possibly remember the terrible fights Bonnie and Guy had before the divorce, Curtis seemed to pick up on any kind of tension in the house. He wasn't as verbal about his feelings as Andy, yet he sought contact with Bonnie by sleeping next to her bed at night. It was as if he was trying to make up for Kayla's withdrawal from the family, as if he knew how much it hurt Bonnie though she'd never said anything out loud to the boys. In the morning when Bonnie would get up, he'd slip back into the room he shared with his brother and sleep in his own bed for the hour before she called to them to get ready for school.

Bonnie mulled over these issues at the office the following day, too lost in thought to see what was on the computer screen in front of her.

Her telephone rang and she answered it absently. "Bonnie Moore. May I help you?"

"This is Charles Brewer. I received your email."

Bonnie had sent an email to him about the incident in which someone impersonating a vice president of security had interrogated her. She'd detailed the use of a vacant office on a hallway where no one should have had access, and her concerns there was a security risk involved. Even though she'd mentioned it to Mr. Brewer earlier, he hadn't done anything about it. In fact, it seemed he hadn't been that concerned.

"Why don't you come to my office, and we'll talk about it."

Bonnie pursed her lips. She'd copied the email to Vivian Walker, the vice president of Kentucky Revenue Services. Either Mr. Brewer wanted to meet with Bonnie to lambast her for going over his head, or he was now taking her concerns seriously.

Bonnie logged off her computer and headed over to

his office. Once there, she waited at his threshold, and he waved her in. "Shut the door, why don't you."

It was going to one of those visits then.

Bonnie shut the door and walked over to sit on the chair in front of his desk. He watched her for a moment.

"I wish you hadn't sent that email to Ms. Walker."

"Don't you think she needs to know someone is squatting in one of the offices upstairs and harassing employees?"

"The office is vacant, Bonnie. Nobody saw those people but you."

"What are you saying? You think I made it up?"

He sighed angrily. "No, I'm not saying that."

Bonnie felt her own anger rising, but she kept her cool. "Then what?"

"It was probably a joke, like I said. You take things too—"

"It wasn't a joke. The guy was trying to get me to tell him something. The entire room was set up like an office. After I got the call, I looked him up in the employee database. He was there—title and everything. So, not only were they able to claim an office under false pretenses, but they were able to enter and delete information in our files. Doesn't that make you uncomfortable?"

"If someone like that had access to our computer files, then why question you? Why not just hack your computer?"

"I don't know."

"What exactly did he ask you?"

Bonnie hesitated. She didn't want to get in trouble, and especially didn't want to get Marla in trouble. After all, Marla hadn't willingly let him use her computer. "He asked how I find missing beneficiaries and if I look at unauthorized files to find out information."

Mr. Brewer leaned back in his chair. His eyes narrowed at her. "What did you tell him?"

"I said I was a model employee, and I didn't like his intimidation tactics. I told him I wanted you to sit in with the interview since you were my supervisor. He picked up the phone, and actually spoke to you, or acted as if he did. But you said you didn't know him, and you didn't talk to him." Bonnie studied him to see his response. Sometimes Mr. Brewer was a hard man to read.

"None of this makes sense."

Bonnie didn't say anything. None of it made sense to her either, but at least now Mr. Brewer was taking her seriously.

Bonnie stood up. "Is there anything else?" Bonnie was hoping Mr. Brewer would say they were going upstairs to meet with Vivian Walker, but he didn't.

"Not right now. We'll see how this plays out."

Bonnie entered her office. Her telephone was ringing.

She reached across the desk and picked up the receiver even as she circled her desk to sit down. "Bonnie Moore. May I help you?"

"I hope so. I'm hungry, and I'd like to take you to lunch."

Bonnie blinked, trying to recover from the shock of hearing Brandt Sherrod's voice.

Or whoever he was.

"Who is this, please?"

His slow laughter made her skin tingle. He knew she knew who it was.

"This is Brandt Sherrod."

"If you are Brandt Sherrod, why did you leave the custody of the security guards the other day?"

"So, no lunch?"

"Why would I go anywhere with you? You could be a serial killer for all I know."

"Or I could be a very nice person."

"A very arrogant person. Why do you even assume I'm available for lunch?"

"Because you haven't given me a reason to assume otherwise."

Bonnie snorted. "When you have some identification proving you are Brandt Sherrod, I will be available to meet with you here in the building. Until then, have a good day. Goodbye."

She hung up the phone wondering if steam were coming out of her ears. What was this guy's deal? If he was Delores's beneficiary, then he needed to prove it. But why go to all this trouble if he really didn't want the money as he claimed? She drummed her fingers on her keyboard wondering if she should call security again. But for what purpose? They'd let him walk away from them while they were supposed to be escorting him to their office. Obviously, either he was a very good ninja, or they were very poor security guards.

A knock sounded on the threshold, and Sheila, Bonnie's friend stood at the doorway. "Ready for some lunch? I'm starving. Rita and Alicia are already in the cafeteria."

Bonnie opened her desk drawer to retrieve her purse.

"You okay? You look mad."

Bonnie shook her head. "Difficult benefits case." She stood, and they walked toward the elevator.

"What?" Sheila cast a sidelong glance at her. "Are they fighting over who gets the money?"

Where should she start? There was no easy explanation, and Bonnie wasn't one for gossip She shook her head. "Not exactly."

The elevator doors opened, and they entered the small space, turning around to face the door that began to close but opened again in defiance of something unknown to either of them. This was an older part of the building, and the elevator sometimes expressed the gremlins of age.

Sheila arched an eyebrow, and they both stepped backward—testimony to conversations of the past blaming proximity to the threshold for the doors flying back open.

A few seconds passed, and the door closed, this time without any reluctance.

"What then?" Sheila asked.

"Let's talk about something else. I'd like to enjoy my lunch break."

"That bad, huh?"

"How's Robby?" Robby, Sheila's husband, had prostate cancer, though they'd caught it early.

"We go next week to see how the radiation is working."

"How's he holding up?"

The question was about his health, but Sheila's glance expressed something more intimate.

"I didn't mean—"

"Oh, honey. It's fine." She placed a placating hand on Bonnie's shoulder. "He's a man. His greatest fear is not being able to...get up with..." She gestured briefly with her fingers to her pants. The naked expression of fear and resignation on Sheila's face brought tears to Bonnie's eyes. She sniffed in an effort to collect herself.

"We're okay. We are." Sheila placed the heel of her hand on one eye then the other. "He knows the most important thing is living, but to live without...." Her voice died away.

Bonnie reached an arm across her friend's shoulders. "I'm sorry."

"No. Don't be. These kinds of things, they show you what's important. Really important, and I'd live a life of a monk only if I could sit across the breakfast table each morning and look at Robby Evans' face for the next fifty years." She stepped away from her friend's embrace. "You're sweet to ask about him."

"You'll let me know, won't you, if I can do anything for you?"

"Of course."

The elevator doors opened on the ground floor, and the women walked into the hallway. The cafeteria was just a few feet ahead. They entered the double doors and perused the selections. With her lunch bag and a fountain drink on a tray, Bonnie followed Sheila a few minutes later across the large dining area to a rectangular table their friends had claimed. Rita waved them over.

They sat, placing their food on the table.

Alicia eyed them critically. "You guys look like somebody shot your dog."

Bonnie could always count on Alicia's lack of tact.

Sheila took it with a grain of salt. "I was just telling Bonnie that I'd rather have Robby here without sex, then not have him at all."

"Aww, Sheila," Rita breathed. "I'm sorry."

"Well, hopefully it's not permanent. It bothers Robby though."

"It wouldn't bother me. I find sex to be a chore."

"Alicia!" Rita's eyes went wide.

"Well, I do. Ted and I can get in the biggest fight right before bed, then he starts rooting around like the pig that he is. But I tell him, 'If you're mad at my face, then you're mad at my tail.'"

"That's brutal," Bonnie said.

"Hey, you're divorced. You don't have to put up with your husband wanting sex after you've worked all day here, then put in another six hours at home taking care of the house and kids."

"Yeah, charmed life right here. Divorced with three children."

"Seriously, Bonnie. Do you miss the sex?"

"If she ever decided to try to date again, she wouldn't *have* to miss it," Sheila counseled.

Bonnie watched her hand holding the spoon stirring her yogurt. "I'm too busy with my life to worry about such things."

"Can't a man be part of your life?" Sheila asked.

"Where is a man going to fit in with my life? I work, and when I leave here, I have three people depending on me to feed, clothe, love, and guide them. Even if a man fell in my lap, he'd have to love my kids. I can barely get Guy to take an interest in them, and he's their father. Why in the world would some man take on a ready-made family just to be with me?"

"Because you're awesome," Rita declared.

Bonnie shot Rita a direct stare. Rita was always the

cheerleader—rooting for the team even when they were losing without any hope of coming back in the fourth quarter. "I'm forty-one years old with children. Statistically, I'm more likely to be struck by lightning than I am to settle down with another husband."

The women sitting around the table were silent. Finally, Bonnie lifted her gaze to them.

Sheila was the first to speak. "If you stand under a tree during a thunderstorm, it's pretty easy to get struck by lightning."

"And why get married again anyway? I tell you, if anything ever happens to Ted, I'm going to paint this town so red, people's going to think it's the Apocalypse."

"This coming from the woman who just said sex is a chore."

"Sex is a chore after I've cooked dinner, picked up Ted's dirty clothes, and cleaned the house."

"There's your problem. Make him pick up his own clothes."

"He's a pig."

"He's a cop. How does he feel about you calling him a pig?" Rita asked.

"He's a pig because he won't pick up anything. He'd wear a dirty smelly shirt before he'd even think about washing it."

Bonnie noticed she'd forgotten a napkin. She glanced around the table and didn't see any extras. She stood up. "I'm going to get a few napkins. Anybody need anything?"

"More napkins sound great. I haven't spilled anything on my shirt yet, so I'm overdue," Alicia stated.

Bonnie walked to the sidebar and pulled napkins out of the dispenser. Walking back toward their table, she saw Tony Meadows from her department rise from a table with his paper bag lunch and head toward the exit. Sitting at the same table, but on the other end directly behind the divider where Bonnie and her group were was....

Bonnie stopped short.

Brandt Sherrod had the blue-plate special in front of

him and was staring intently at his cell phone. He punched the screen with his index finger as if he were texting.

Why was he here?

Chapter Five

Bonnie continued on to her table, uncomfortably aware he could probably hear everything she and her friends were saying.

Had said.

She sat down at the table.

"Bonnie," Rita said. "We think you need to cut loose and just go out with us, and we'll find you a cute guy to dance with and—"

Alicia interrupted. "A younger guy."

"Shh." Bonnie glared at them.

"Why? Don't you think—"

Bonnie leaned forward. "There's a man back there. I don't want him hearing anything."

All three of them craned their heads to peer over the divider.

"Stop!" Bonnie hissed.

"Who is it?" Sheila asked.

"It's someone I'm involved with in a—"

"You're involved with somebody!" Rita crowed.

"No. Be quiet, would you? A case. A beneficiaries case. He's…" Bonnie shook her head.

Alicia jumped up and trounced off toward the napkins. Bonnie reached to grab her, but the woman was too fast.

"Oh, darn it. I want to see too," Rita complained.

Alicia came back with an angry expression on her face. "What is this, a joke? The table's empty."

"What? No. The table right behind us." Bonnie stood and peeked over the divider. The table was empty. She scanned the room. He was at the self-service bar refilling his drink. "Oh," she said. "There he is." She sat back down, and the rest of the women all turned their heads in unison to see him.

"Oh, my gosh, he's good-looking. Why aren't you having lunch with him?"

"Because you asked me first."

"What!" Rita reared back. "He asked you to lunch?"

"Look. He just appears and disappears. It's kind of creepy."

"If that's what creepy looks like, I want creepy too."

"No, you don't. You think it's an accident he just shows up here?"

"You think he's stalking you?"

Bonnie raised an eyebrow at the people sitting around her. "He was sitting directly behind us. What do you think?"

"Go talk to him."

"Yeah, don't let him get away with it."

"Hurry. Before he disappears."

Bonnie huffed. Her friends were trying to set her up with a creepy stalker. So what if he was good looking? She scooted back her chair and walked over to where he stood at the kitchen window placing his tray and dishes in the return. He turned and met her eyes as if he knew she had been behind him.

"Hello, Ms. Moore."

"What are you doing here?"

"Having lunch."

"You're following me."

"I was actually here first. I called you, and when you refused, I bought lunch and sat down. It seems you are following me."

"You don't have any business here except with me."

He nodded and reached behind him. Pulling out his wallet, he opened it, slid a card out of a sleeve, and offered it to her.

"What's that?" she asked suspiciously.

"Proof."

She peered at it. She didn't have her glasses, but from

this distance it appeared to be a driver's license. She snorted. "Right. I bet it's fake."

"Well." He shrugged. "No, actually that one's real." He gestured her to take it, but she didn't.

"Why did you ditch the security guards?"

He placed the license back in his wallet and pocketed it. "Because I had no ID and couldn't prove who I was. What would be the point of wasting my time and theirs?"

"They wasted their time looking for you. What you did was rude and very unprofessional."

He bit his lip in mirth. "I guess it depends on one's profession."

"There's no such thing as a ninja. That's ridiculous."

"Okay." His tone expressed he found her proclamation amusing.

Bonnie put her hands on her hips. "Did you want to meet with me?"

His eyes flicked to her hands then back to her face. He nodded.

She dropped her hands and straightened her spine. Why did he make her feel so…aware of herself? Every posture and stance? "Fine. I'll be available at one o'clock. Do not go to my office. I don't like you creeping around in secure locations. I'll meet you in the lobby."

He wisely did not comment about how unsecure the secure locations were.

"Oh, forget it. You made me lose my appetite. Let's just go now and get this over with."

"May I have a few minutes? I want to get one more thing from the self-serve bar."

"Fine. I'll get my stuff and meet you in the lobby." She pivoted and marched over to where all three of her friends were watching, their heads visible above the divider. Rolling her eyes at their antics, Bonnie approached the table and began gathering her lunch.

"Don't say anything. He's a benefits case."

"I wouldn't mind taking advantage of his benefits," Alicia commented.

"For someone who thinks sex is a chore, you sure got a saucy mouth."

"Where are you going? Are you going to eat with him?" Rita asked. She clapped her hands enthusiastically.

Alicia grabbed at Bonnie's lunch bag. "Make him buy you lunch. Geez, he just dropped a few points if you've got to provide your own food."

Bonnie pulled her bag out of her friend's reach. "I'm not eating with him. I'm meeting with him so I can hopefully get this case resolved."

Sheila's head whipped around. "Where did he go? I didn't see him leave."

"See what I mean about him? He needs a bell hung around his neck."

"And speaking of hung—"

"Don't you dare finish that sentence," Bonnie growled. "Whatever you're going to say, I don't want to hear it. I'll see you all later."

Bonnie strode across the room and pushed open the door. She noted he wasn't in the lobby yet. She claimed a spot in the corner where she could see all three entrances to the lobby. He wasn't going to sneak up on her.

In a few minutes a small group of people exited from the direction of the cafeteria. Her eyes skimmed them before jumping to other door. But her skin on the back of her neck prickled, and her attention returned to the group.

Brandt meandered on the periphery. He was good at blending, even as attractive as he was. When he broke away from the group, his countenance changed. He walked taller, and his eyes focused.

On her.

Bonnie's heart thumped hard in her chest, and she lost her breath for a second.

What is wrong with me?

He was a liar and possibly a thief. He was too smooth and too arrogant.

And much too attractive.

Gone was the suit he had worn when she'd first met

him. Today he wore a pinstriped shirt and dark pants. No tie. He dressed like most of the other male state employees, but none of the other male employees made her knees feel like goo. The Styrofoam cup he had been carrying was gone. Now he held a white take-out bag, and Bonnie wondered what was in there.

The corner of his lips crooked upward, and Bonnie realized she was staring.

Fine. She had the right to stare at him in case he tried to pull something. She raised her arm and indicated that he should go toward the elevator.

"Ladies first," he said.

"I don't think so. You go first so I can keep an eye on you."

He bent his head in acquiescence, turned and walked toward the shiny doors. Bonnie noted his broad shoulders under the wrinkle-free shirt.

Obviously he took his shirts to the dry-cleaners. No one could have a shirt that crisp and line free without commercial starch. She sniffed and detected a sweet aroma, which reminded her of the tobacco her grandfather had smoked in his pipe.

Did Brandt smoke a pipe? How odd. She didn't know men under seventy did that kind of thing.

He pressed the up button, and they stood there for a moment. A hundred questions ricocheted through her head. How had he slipped away from Steve and Luke? How had he known she'd gotten into Mrs. Tackett's computer? How had he acquired a custodian uniform, and had he only done it to try to get the beneficiary money?

A bell sounded, and the doors slid open. Brandt walked in and turned around to face the opening. He wore a smug smile on his face as he watched her follow him. She positioned herself in front of the buttons and pressed the correct number. When the doors closed, the room immediately closed in on her.

They were alone in this tiny space.

The sweet aroma she'd detected earlier lingered in the

air. She inhaled, enjoying the familiar scent of her granddad. They'd sit on the front porch at his house in the dusk of the day. He on his chair, and her on the swing pushing her feet back and forth until the blinking of the lightning bugs drew her into the yard. Oh, the fun of catching them in the empty mayonnaise jar her granny provided. Then later she'd lie in bed and watch the multitude of blinking lights encased in the glass. Sometimes on the cusp of sleep, she'd detect the sweet tobacco scent of Granddad as he entered the room, picked up the jar, bent down and kissed her forehead goodnight, then took the jar outside to set the bugs free so they could continue their luminary courtship on into the night. The tender memories warmed Bonnie in spite of her present suspicions of the man with her.

"Do you smoke, Mr. Sherrod?"

"Do I smoke what, Ms. Moore?"

His low words spoken close to her ear almost made her jump. He'd moved after she turned to face the doors. She glanced over her shoulder and found him standing there. She stepped away and pivoted toward him.

"I smell pipe tobacco."

"Really?" He sniffed. "I believe I do as well."

"So, it's not you?"

His brown gaze dropped before meeting hers. "Does it offend you?"

"No, actually. I…appreciate the aroma. I haven't smelled anything like it in a long time."

"Ah." He nodded.

The motion of the elevator ceased, and the doors swooshed open onto her floor. She didn't move. For a few seconds, he didn't either. She folded her arms across her chest and crooked her head toward the door.

Go.

He did, strolling across the wide space and toward her office in that nonchalant way he had, as if he belonged here.

Bonnie trailed him until she reached her office door. Stepping in front of him, she slid her badge across the lock.

Since she'd discovered him in her office, she'd started locking the door. She didn't have to look behind her to know he was still there. Every one of her senses knew it—all five standing at attention, even her sense of taste, as memory receptors from childhood reminded her of the time she'd chewed on one of granddad's tobacco leaves. The buzzy sensation had gone to her head.

She opened the door and took her place behind her desk. She needed to put something between them—a barrier. "Sit down, please." She grabbed the folder from the drawer where she kept current open cases, and set it down in front of her.

"May I see your identification?"

With one hand, he moved the chair closer to her desk. Great. They'd be all cozy across from each other. He reached behind him for his wallet, and Bonnie purposely looked away. No sense in ruminating on how his slacks fit so well on his hips or the kind of belt buckle he had, or… Nope. No sense in thinking any of that. She scanned her desktop for her cheaters but didn't see them. Pulling out the wide middle drawer of her desk, she didn't see them there either.

He slid the license across the desktop toward her.

She picked it up and held it reading distance, squinting for a better view.

A pair of reading glasses appeared in front of her, and Bonnie lifted her gaze to them then to the man who held them.

The smirky expression she expected wasn't there. Instead, she recognized the resignation of being forty and not being able to read small print without aid.

"How long have you needed glasses?" he asked.

"Two months after my fortieth birthday." She pinched the stem and glanced through the lenses briefly before sliding them on her face.

The plastic frames felt warm against her skin.

Don't think about it.

The letters came into focus.

"How about you?" she asked.

"About six months ago. I was almost captured in Kazakhstan because I couldn't see the fine print."

"What?" She watched him over the lenses. "On one of your spy missions, I suppose. You couldn't read the instructions on the side of a bomb?" She turned back to his license. Running her thumb and fingers over it, she judged it to feel authentic. Reaching down, she fished her own license out of her purse and compared the two.

"Bombs don't have instructions on the side."

"Or at least not that you can see without your cheaters, right?"

He expelled a burst of laughter.

His license sure looked real enough.

Still.

"Why were you in here emptying my trash?"

His gaze didn't waver from hers. "I wanted to know if you were who you claimed you were, or if it was a ruse to ferret me into the open."

"Why would someone need to do that unless you're hiding from law enforcement? The fact that you disappeared when you knew the police were going to get involved the other day leads me to believe you're a fugitive."

"Do you run criminal background checks on every beneficiary?"

"Only the ones who go through my trash."

He opened his hands in a helpless shrug. "I don't really want Delores's money. I appreciate that she wanted to leave it to me, but I wasn't family. Give it to her sister."

Bonnie sighed. Perhaps he was acting reluctant so that it would lower her suspicions of him and she'd insist he take the money.

She pulled out the acquisition form, turned it over, and slid it to him. "Fill out this form."

He quirked an eyebrow at her.

"What?"

"I'm going to need my glasses back."

She slipped them off her nose and placed them on the paper. Pulling a pen from her holder, she placed it next to both items. Sharing eyeglasses seemed intimate. Too intimate.

He put them on and read the form. He glanced at her over the frames as she had done to him. The glasses made him seem more human and less the crook she suspected him to be.

His pen rested on the first blank.

Was he having trouble remembering the lies he'd written on his tax form or the lies he'd told her? "What's wrong?"

"Nothing." He shook his head and wrote.

He was left handed. His handwriting was neat. In a few minutes, he gave it to her. "Thank you." Without reading it, she placed it in the folder and closed it. "If there are no problems with the information you've provided, the check will be mailed to the address you've given."

He took off the glasses and pocketed them. "Very well." He stood and held out his hand. "Thank you, Ms. Moore."

She stood as well and took the hand he offered. His grasp was warm and firm. She ignored the tingles from the contact and pulled her hand away quickly.

"I'd still like to take you to dinner."

"No thank you."

"Why not?"

"I don't trust you."

"Is that the only reason?"

Bonnie thought of Kayla, Curtis, and Andy. "There are a few others, but that's reason enough."

"Your children."

Bonnie pinched her lips together in irritation. She didn't like how easily he'd read her thoughts. Or that he'd listened in on a private conversation with her friends. "So you *were* eavesdropping on our conversation."

"It wasn't difficult. Your friends are loud."

"You could have moved."

"You intrigue me." His voice dropped when he said it, as if he were disclosing a secret he wasn't quite comfortable with.

A little shudder skittered along her spine. "What?"

"Your friends said you needed to cut loose and go out dancing."

"With a younger man. That wouldn't be you." Actually, she was older, but only by a few months, and she wasn't going to share that with him. "And this conversation is extremely inappropriate. You are a beneficiaries case."

His eyes sparkled, but it wasn't from humor this time. "Delores Parks, who was the closest thing I had to a mother, died last year. This may be just a case to you, but she was a dear woman with a very big heart who loved a bitter kid more than he deserved." He closed his eyes for a moment. "Goodbye, Ms. Moore. If you change your mind about dinner, call me. My number is on the form." He nodded to her then turned and walked out of her office without looking back.

Wait!

Bonnie wanted to call out to him, but she didn't. Shame drowned out the suspicion she'd harbored against the man since she'd met him.

Chapter Six

Get out.
Just get out, and don't think about it.
Don't think about her.

Brandt stalked to the elevator and pushed the button. It opened immediately, and he stepped in. His mind went white, a trick he'd trained himself to do when things got too intense. It's what had helped him to focus on his objective, get in and out without detection, to survive.

An image of Bonnie Moore shattered the white, her blue eyes glaring at him over his own readers, their frames resting low on her cute nose. All business and efficiency—he was used to the women in operations, but they were hard, all angular and tight, even their curves, contained to draw the eye away instead of entice. Then there were the other women Brandt ran into—sensual, yes, but they used their sexuality like a weapon. They were harder still, like marble, and they were ruthless. Brandt learned long ago to stay away from them unless they could help him with his objective. He would put up the white wall, accomplish his goal, and leave making sure he watched his back in case somebody wanted to stick a knife in it.

And then there was Bonnie. Softness and domesticity clung to her like the aroma of chocolate chip cookies in Aunt Louise's kitchen. But Bonnie wasn't weak or shallow, like he'd seen elsewhere. She was competent. He liked that, really liked it.

"Hi."

A woman who just entered the elevator smiled at him. He recognized her from the cafeteria. One of Bonnie's friends.

I'm losing my edge.

This woman shouldn't have been able to sneak up on him, much less even notice him.

Bonnie had him distracted.

"I'm Rita. I'm a friend of Bonnie's."

Brandt nodded to her.

"Bonnie Moore, the bloodhound, I mean, the beneficiaries manager."

"Yes, I know who she is." The nickname intrigued him. But she'd located him, hadn't she? Brandt reached out to shake Rita's hand. "Nice to meet you."

A cloud passed over her expression. "You're not married, right?"

A shocked laugh burst from him. "No. Are you?"

Her eyes widened. "Yes. Happily. I'm asking for Bonnie."

"Bonnie wants to know if I'm married?"

Rita snickered. "What am I thinking? Of course, she has already found that out. Bloodhound, you know. She just didn't say specifically, but I guess since she's interested…."

"She's interested?"

"Well, she denied it, but I believe in Shakespeare's adage, 'The lady doth protest too much.' Know what I mean?"

Brandt grinned. Oh, he loved this. Ms. Moore was interested, yet she was in denial. But she hadn't fooled her friends. "What was the protest?"

"It wasn't so much what she said, but how she said it. A little flustered. That's not Bonnie."

He hadn't seen her flustered. He'd seen cool as a cucumber. He'd seen distrust and disdain, but not fluster, although he'd sure like to.

"So, if you're free Thursday night and you'd like to…see Bonnie, we'll be at the Barefoot Café around six. We go there once a month from six to eight."

****

It was nearly eight, and Kayla wasn't home yet though

she'd texted at five and said they were practicing late again. What was going on with band? Why were they going late every night? She picked up her phone and called Hannah Bradley's mother. Maybe she knew why the band needed extra practice. Fran picked up on the second ring.

"Hi, Fran, it's Bonnie."

"Hey, what's up?"

"Do you know why the band practices are running long this week?"

"I didn't know they were running late. Just a minute. Hannah? Are you all having late practices?"

Hannah? Why would Hannah already be home if Kayla was riding home with her?

"She said they went a few minutes late Tuesday, but that was it."

It was on the tip of Bonnie's tongue to have Fran ask her daughter if Kayla was riding home with her, but Bonnie already knew the answer.

Rex.

Damn you.

The front door opened and closed.

"Thanks a lot," Bonnie said into the receiver.

"Is anything wrong?"

"No, not at all. I'll talk to you later, okay?"

"Sure."

Bonnie hung up the phone just as Kayla walked into the room, grabbed a bottle of water from the fridge, and began to walk out again.

"Hey, kiddo. You must be hungry."

"Not really."

"I didn't hear Hannah's car in the driveway."

Kayla shrugged. "I had her drop me off at the street. That way she doesn't have to pull in, then pull back out."

"She's not giving you a hard time about riding home with her, is she? I didn't think she minded."

"Get off my back, Mom. Geez. It's fine," the young woman snapped before stalking through the kitchen door into the den.

Bonnie knew it definitely was *not* fine. She followed her daughter. "Tell her I'll pick you up from band practice tomorrow at five. It's my girl's night out, and I don't want to be late."

Kayla stopped and turned toward her mother, shooting her a murderous look. "I can't just tell Mr. Headly I have to leave early. We have to stay until seven this week."

Or eight, but who's keeping track? Obviously, the stupid idiotic mother who trusted her daughter to be truthful. "Well, I guess I'll have to call him and talk about it. I find it unreasonable that he's keeping all of you so late, here with midterms coming up."

"No. Don't call him." Kayla raised her hand in surrender then higher in fury. "God, I hate it when you blow everything out of proportion and start calling the school."

"Two hours of practice a day in addition to the thirty minutes he has you during school hours should be enough." Bonnie knew she was losing her temper. She worked to rein it in.

"Okay. Okay. I'll just ride home with Cindy."

"No. If they go late tomorrow, I don't want to have to go back over there to pick you up. You're on my way home from work. I'll just leave a little early to get you."

"I'll get a ride with someone else."

"Like Rex? I don't think so."

Something flashed in her eyes. It almost looked like fear. Of being caught? Then the anger was back. "Why do you hate him so much?"

"Because he's…" *corrupting you.* Bonnie didn't say it, knowing how Kayla would react. "He's bad news, Kayla."

Kayla turned and stalked up the stairs. Bonnie resisted the urge to command her to stop and turn around when she was talking to her.

She followed her daughter. "Don't you see what he's doing? You can do so much better than—"

Kayla turned on the landing and glared down at her mother. "You're just jealous because you don't have anyone. You and Dad screwed things up, and now no one wants you because you're old. Well, I don't want to be like you. Rex and I are in love—"

Bonnie continued upward toward her daughter. Kayla stood there glaring at her. She was as tall as Bonnie now. Bonnie reached out to touch her arm, and Kayla flinched away. Not in anger, though, in pain.

"What's wrong with your arm?"

Kayla rolled her shoulder a little stiffly. The movement seemed to illicit more anger in her. "Nothing. Would you just get out of my life!"

"Let me see."

Kayla shook her head and strode to her bedroom. She put her hand on the doorknob. "No. Don't touch me."

"What is wrong with you?"

"You're what's wrong with me," she yelled. She opened the door, getting ready for her big exit line. "You're pathetic, and I hate you."

Slam!

And there it was.

Bonnie blew out a breath. A small sound drew her attention down the hall where two sets of eyes peered at her around the door facing of the boys' room. Big scared eyes.

Bonnie walked toward them and breathed in and out a few times like she had learned in her mindfulness exercises. She walked in their room and lay down on the floor. They looked back at her with troubled expressions on their faces. "Well, boys, all that yelling wears me out."

Andy's nose wrinkled up as if he smelled something bad. "Does Kayla really hate you?"

Curtis walked over and folded his legs under him as he sat next to Bonnie. Bending his head down, he rested his forehead against her hip, and Bonnie caressed his hair. As much as she didn't like their father, she couldn't help but be grateful to the man for his part in creating these children.

"She probably feels like she does right now."

"If she hates you, then I hate her."

Bonnie cupped Curtis' head and rolled to her side. She bent over and kissed the crown of his head. "She needs us to love her now more than ever."

"But she said she hated you and stay out of her life," Curtis reminded her.

"You think she really means it, Mama?" Andy asked.

"No. I don't think she really means it."

"We're supposed to go to Dad's tomorrow. What if she doesn't come back with us Sunday?"

Bonnie suppressed the *harrumph* that rose in her throat. As if Guy would agree to that.

"I think she'll come back. After all, all her stuff's here."

"But she hates you."

"Tell you what. If she goes to live with your dad, Andy, you can move in her room, then you guys wouldn't have to share a room anymore."

A sparkle shone in Andy's eyes. He'd expressed interest in wanting his own room for a couple of years now. A little grin surfaced on his lips. "Can we go get ice cream?"

Bonnie smiled and sat up. They had a tradition of going out for ice cream to celebrate something. Like getting one's own room. "Don't start moving your stuff yet. She's not moving in with your dad no matter how much she hates me."

****

She hates me.

Nearly sixteen years ago Bonnie lay in a hospital bed in the maternity ward holding this perfect baby with her ten fingers and toes, her pink bow mouth, and her inquisitive gaze that made her look more like a wise sage than a day-old baby. Bonnie had gazed in that face for hours memorizing every feature, the hope of a lifetime of dreams all in that tiny, beautiful face.

I did this. Me. Well, me and Guy.

But it was my body, which had nurtured this perfect child for nine months, which had provided a place for her to develop and grow until she could survive the outside world, breathe the air, eat and drink, sleep, and grow into an adult.

Me.

Bonnie remembered those moments of wonder. Sitting by the crib nights gazing at her sleeping daughter, Bonnie never imagined those tender maternal moments would graduate to this moment—nursing a margarita at the Barefoot Café, thinking back to the night before when that perfect baby, fifteen years later, flung angry words at her.

I don't want to be like you. You're pathetic, and I hate you.

"Bonnie? Where are you, hon?"

Bonnie blinked, Rita's words bringing her back to the present. The boisterous atmosphere of the bar and grill finally pricked her ruminations. Bonnie focused on her friends sitting around the table. Rita, Alicia, and Sheila all watched her, their own favorite drinks sitting on the table in front of them.

"I told you I wouldn't be good company tonight," Bonnie said.

She had told them. Guy picked up the kids from school, including the hater. And even though Bonnie hadn't let Kayla see it, her words hurt. They'd hurt very much. And all Bonnie wanted to do was to stay home and be alone with her misery. But when she hadn't shown up for the six o'clock meeting time at the café, Alicia had called her—and called her on not showing up.

"Get your ass down here. If the rest of us can leave our miserable lives to come and drink and make merry, you surely can, too."

"Tell her to put on something pretty before she comes." Bonnie heard Sheila say in the background.

"Yeah," Alicia said. "And put on that sleeveless number you have. The red one."

Bonnie had refused, and twenty minutes later, Rita had shown up, dismissed her excuses, pulled out the red dress, and driven her over here.

She stirred the margarita with the little straw that had come with it and took a sip, then another. At least, she didn't have to worry about driving home. Her friends' insistence she live out the aphorism *misery loves company* meant she had a designated driver tonight. It would serve them right for her to get drunk out of her skull and make them put up with her. But of course, she wouldn't. Bonnie didn't do things like that.

She studied the glass in front of her and the ice cubes in it. Their food hadn't arrived yet, and she'd already finished her cocktail. And since Bonnie didn't get drunk out of her skull, didn't make her friends put up with her, and wouldn't be a burden to anyone, she'd order ice tea when the waiter came back. She sighed and pushed back her chair a bit. Standing up, her head swam a little.

"Where you going?" Sheila asked.

"Bathroom."

"Want me to go with you?" Rita asked.

"Nope. I'm a big girl." Bonnie thought she might have swayed a little bit and hoped no one noticed. She stepped around the chair and concentrated on walking a straight line. She had to walk through the bar to get to the restrooms, and three large televisions displayed three different channels—news, a crime drama, and a football game. Who played on a Thursday night, she wondered as she gave the screens a curious glance. Once she'd visited the bathroom, she threaded her way through the bar again. A commercial played on one of the screens, its picture reflected in the angled mirror over the bar. A man sat by himself on one side of the bar, his face shown clearly in the reflected glass, and his eyes met hers. Bonnie gasped.

Brandt Sherrod is stalking me.

She marched over to him, and his gaze followed her. They watched each other in the mirror for a few seconds.

Though it felt like days.

She grabbed the raised back of the barstool and turned it, sitting down, not breaking eye contact. Bonnie shook her head. "You're going to stop this."

One side of that perfect mouth turned up. "Stop what?"

Bonnie snorted. "Following me." Her attention strayed to the beer glass in front of him. It was nearly full.

"Once again, I was here first." He turned to her. Tonight he wore a knit shirt with blue jeans. The more casual look was just as appealing as his more formal daytime attire. "You seem to be following me."

"Come on. I don't hardly believe you and I just happen to be at the same place at the same time."

"It does seem like an awful big coincidence."

"I don't believe in coincidences."

Brandt's gaze turned away from her toward the bartender who stood in front of them. He nodded to the young woman who turned her back and in a minute, placed a margarita on the rocks in front of Bonnie.

"Me neither. That comes from working in stealth operations. They create situations which appear to be coincidental but are actually opportunities."

"Who are *they?*"

He smiled again, but this time the amusement, which had lit his eyes, was gone. "The people I work for."

"The government," Bonnie supplied.

Brandt shrugged. "Kinda sorta."

"What kind of answer is that? The CIA, right? That's why all the secrecy and your spy attitude."

Brandt's gaze flicked around before coming to rest on her. "No. Not the CIA. I told you, I'm a ninja."

"Yeah, and you're about two centuries past your prime. Also in the wrong country and culture, not to mention ethnicity."

"It's the quality that's the descriptor, not the context." He glanced at the drink. "It was a margarita, right?" His eyes went up to the mirror, and Bonnie followed it and noticed a perfect view of their table from his vantage point.

"Prove it to me that you're a ninja."

A speculative expression settled on his face.

The television closest to them showed the Kentucky governor in his office in Frankfort. The closed caption flashed across the bottom of the screen about the commonwealth budget. On a shelf behind him was an autographed basketball in a Lucite cube. The would-be governor's passion for the game had been the main reason her ex-husband had voted for the man. Bonnie shook her head in derision at the memory.

"What are you thinking?" Brandt asked.

She gestured toward the television. "My ex voted for him because he was a forward for UK the year they got the national championship."

Brandt watched the television for a minute. "You think the basketball is from his championship year?"

"I'm almost sure of it."

Brandt squinted at the screen, and a lecherous grin spread across his lips.

"Don't tell me you bow to the basketball god too." Bonnie rolled her eyes. Men and their silly pastimes. "It's sad all of the energy and money you boys spend caring that a big ball goes through a metal ring."

"Everything we boys spend our time and energy on is more than sad. It's absurd."

"So, proof," Bonnie said returning to their earlier topic.

He held up his hands in surrender.

"Have you ever killed anyone?"

He held her gaze steadily, not a flicker of anything. "Nothing I do is available for barroom bragging."

"What a shame." Bonnie looked at the glass in front of her. With her index finger, she wiped the condensation off the side up to the rim where she swiped it and put the digit in her mouth. "How are you supposed to impress a woman if you can't tell her of your violent exploits in an effort to rid the world of the bad guys?"

"Does the woman want to be impressed?"

Bonnie turned her attention to Brandt. His eyes watched her mouth, and she realized she was sucking on her finger. She lowered her hand and folded it in the other one in her lap. The skin burned on her face from embarrassment. "Well, not me, of course. I'm not...you know…" She pulled her eyes away from his dark mesmerizing ones to her margarita.

It was empty save for the ice cubes.

"You're not what?"

"I'm not into…the dating scene and all that. I have kids and a…a mortgage."

"And a husband."

"Well, no. I don't have one of those anymore."

"He's the ex who votes for basketball players."

"Yes."

The bartender came by and replaced her empty glass with a full one. "No, thank you. I've had my limit."

The bartender shrugged indifferently. "It's already made, honey. Don't drink it if you don't want it."

"Oh. Okay. Well, I don't want to pay for it. I didn't order it."

"No. You didn't order it," she agreed.

Bonnie looked at Brandt angrily. "Are you trying to get me drunk?"

He shook his head. "I didn't order it." He arched an eyebrow and his eyes shifted upward, and Bonnie looked in the mirror above their heads. Her friends' faces turned toward the bar, in open interest.

The traitors.

Bonnie glared at their treacherous reflections. "I've a good a mind to leave with you. That would show them."

"Yeah. That would show them," Brandt repeated with a grin.

"And then when you kill me and leave me in a ditch somewhere, won't they be sorry."

His smile fell a bit. "Ouch. That hurts. You think I'm Ted Bundy."

"I'm not really sure who you are. But it would serve them right."

"Except in your self-righteous fantasy, you'd be dead, and your children are deprived of their mother."

"One of those children would probably be happy about it. My daughter hates me."

"Oh? How old is she?"

"Fifteen." Bonnie turned and slid off the chair, holding onto the edge of the bar as she did so. "It's this guy. He's corrupting her." She watched her shoes walk toward Rita and crew.

When she arrived at the table, she pulled at her purse strap hanging over the back of the chair. "Good night. The ninja is taking me home. If you never see me again, just know it's your fault."

Rita and Sheila's mouths fell open. Alicia sniggered. Without looking back to see if Brandt was following her, she walked toward the door, at least where she thought the door was. Once outside, she breathed in the cool air and patted her flushed face. The door opened behind her, and then Brandt was at her side.

"May I?" he asked.

She closed one eye because there was two of him. "May you what?"

"Take your arm to walk you to the car."

"Are you going to give it back?"

He chuckled. "Yes." Warmth at her elbow alerted Bonnie that Brandt had placed his hand there, and he tugged her forward. "You're funny. It's a side of you I haven't seen before."

He led her to a sleek sports car, black as an ace of spades.

Bonnie blinked at it. "Does this car have seatbelts?"

"Yes. One for each of us." The headlights flashed briefly, and the interior light came on. Brandt opened the passenger side door, and Bonnie hesitated.

"I don't know. This looks too fast." She grasped his forearm and squeezed it. The soft material slid over his flesh, and she wondered briefly if he had hairy arms and a hairy chest and back like Guy did. Guy had been bad about speeding when they'd dated.

Not that this was a date or anything.

"It's not moving. Zero miles per hour."

"No. I mean, when you drive it." She bit her lip

anxiously. "You shouldn't break the speed limit, but you probably can't help it in this car."

"I can help it. I'm a very safe driver. No speeding tickets."

"Not ever?" Bonnie looked at him suspiciously.

"Not in about ten years or so, but I don't want you jinxing it."

"Yeah. You should knock on some wood. Any trees around?" Bonnie looked around the parking lot. No trees in sight. Wasn't there a song about that? Her attention returned to the car—a two-seater, of course.

"So, tell me about your daughter who hates you, and the boy corrupting her."

Bonnie sighed, as an image of Kayla swam across her mind. "He's seventeen. An older boy who has a car." Not like this one, but still.

Brandt took her hand and guided her to sit in the passenger seat. The door closed with only a soft snick. Bonnie leaned back on the leather seats sighing. Oh. Nice.

In a moment Brandt was beside her, and the engine started up. Bonnie looked at the console separating them. "What do those buttons do?"

"Ejector seats. Don't press them."

Bonnie shot him a startled glance.

"I'm kidding. It's really the missile launcher which pops out of the rear of the car and launches at anyone chasing me."

Onto his joke now, Bonnie nodded. "It explains why you haven't gotten any speeding tickets lately."

"Exactly." He paused for a beat. "You didn't eat inside. Would you like to stop somewhere and get something?"

"Can we get it to go? I'd like to go home."

"Where do you live?"

"You're a spy. I thought you would know these things."

"I'm a ninja. Not a spy. I sneak into places and back out. I don't find out where retirement benefits ladies live.

It's an invasion of privacy."

"What about the privacy of the places you sneak into?"

He crooked his head in a shrug. "When it's my job, it's a different set of rules."

The car was idling at the edge of the parking lot. Bonnie gave him her address, and he put the car in gear and pulled into the street. The car rode smooth.

"This doesn't seem the kind of car you could sneak around in."

"No. It doesn't blend well, does it?"

"So, what are you working on with your ninja job?"

"I'm waiting on an assignment, but my phone is shut down because of a security issue, so I don't expect to hear anything before tomorrow."

"Where's your phone?"

Brandt reached inside of his jacket and handed it to her.

She looked at the screen. "You've got it locked." She touched the screen and held it up to his face.

"Hey, what're you doing?"

"Face recognition, right?"

The phone didn't unlock. "What's the code?"

He snickered and shook his head. Reaching for it, he held it in his hand then handed it back to her.

She hadn't seen him tap the screen at all. "How'd you do that?"

"Embedded microchip."

"Embedded where?"

He arched an eyebrow at her but didn't respond. She dismissed his secrecy and began playing with the phone. "You can make calls on it."

"It *is* a phone."

"Where's the ninja icon?"

"You don't really expect me to tell you, do you?"

Bonnie surfed through the pictures on the phone, pressing each one and not getting anywhere. She looked in settings and went through his ringtones. Nothing ninja. It had to be something convenient, but unexpected. What would that be? She went to the second screen and tried the icons there. Nope. "Is it voice recognition? A secret word you have to say?"

He didn't say anything.

"I suppose not because then someone could hear you." She touched a blank part of the screen then tried another blank part. The screen blinked then letters appeared.

Hello HKAVMJ

"Oh. I think I found it. What does HKAVMJ mean?"

Brandt held out his hand. "All right. You've lost phone privileges. Let me have it back."

Bonnie grinned and placed it in his hand. "I impress myself. I found your secret message screen. All of my skills I've learned as the mother of a teenager have come in handy."

She settled back into the cozy seat and closed her eyes with a satisfied expression on her face.

"What kind of food are you in the mood for?"

Bonnie named a fast food place, which had good salads. Brandt went through the drive-through, and she noticed he didn't order anything for himself.

In a few minutes Brandt maneuvered the car into a sharp, but smooth, turn and cut the engine. Bonnie opened her eyes and saw he had parked in her driveway. A pang of uneasiness rose in her chest.

"Brandt?"

"Yes?"

"My children are not home."

The silence in the car thrummed in her ears.

"I'm telling you this because it's the only reason I'd allow you to drive me home. Do you understand?"

"Yes. You don't want me to meet your kids."

"Exactly. Are you okay with that?"

"Sure. You still think I might kill you and throw you in a ditch somewhere, and you want to keep your kids safe. Even though your thinking is a little skewed. After all, if I'm going to murder you, why would I abide by your wishes to keep away from your house when your children are home?"

"I was joking about you killing me. If I was really concerned about it, I wouldn't have left the restaurant with you."

"What makes you think you're safe with me?"

"Because Louise Tackett thinks you're a good boy."

She depressed the handle on her car door, but before she could step out of the car, Brandt was there on the outside taking the to-go bag from her fingers and lifting her hand to help her out. Bonnie liked the feel of his hand on hers. It had been a long time since she'd held hands with anyone but her kids. When they arrived at the door, she loosened her fingers from his regretfully. Fishing into her purse, she pulled out her key ring and unlocked the door. Pushing it open, she flicked the switch, and the foyer light came on.

She turned to Brandt and looked up in his face. Her heart beat hard in her chest. *I'm alone in my house with a man.* "Thanks for the ride." She gestured for the food bag he still held, and he surrendered it to her.

"You're welcome." He didn't move toward the door.

"I'm just going to sit on the couch and watch an old movie. Very boring."

"It sounds like it."

"Want to stay?"

"Absolutely."

Chapter Seven

Bonnie rolled over in bed and groaned.

Oh, my head.

She pushed in on her hair with her hands. Hoisting herself on an elbow, Bonnie sat up. The sheet fell down to her waist.

Ooof! Where are my clothes?

She looked toward her open closet door where the dress she had been wearing the night before hung. She'd changed into it at Rita's insistence. They'd gone to the restaurant. She'd....

Oh, no. Brandt!

Brandt had been here last night.

They'd settled on the couch. She'd found a classic movie, and they'd watched it. Then they'd watched another one.

And nothing else had happened. Well, except she'd fallen asleep, and he'd nudged her awake. She'd shot off the couch and away from him, staring at him suspiciously. He stood and offered to help her to bed, but she'd laughed at him. And he'd laughed in response.

"Yes. It is funny, isn't it? The ninja is going to tuck me in."

"One thing about you, Ms. Moore. You know how to toughen up a guy's skin."

"Oh, call me Bonnie. After all, you've sat on my couch."

"Sure I can't walk you to your room?" He bounced back on his heels, watching her as he did so.

"I'd like to think you're propositioning me, but I'm forty-one, and you drive a Porsche."

"I'm also forty-one, and it feels like you're insulting the Spyder."

"You have a name for your car?"

"The company does. That's the model name."

They stood there at the apex between the living room and the foyer. She'd taken off her shoes, and he seemed even taller when she looked up at him. There was a presence about him, a calm watchfulness, which tonight put her at ease. In her office, it made her nervous, but here he seemed less…what? Predatory. "It seems silly to be talking about this."

Brandt was closer now. He bent down and kissed her forehead then walked to the door. "Good night, Bonnie."

Good night, Bonnie.

That had been the climax and conclusion of their night together.

****

Bonnie walked toward her office later that morning waiting for her friends to pounce on her about Brandt. She'd gotten no calls last night. No texts. She was irritated and amused at the same time. They hadn't checked to see if she was okay, but it was probably because they hadn't wanted to bother her if she and Brandt were having fun.

Whatever fun was, to a woman her age.

Sitting on the couch eating a salad and watching a movie, apparently.

From her peripheral vision, she saw movement.

Alicia barreled across the room, then Rita joined her. They were making a beeline for Bonnie, and from their trajectory, it looked like the three of them would intersect about the time they reached Bonnie's door. Alicia had her cell phone to her ear, and Bonnie could read the words on her lips.

She's here.

Bonnie would bet the person on the other line was Sheila. Opening her office door, she hoped she could at least get her purse put away before the Inquisition descended upon her. She closed her desk drawer as Rita and Alicia filled the doorway.

"Well?" Alicia demanded shutting the door to contain the gossip.

Bonnie shook her head. "No."

Their excited expressions fell in unison.

Rita hurried across the room and gripped the edge of the desk. "Ah, come on, Bonnie. Please tell us what happened. We saw you two drive away in his Porsche." Her eyes sparkled. "His Porsche!"

"He obeyed the speed limit," Bonnie said defensively.

"At your request, I'm sure," Alicia observed.

"Where you'd go? His place? I bet he has a penthouse somewhere." Rita sighed. "It's just like a movie."

"They don't make movies about forty-something-year-old divorced mothers. At least not the kind of movies you're talking about." Bonnie sat back and watched her friends in amusement.

"Yeah. Movies about your age bracket tend to be about women killing their husbands for cheating on them—or being cougars."

"Is he younger than you?"

Bonnie shook her head in a refusal to answer.

"Where did you go?" Alicia asked.

"He took me home."

"Oh, my gosh. Your kids aren't there on Thursday night. What happened?"

"Nothing really. We watched a movie, and he went home."

"You watched a movie?"

"Yeah."

"What movie? A romantic comedy? Those are great date night movies."

"No. A war movie. *The Bridge on the River Kwai*."

They blinked at her like two owls. A knock sounded on the door, and Sheila slipped inside with a big smile.

"Might as well wipe that grin off your face." Alicia groused. "They watched a war movie at her house, then he went home."

Sheila looked at Bonnie for confirmation, but her smile remained. "How did it feel having a man in your house again?"

"Strange."

****

Bonnie settled in bed and closed her eyes hoping she could go to sleep, but doubted it would really happen. There'd been another argument with Kayla. She'd cut class today, and the only reason Bonnie had known was because of the cameras she'd installed in the house. When she'd seen Kayla on the camera feed, she'd hardly believed her eyes, so she'd called Kayla's cell phone and lied, saying the school had called her to find out why she wasn't there.

"I'm sick," she snapped.

She didn't sound sick. "Then why didn't the school call me to ask if you could check out? Where are you?"

"I'm home."

How did she get home? Did Rex take her? "Did you even go to school today?"

"Does it matter? I don't feel good."

"What doesn't feel good? Stomach? Head?"

Kayla huffed. "Everything. Leave me alone. I just want to go to sleep."

It was on the tip of Bonnie's tongue to lecture her some more, but the dejection in her daughter's tone stopped her. Throughout the morning, she'd kept the video feed on her computer and had seen Kayla in bed.

At lunch time, Bonnie had gone home and checked on her. Opening her bedroom door, Bonnie walked in the room and stood next to the bed. She touched a hand to Kayla's forehead.

No fever.

Kayla opened her eyes and cast a glare toward her.

"What's wrong, honey?"

"I told you, I'm sick. Just leave me alone."

"Did you and Rex get in a fight?"

Kayla turned over in bed with her back to her mother. The movement stung, like a rejection.

"Mama?" Curtis asked, bringing Bonnie's attention back to the present. He stood next to her bed, looking at her with those soulful eyes.

She scooted over to make room for him. "Yeah, babe?"

He picked up the pillow. "Can I lie down for a little while?"

"Sure. You can lie down on the bed."

"No. I like the floor." He settled down on the far side of her bed.

Bonnie moved to that side and peered down at him. "Want to talk about anything?"

His little boy sigh echoed through the room. She reached over and patted his head. "I love you. You know that?"

"Yeah. You have to though, 'cause you're our mom."

"I suppose, but I love loving you."

"Ugh. Can I go to sleep now?"

Bonnie smiled. "Yes." She closed her eyes and listened in the stillness to her son's breathing.

The next morning Bonnie congratulated herself. She'd found the company who had delivered office furniture to the office where David Bentley, or whoever the man was, had grilled her. The same company had delivered and picked up the rented furniture. Sheri Stillthorpe's name was on the account. That had been the secretary's name in the outer office. Bonnie had looked for the name in the employee database but hadn't found the woman. On Bonnie's lunch break, she'd visited the store and obtained a copy of the order form. Reading it, Bonnie smiled.

She had a phone number.

Once back in her office, she did a search and found it was a Virginia number. She called it.

"Hello?"

"Hi, may I speak to Sheri Stillthorpe, please."

There was a slight pause. "Whom should I say is calling?"

"This is Bonnie Moore. I work for the Kentucky

Commonwealth Retirement Systems. I'd like to send Ms. Stillthorpe some paperwork; may I have your address please?"

"What is this about?"

"Some furniture was rented and placed in a Kentucky office building. I need to send the bill of lading to her."

"You do, huh?" The woman on the other end chuckled briefly. "Miss Stillthorpe isn't available, but if you'll give me your telephone number, I'll call you back with an address to mail the bill of lading to."

"That would be great, and what's your...name?"

The line went dead, before Bonnie could finish her question. She walked out of her office to get a cup of coffee from the break room. The trip there and back couldn't have been more than five minutes. She entered her office and stopped.

A basketball in a Lucite cube sat on the shelf behind her desk.

It couldn't be. She strode over to it. The ball had signatures on it, including...Bonnie gasped. The governor's name.

Brandt. He'd been here. Had to have just been here since she knew that ball in a cube hadn't been here when she'd left for coffee.

She looked behind her attempting to catch a glimpse of him.

The thief had stolen the governor's championship ball and put it in her office.

****

The officer—Patton was what his nameplate said—looked at her quizzically. "No one asked you to wait in the lobby."

The elevator doors opened, and she and the two officers stepped out. "Yes. Sergeant Weeks called me and asked me to wait down in the lobby for you guys." Bonnie led the way to her office. The door was open, and she gasped.

"There is no—"

Bonnie glared at her bare shelf. "No Sergeant Weeks, right?"

"No ma'am."

She turned to the two men. "I'm sorry. I think I've wasted your time. There was a college championship ball in here, but it seems to have vanished."

They looked at her then around the walls of her office. "Do you want to tell us what happened?"

Bonnie sighed in frustration. "There was a ball in here that wasn't mine. It looked like the one in the governor's office. But it's not here now."

They were giving her let's-humor-the-crazy-woman stares.

Officer Patton cleared his throat. "Who do you think stole the ball, put it in here, then took it out again?"

Bonnie shook her head. "What's the point? I'm sure you have more important things to do than chase after phantoms." *Or ninjas, as the case may be.* She walked back out of the office.

They didn't follow her.

"Did you take the ball?"

"What? No!"

They stood inside her office and watched her. She walked back in the room. "I'm the one who called you about it. Why would I steal the ball, hide it, and then call you?"

"I don't know. Why would you?"

"I wouldn't."

"Then where's this ball?"

"I don't know. I suppose he took it after he made sure I saw it."

"Who's he?"

"Brandt Sherrod. He says he's a ninja."

"A what?"

"A ninja. Isn't that ridiculous?"

"Yes. Where's your ninja now?"

"He's not *my* ninja. I think it's as crazy as you do. Ninjas don't exist."

They didn't reply, but Officer Patton crooked his head as if he were deciding whether to call someone to bring a straitjacket.

Obviously, this was only going to mean trouble for her. She walked back to her desk. Sitting down, she folded her hands. "Look. Obviously, I'm the butt of someone's joke. I'm sorry that I brought you into this."

"We'll take your name and number, and if anything comes up, we will call you," the other policeman said.

He was placating her, Bonnie felt sure.

Instead of arguing with him, she nodded. "Thanks."

The policemen left, and Bonnie was about to get back to work when her telephone rang. It was Tammy, the receptionist from downstairs.

"Hi. You've got some flowers down here, and they're gorgeous."

Bonnie sat back in disbelief. "Flowers? I don't think so."

"Bonnie Moore. It says as clear as day."

Obviously it was a mistake. All of these interruptions were making work impossible. Walking around the desk, she went to sort out the mess. Downstairs she stood in front of a colorful bouquet of roses, lilies, and delphiniums cascading over a glass vase. It was gorgeous, but this couldn't be right.

Bonnie plucked the card from its holder.

My number is in your file. Brandt.

"Of all the arrogance! The audacity!"

"What? What does it say?" Tammy stood and craned her head attempting to read the card Bonnie had waved around in her rant.

Bonnie slapped the card down next to the vase and marched to the elevator. "Who's Brandt?" Tammy called after her. Bonnie didn't answer. She was too incensed.

It was nearly lunchtime when her friends entered the office with the offending flowers in hand.

"I don't want those in here," Bonnie said.

"Did you call him?" Rita asked.

"No, I did not, nor do I plan to."

Alicia set the vase on the corner of her desk. "Aw, come on, Bonnie. Call him. These are gorgeous, and he's obviously interested." She fingered the coral-colored petal of a rose.

"I'm not."

"Why not?"

"He's playing games, and I don't like that."

"Come on, honey. Live a little. Didn't he behave himself the other night at your house?"

"He attempted to solicit an invitation to my bedroom after plying me with drinks at the restaurant."

"*We* were plying you with drinks. Don't blame him for that."

Bonnie retrieved her purse from her desk. "Are we going to lunch? If so, the topic of Brandt is off-limits."

They responded with a chorus of groans.

****

Three days went by, and the flowers, sitting on her desk, still looked as fresh as the day they had arrived. A tender feeling tugged at her heart. He'd probably paid a lot for the flowers, an apology, she supposed, for pulling a stupid stunt like stealing the governor's basketball and placing it in her office and making her look like a fool in front of the police.

The telephone on her desk rang, and she picked it up. It was a summons from Vivian Walker.

What now?

When Bonnie arrived at the woman's office, the door was ajar. From inside, a man spoke, and Vivian laughed. Bonnie raised her hand and knocked on the doorframe.

"I bet that's Bonnie," Vivian said. She appeared at the door, her expression friendly and relaxed. She opened the door wide and stepped back. "Hi. Come on in."

Come on in?

Bonnie walked through the threshold spotting Vivian's vacant desk and the chair in front of it. She had enough clout that there was a little sitting area in the far corner. On a snow white love seat sat Brandt Sherrod in suit and tie. Bonnie looked back at Vivian, who had shut the door.

"Have a seat, Bonnie. You know Brandt," Vivian said as she herded her over to the sitting area.

Brandt didn't change his comfy pose.

Bonnie chose the chair furthest away from the snake. His eyes crinkled at the corners and his lips widened in a smile, which Bonnie didn't trust.

"What's going on?" Bonnie asked.

Chapter Eight

"I came to explain what's been going on and to apologize," Brandt said.

Bonnie hid her surprise.

"Brandt told me that he was behind the vice president of security office stunt, and why he did it."

"It was never my intention to cause any problems. In my work, I have to be sure there aren't any security issues so I just did a little investigating to be sure you were actually looking for Delores Park's beneficiary and it wasn't a front for something else."

"What is that work exactly?" Bonnie asked. "And how is it that you are able to steal property from the governor and get away with it?"

"I thought it was the lieutenant governor you were buddies with," Vivian purred.

Bonnie rolled her eyes. "Look. I don't care what business he's in, who he's friends with, or what line he's fed you. Don't you see he got access to our files, and he was able to put false information in there? That means our digital security is vulnerable. We deal with people's retirement benefits. If he can create a person in the employee database, he can probably access the financial records too."

"Oh, I don't think so. Those are much more secure. Besides, Brandt has assured me that it was an A security breach, and it was done with permission by the lieutenant governor."

"An A security breach? I've never heard of that." Bonnie turned to Brandt. "What did you do, make it up?"

"I'm sorry, Bonnie. I didn't mean to make any trouble.

I just had to be sure you were who you claimed to be."

"So, you were behind Sheri Stillthorpe and David Bentley squatting in the vacant offices upstairs?"

"Yes. They work with me."

"They work with you at your ninja company in Bellini, Kentucky."

"Well, we tend to be known as a consulting firm." He conceded.

Bonnie wasn't falling for his act. "That's a lot easier to believe than the ninja story."

He nodded with a twinkle in his eye. "Yeah, I know."

"So, Bonnie, this solves the mystery of who those people were and why they set up an office in the building," Vivian said.

Bonnie turned to her. "Which they had no business doing. Are you going to let him get away with this? Let's call the police right now."

Vivian shook her head. "No. He has clearance from way above my head. I've already checked out his story, and it's been verified."

"Really? I bet if you call tomorrow, the number will be disconnected." Bonnie knew now she had said it, Brandt would make sure it wasn't, making her look, once again, like an idiot.

Brandt arched an eyebrow at her but kept his quirky smile. He cut his gaze to Vivian, and so did Bonnie. Vivian was studying her. She looked at her watch then back at Bonnie.

"Why don't you two go out to lunch and sort this out?"

"What? No!"

"Yes, go ahead. But be back in an hour, all right?"

Brandt stood. "Thank you, Viv. I think that sounds like a great idea."

Bonnie put her hands on her hips. "It doesn't sound great to me. Why don't you go with him since you're so chummy."

Vivian tapped her chin. "Brandt, do you mind waiting

outside for Bonnie?"

"Not at all." He walked toward the exit. He had something tucked in his hand—tablet perhaps? Bonnie noticed Vivian watched his graceful stride across her office. Gross. She was at least ten years older than he was. The woman was a cougar. No doubt about it.

When the door closed behind him, Vivian turned toward her. "Go with him."

"I don't want to. Why don't *you* go with him?"

"Because even though he is extremely charming, he's also a little too smooth. Find out what you can. I want to know how he breached our computer system. You have a knack for computers. I think you can be very…beneficial for the Commonwealth. Find the back door, so we can close it. Do you understand?"

Bonnie huffed. "I'm not good at this."

Vivian pinned her with a suddenly serious expression. "You're very good at this. You're the only one who tried to blow the whistle on someone who not only breached our computer security, but was able to set up shop on a secure floor, and was unnoticed by anyone else. I don't like this at all, but he's got connections, and I wasn't able to do anything about it. I want to be sure this doesn't happen again. Got me?"

"Yes."

"Good. Take two hours if you need it."

"This is more than a lunch project. It took me a couple of months to find him, and he's just such a liar."

Vivian tucked her chin in. "This is top priority."

"Surely there is someone else you can bring in to find out."

"I just had the lieutenant governor call me and threaten my job, one of those offers-I-couldn't-refuse kind of thing. I don't like that, especially since I didn't vote for that clown. Do me a favor and help me find the gap, so I can close it."

"I'm no Mata Hari. This is crazy."

Vivian watched Bonnie for a moment. "No, you're not

a Mata Hari. He knows those types. He likes you, and he thinks you're all integrity and apple pie. I think he'll tell you how they got in the system. Just keep being who you are. You'll have him eating out of your hand."

"I don't think so."

"Bonnie, do you realize he met with me and disclosed his culpability in this little stunt because he thought your reputation was at risk? There was no other reason for him to come here today because no one really believed you. Until now."

"I think there's more to it."

"Perhaps there is. Good luck." She turned and propelled Bonnie toward the door. Opening it, Vivian motioned with her head for Bonnie to leave. The older woman's eyes sparkled with a hunger that worried and intrigued Bonnie.

Maybe Vivian herself had some Mata Hari in her.

Brandt was leaning against the wall with his arms folded across his chest a small black tablet tucked under one arm, starched shirt and classy tie, razor straight crease down his pants, and one leather Oxford crossed over the other—the epitome of suave business, except for that small bump on his nose that hinted at a darker side.

One side of his mouth crooked up in what some women would consider a flirty hint of a smile.

"So," Bonnie said as she took a few steps toward him. "Who thinks I'm all integrity and apple pie? Were those your words or hers?"

Brandt laughed softly. "Not apple pie. Not you."

"What's wrong with apple pie?" Not that Bonnie was a fan, but the description bothered her. It seemed so…domestic and wholesome.

"Somehow you don't strike me as the kind of person that likes to be compared to food. You're too practical for that nonsense."

Ugh. He made her sound so boring. But she probably was, which was why this fishing expedition was not going to work.

"Yeah, that's me. Practical Bonnie. I have to go and get my practical purse from my practical office." Bonnie walked past him to the stairwell. It was three flights down, but she was irritated enough to want to stomp down the stairs instead of having to share an elevator with the ninja.

He followed her, but she ignored him. When she reached her office and unlocked the door, he accompanied her into the room. She opened her desk drawer and withdrew her purse.

"Lemon," he said.

"What?" She walked past him then held the door so she could lock it after he left the room.

"If I were to compare you to a dessert, it would be lemon." He stood just behind her as she tested the knob to be sure it was locked, but it moved under her touch and the door opened.

"Gee, thanks. Lemon pie, a dessert that is sour and fattening."

"No. Not a pie, a tart."

Bonnie snorted. "Well, there's a first. Wait until I tell my daughter I got called a tart today. She thinks I'm a shriveled up old witch."

"She's young and your daughter. She doesn't see what I do."

"And you see a lemon tart. Now there's a line."

"Here's another one: a crisp outer shell, and on the inside a filling that is tangy and sweet blended together just right on the tongue." His voice reverberated just above her shoulder, his breath tickled her hair. She jiggled the key, but it wouldn't release from the lock. She bit her lip, determined not to get distracted by the effects of anything on anyone's tongue.

"Do you mind taking a few steps back? The lemon tart is trying to lock her office door against thieves and bandits."

****

Outside the building, Bonnie walked toward the garage.

"I'm parked over there," Brandt said from behind her.

"I'm driving." She tossed the words over her shoulder without pausing. Vivian might insist Bonnie eat lunch with Brandt, but she didn't say Bonnie couldn't get it to go and eat it in her office at her desk. That way Brandt could show her how he'd gotten into the Commonwealth's computer system.

She expected a fight, but in a few seconds he had caught up with her. They walked side by side on the walkway, and when they reached the garage, he reached in front of her and opened the door, then stood aside as she walked through the opening. She walked up one flight, and once again he reached in front of her and opened the door.

They walked without speaking toward her car. Bonnie paused before she reached it. She studied the man next to her. "Which one is mine?"

"Blue SUV." He held up his hands in a gesture of innocence. "Now don't look at me like that. It was in your carport when I was at your house the other night."

"Oh."

She pushed the button on her key ring, and the car chirped in response. He opened the driver's side door, and she hesitated just a moment before sitting down inside the car. She glanced around the interior of the car. There was a French fry, a Lego, and a ponytail holder on the passenger side floorboard. The rest of the car was in a similar state.

Welcome to my world, Brandt Sherrod.

"I decide where we go eat," Bonnie declared once he sat down and put on his seat belt.

Bonnie waited for him to argue. She knew his type.

Arrogant. Controlling. God's gift to women and all that.

Brandt turned to her. "Great. Do they serve lemon tarts?"

Bonnie couldn't help it. She laughed. Starting up the car, she backed it out of the parking space and followed the exit path through the garage.

I'm taking a man to lunch, and he isn't picking where.

Unless he was still going to try to influence her decision. Guy was never so subtle, but Alicia's husband would pout if he didn't get his way. Alicia talked about it frequently.

In ten minutes, Bonnie maneuvered the car into the parking lot of a local doughnut place. The owner was Greek, and a few years ago, he had expanded the kitchen and started serving gyros. Bonnie loved them, though the kids didn't like the idea of eating lamb so she didn't eat here often.

Once again, he held the door for her as she walked through. "Do you like Greek food?" She asked stepping over the threshold.

"Yes, though I didn't realize doughnuts qualified as Greek food."

Bonnie walked past the display of doughnuts behind the long counter and toward the corner that had a second menu. "Two gyros, please. To go." She glanced over her shoulder at Brandt. "Water okay with you to drink?"

"Sure."

"And two bottles of water."

Brandt pulled his wallet out and opened it.

"No," Bonnie said. "My treat." She handed her debit card to the cashier and noticed out of the corner of her eye that Brandt stepped away from her.

"Do you mind if I get us a few pastries?"

"Just so you know, they don't serve lemon tarts."

Brandt grinned widely. "They just did. Just so *you* know." He winked and turned to the shelves in front of him encasing doughnuts. "One of each, please. To go."

"What are going to do with that many doughnuts?"

"Probably share with your coworkers. We are going back to your office, aren't we?"

Bonnie sputtered. "Well, yes." How could he have known? She hadn't said anything to Vivian. She'd only thought it.

Soon they were back in the car with the boxes of doughnuts in the backseat next to the bag of gyros. She directed the car toward her office building. "How did you know I'd want to go back to work to eat?"

"Because you didn't want to go with me in the first place, and you want to be able to interrogate me on your own turf. It gives you an advantage that way."

"Who says I'm going to interrogate you?"

"I say so, because you want to know if that basketball really belonged to the governor and how I got it in and out of your office. You probably have a few other questions, but I imagine those two are pretty high up on your list."

"Why don't you tell me right now."

"Yes, it was the governor's ball. I carried it in the building in a copier paper box. I picked the lock of your office and put it on the shelf. After you called the police, I figured I needed to get it out quickly, so—"

"How did you know I called the police?"

"I have a police scanner."

"Where is the ball now?"

"It's back at the capitol building where it belongs."

"How do you beat security at the capitol building?"

"It's my job to sneak in and out of places undetected."

"To break the law."

"If it makes you feel any better, most of the places where I go without permission by the owner are owned by people who are themselves breaking laws or breaking treaties."

"Treaties," Bonnie said in disbelief. "As in international espionage?"

"I don't work for the government. You know that. You've seen my tax return."

"Yes, I saw it, and I still don't believe it. I don't understand how you are getting away with lying and…and stealing."

"I didn't steal the ball. I borrowed it."

"It's stealing if you didn't ask permission."

"How do you know I didn't?"

"Did you?"

"I asked permission to attempt to break in the capitol.

I let them use it as a test of their security. And as you know, they failed, so they have some work to do."

Bonnie mulled over his words. Could she believe him? And if so, would he also disclose to her how he had been going in and out of their office building like it was his own house?

"I want to know how you got by our security."

Brandt laughed. "No offense, but your building doesn't have any security."

"We have locked doors and a security system."

"None of which have been updated in at least ten years. It's a joke."

"We have security guards."

"Yes. They did such a *great* job of keeping track of me."

Bonnie shot him a glance. An expression of annoyance crossed his face.

"Shouldn't you be happy about that?" she asked.

"It was too easy. I felt like I was in a Laurel and Hardy routine. And anyway, even if their presence did deter someone, they aren't there 24-7. They come in shortly before the building is open and leave half an hour after office hours. Housekeeping works eight to midnight without any security whatsoever, and they're paid minimum wage with access to every office."

"What are you saying? That our housekeeping service people aren't trustworthy?"

"I'm saying that type of set-up creates vulnerability."

"It's not like they can get into our computers. Each employee has to have a log-in code. Otherwise you can't get on."

Bonnie didn't volunteer she accessed files she didn't have clearance for. It wasn't her fault people like Marla rarely logged out of their computers when they left their desks.

"Yeah? Except I didn't have a log-in code, and I had no trouble getting in at all."

"Well, you're a professional."

"You think it's only amateurs who would try to break into the Commonwealth's retirement files?"

Bonnie sighed. "Good point." She turned the steering wheel to the right, toward the river.

"Where are we going?"

"To Riverfront Park. I don't like being predictable."

Bonnie slowed the car as it bumped over the railroad tracks and crossed through the gate of the floodwall, built before the locks on the river. She followed the road down to the riverside and parked. Cutting the engine, she released her seatbelt.

"When was the last time you had a picnic?" she asked.

He shook his head.

"Never?"

"I've eaten take-out food in my car plenty of times."

She opened the door and exited the car. Opening the trunk, she picked up a plastic-wrapped package. She heard Brandt open the back door. When he rounded the back of the car, he held a box of doughnuts and the bag with their gyros and bottled water.

"Is that a table cloth?" Brandt asked, his eyebrows high in surprise.

"There are a lot of picnic tables around, but I don't trust the cleanliness of the surfaces, so I usually keep a few of these in the trunk. They're disposable." She shut the trunk, and together they walked toward a grassy copse where several wooden tables sat.

"Wow. You believe in being prepared."

"That's the mom in me."

"What else do you keep in the trunk?"

Uh-huh. I'm the one doing the interrogating. "What do you keep in your trunk?"

He laughed, that low sexy laugh she'd heard a few times now. If he thought he was going to distract her with it, he had another think coming. Bonnie ignored the little shift of her heart in her chest. She was too old to fall for his Casanova routine, even if he did look handsome in his suit and loosened tie with the tiny top button undone.

Bonnie stopped at a table and tore open the plastic encasing the tablecloth. Brandt placed the boxes and the sack on the bench.

"So, what is in your trunk?"

"Nothing." He took the end of the cloth when she shook it out and helped her spread it across the table. Bonnie ignored the domesticity of the act. He was a rolling stone, obviously, playing a part. What did he want from her anyway?

"Not even a stray French fry?"

He smiled. "I rarely eat in there."

"No. You keep the fries in the trunk, so you're not tempted to eat them on the way home."

"Why would I take food home to eat it?"

He lived alone. She had already figured that. Everything about him screamed loner. "Where is home?"

The cloth was in place. He removed the bottles and set them on the table. "I see why they call you the Bloodhound."

Bonnie let that pass. "So do you live in Bellini, Kentucky, the same place where your home office is?"

Next he removed two of the wrapped gyros and handed one to her. "I thought you said Bellini was made up."

"No, I said the zip code was fabricated." Bonnie took the gyro and settled down on the bench across from him. "I've never been to a town with a letter in the zip code. I'd like to go there, although interestingly I can't seem to find it on my GPS or any social media map site I've looked on, or even my atlas."

He unwrapped the food and studied the meat and vegetable wrapped pita. "They were generous with the onions, weren't they?"

"They're mild."

He bit into it, and Bonnie noted the expression of pleasure on his face.

"It's good, isn't it?"

He nodded as he chewed. Then he spoke. "Very

good."

"Do you live in Bellini?"

"I don't stay home much. Not a lot of ninja jobs in Appalachia."

Bonnie scoffed at his non-answer. "I just want to know where a town is that doesn't seem to exist anywhere but on your tax form."

"I could take you there."

"I suppose I'd have to be blindfolded for the trip." She bit into her own gyro, loving the taste of it. A dollop of tzatziki sauce fell on the open wrapper on the table, and she wiped the gyro through it before taking another bite.

"Yeah, I can see you agreeing to that."

They ate for a few moments in silence. Bonnie drank from the bottle of water. "Could we get there and back in a day?" she asked, picking back up their conversation

"Yes."

"Do I need a passport?"

"It's Kentucky. You don't even cross a state line."

"Except Kentucky only uses numbered zip codes. I can't believe you've been able to get away with this, for years, I bet."

"Get away with what?"

"Whatever you're doing. Breaking and entering. Stealing. Lying. Trespassing. Impersonating people."

"I do a really good impersonation of Sean Connery. Want to hear it?"

"No." Some of the sauce had dropped on his tie. "You've got food on your tie."

He looked down. "Well, there goes my suave image," he said in a convincing Sean Connery voice.

Bonnie handed him a napkin and watched him wipe at the spot. When the stain remained, he took off the tie, laid it on the table, and released another button on his shirt. Bonnie strayed a glance to the triangle of skin he had uncovered. It was just a small patch—that indentation at the base of his neck, but it felt intimate, as if he were revealing to her a piece of himself that most people hadn't seen.

"Would you say you've slept with more than fifty women in your lifetime?" It was a bold question to ask, sure, but Bonnie wasn't getting anywhere with the other questions.

Brandt stilled, his dark gaze fell on her drawing open something inside her like the petals of a morning glory in the sunshine. Bonnie resisted the feeling. She couldn't get distracted by his sex appeal.

"I wouldn't say that to you."

"Well, James Bond sleeps with a lot of women. It's part of his appeal, I think."

"I was always more intrigued by the cool spy gadgets."

"Which ones did you use to break into the retirement system?"

He turned his head and looked out toward the river. "Just when I think you're flirting with me, you go back to treating me like a benefits case."

"When you can't sneak into some place in secret, you use your charm to walk right through the front door."

He nodded. "That about sums me up." He took the last bite of the gyro and balled up the wrapper. He drank half of the water in the bottle and wiped his mouth with a napkin.

"But it's not all of you. I'd like to meet the person who Delores Parks knew, the one who made it home by curfew and captured the heart of a retired teacher, so much so that she wanted to make him her beneficiary."

Bonnie watched his profile. He wasn't going to give it up. But he might yet tell her how he had gotten into the computer system. He reached inside his jacket and pulled out a pair of sunglasses, which he put on. Was this his way of covering up so she couldn't see the expression in his eyes?

"Is the sun bothering you?"

"A little. My pupils don't dilate well. It's a condition I've had since a kid. It's why I can work so well in the dark, but after being outside in the sun for a while, I tend to get headaches."

Bonnie digested that piece of personal information, thinking his disclosure was a victory of sorts.

"Do you have a headache now?"

"Not yet. I can usually feel one coming on."

"Should you take something for it?"

He smiled. "I'm touched that you're concerned."

The turn of the conversation began to feel too close. Bonnie decided to get back on track. "If you help me with the security at work, then it will protect the benefits of people like your foster mom."

"You're going about this the wrong way, you know." He pivoted his body and stood up. He began to gather the refuse from their picnic, and she wrapped up her unfinished gyro.

"What do you mean?" She grabbed the edge of the table and swung her legs over the bench to stand. She brushed any dirt off her skirt.

"My motivation to help you. You should appeal to my baser instincts."

Glancing behind her, she brushed the back of her skirt too. "I fed you. It doesn't get more base than that."

"It *definitely* could be more base than that."

His silky tone snagged her attention, and she looked at him. His lips turned up in a sexy smile that curled her toes. She tamped down the teen yearning and shot him her best I-mean-business glare. "The charm doesn't work on me. I've had my heart stepped on too many times."

"I suppose I have to work harder then."

"Or give me what I want."

"Can I give you a rain check? I need to go."

"Go?"

"Yes." He reached into the pocket of his slacks and pulled out his cell phone. His face turned to the screen then at her.

"All right." She began to walk toward the car.

"I'm not going to ride back with you."

Bonnie turned to him. "Why not? Did I offend you?"

"No. I need to take care of a few things. Close by."

"Oh." Bonnie ran through a mental list of buildings close by and what business he might have in any of them. There was a federal building two blocks up.

"You don't mind taking the doughnuts back, do you?"

Bonnie shrugged and headed toward the car. "I suppose not. I hate to take credit for your bribe though."

"Funny. I'll see you later, okay?"

"Sure."

Bonnie unlocked the car and opened the door. Sitting down on the driver's seat, she craned her head over her shoulder and saw the doughnut boxes. But that wasn't all. Brandt's jacket and his tablet were also back there.

She exited the car. "Hey, you forgot—"

Where was he? Bonnie looked around the park. He had been standing just beyond the picnic table. The floodwall separating the park from the rest of the town was at least fifty yards away. He couldn't have walked there that quickly. Could he?

Oh, well. She eyed the tablet and couldn't keep the grin off her face.

He'd show up again when he realized he left his jacket and tablet with her.

In the meantime, it might be fun to see how secure *his* security was.

Chapter Nine

Brandt eased through a stairwell door seconds before it clicked shut and sprinted up three flights of stairs to another door. He passed his phone over the electronic pad, and the lock clicked. He had four minutes to change clothes and get to the roof. Slipping into a storage room, he toed off his shoes and slipped on the scrubs neatly folded on the shelf. With his shoes back on, he grabbed two disposable shoe covers and a cap.

With a minute to spare, he was in the helicopter attending a no-publicity patient who needed security more than she needed the EMT even if the hospital didn't agree. He nodded to the pilot, and they lifted off. Shielding her with his body, he scanned the nearby buildings and the tree line as they continued their ascent. By air, they'd be at their destination in an hour, then he'd be flown back to Andersonville—at his request.

His unscheduled lunch with Bonnie Moore had made him really scramble to keep to his timeframe. Her unexpected picnic location had been providential. He couldn't have planned it better, actually. Because he was still driving the Spyder, and as much as he loved the car, it stuck out like a sore thumb. But not when she insisted on driving so he was able to leave it on the street in a much busier location. He'd get a ticket, but if anything, that just provided an alibi for where he was if it ever came up. All he'd have to do was show back up at her building and kill a little time with her in her office.

Once his project was complete, he sat in the copilot chair and scrolled through his cell phone while they flew over the wooded landscape of rural Ohio.

What was this?

Four alerts that someone was attempting to access his tablet. The fifth notice acknowledged she'd gotten in.

Wow. She's good.

She'd never get past the second firewall—not unless she somehow could mimic his encoded biological rhythm and had a perfect replica of his palm print with the embedded chip, a technology his company used for added security.

Still.

He wouldn't have thought she could have been able to get as far as she'd gotten. Sheri kept telling him he needed to be more careful. Guess she had a point.

By five minutes after four, he was back in his suit and was climbing the stairs to her floor. He dialed her office number, and it rang twice before she picked up.

"Hello, Ms. Moore."

She paused before responding. She was still working on getting in his tablet. He'd bet his Spyder on it.

"Hi."

Brandt had yet to hear her call him by his first name.

"Do you know who this is?"

"I know who you've told me you are... Brandt Sherrod."

Bingo.

"I'm on my way to your office."

"All right. I'll meet you in the lobby."

"Try again, Bonnie. I'm about twenty feet away from your office." He exited the stairwell passage way and strode across the carpet. Her door shut ahead of him, and he chuckled before hitting end on his cell. He stopped and knocked. A minute went by before she opened it.

Guilt flushed her cheeks, and she didn't quite meet his eyes. "I thought I told you not to come into secure sections of our office building without an escort."

"Well, you didn't say that exactly." He leaned against her doorframe, and she took a step backward. "I left some things in your car. Did you happen to see them?"

She turned on her heel and marched to her desk. Skirting its corner, she settled on her chair and straightened some papers then set them aside. Brandt walked into the room. "Is it okay if I shut the door?"

"Sure."

The door snicked closed behind him, and he held the back of the chair in front of her desk and pushed it back a few inches before sitting on it. "Are there any doughnuts left?"

"I... I haven't checked lately."

I'll just bet you haven't. You've been too busy, you little sneak.

"So, did you find anything of mine in your car?"

She squirmed a bit, then he saw her shoulders straighten. She was composing herself.

"As a matter of fact, yes. Your jacket." She raised her hand and pointed to the corner, where it hung from a hanger on a coat tree.

He nodded but didn't follow her gesture with his gaze. Instead he watched her and waited.

The blush staining her cheeks deepened. She opened her desk drawer and withdrew his tablet. "This too."

He dropped his gaze to it, then back to her face.

"Great. I'm glad it was in good hands."

"Does it really matter?"

"What do you mean?"

Her gaze flicked to him, and the tension dropped from her expression. A self-deprecating smile creased her mouth. "I tried to get into it, okay? But I only got as far as your games, so good job on your security. It was dumb of me to think I could access it. You being a self-proclaimed ninja, and all."

"Ninjas haven't been about digital and electronic security until the last few years or so. I'm a little too set in my ways to be on the cusp of this cloud information security. You know what they say about old dogs and new tricks."

"You're a has been," she said in a disparaging tone. "At forty-one."

"Apparently."

"So, what will you do?"

Brandt shrugged. "Work until they put me out to pasture, or I get too old and crippled to slip in and out of places. I have to stay limber for some of these jobs, and it's not as easy as it used to be." He stood and approached her desk. "So, you want me to show you how I accessed the Commonwealth files?"

Her startled gaze flew to his. "Really?"

"I'd like to set a couple of conditions first." Coming to the side of the desk, he perched on the edge of it. "Make a deal, as it were."

"What?"

"I want you to help me with something."

Her eyes flashed at him. "I'm not doing anything illegal."

"Not illegal. I want to find someone. You're really good at that."

"Who is it?"

"I only have a copy of a birth certificate. I know the last time I saw him. He might have been adopted."

Bonnie shook her head. "It could be impossible to find him. It's a start that you have the birth certificate, but unless the adoptive parents and the child have registered with some of the adoption contact sites, you're probably not going to have any luck."

"You could find this person." Brandt tried to temper his excitement, but she was good at finding people. She had found *him*.

"Who is this person to you, Brandt? Because I'm telling you, if this is something dangerous that's going to put my family in harm's way, I just can't be a part of it."

"It's not. It's just this little project that I've been working on, and I keep hitting dead ends on it."

She sighed and reached over, putting her hand on the computer mouse and moving it across the desk's surface.

"Bonnie?" he murmured, allowing the appeal in his heart to color his tone. "You could find this guy, and in exchange, I'll help you close the security holes here."

He watched her fingers toy with the mouse, caress it.

"I'd really like to work with you." He dropped his voice a little more, and her lips parted. Her blue eyes met his, and he saw there her capitulation.

Oh, yes. He had her. Right where he wanted her.

Brandt leaned toward her, moving in to seal the deal. It was slight, but she swayed in his direction. It was going to be sweet, he knew.

Movement from the computer monitor drew her attention, and her back straightened. Her chair squeaked as she focused on whatever was happening on the screen.

"*Ooof!* I knew it. I knew it!" She balled up her fist and pounded it on the desktop, and with the other hand, she moved the mouse and clicked it rapidly.

"Bonnie? What's wrong?"

She wrenched open a drawer and pulled out her purse.

Standing up, she hoisted her purse straps over her shoulder. "I can't play spy with you. We're out of toilet paper, and I've got a juvenile delinquent trying his best to make me a grandmother at forty-one."

She shoved back her chair and marched across the office and didn't even look back at him as she headed for the door. Fury rolled off her, and Brandt wondered what in the world had turned her madder than a wet hen so quickly.

He settled in the chair Bonnie had just vacated watching with interest the computer screen. Three pictures of the inside of a house—two entryways and a bedroom.

From his evening spent with her, he recognized the inside of her home.

Brandt grinned as two teenagers walked into the bedroom, shut the door, and immediately started kissing. *Bonnie Moore, you conniving mother, putting a video camera in your daughter's bedroom.* The woman's brilliance impressed him. Not an easy thing to do in his line of work.

Yes.

He had found the woman who would help him find his brother.

****

That lying little….

Even in her mind, Bonnie couldn't finish the sentence.

Her daughter! Her daughter was probably having sex with that little piece of crap right now. In Bonnie's house! *What if she gets pregnant?* No way that jerk would even think about practicing safe sex. He'd have to actually have a brain in his head instead of in his….

Had she already been having sex with him?

No!

The images on her computer screen played over in her mind. That wasn't a first time kind of interaction. Maybe she was pregnant already. What if she had some kind of venereal disease? Rex had probably slept with half of the school. *Oh, Kayla, what are you thinking? You used to have some common sense, girl.*

Blue lights flashed at her from behind, and a siren invaded her brain.

Great! This is all I need. I don't have time for this. I've got to get to my house now.

Bonnie pulled to the side of the road and jumped out of the car even before the police officer had opened his door.

"Please!" she said as he opened his door with his hand on his holster. "My daughter. She's at my house. If you want to give me a ticket, okay, but can you just wait until I get home?"

"Is your daughter in danger?"

"She and her…boyfriend are…were… She's only fifteen. They're at my house, and he's…he's… I can't… I'm sorry. Can you just follow me and let me get there? I swear, I'll pay the ticket, but—"

"Where do you live?"

Bonnie rattled off her address to him.

"Okay. Follow me."

Then Bonnie was back in her car following the police car with lights and siren going. The officer pulled in front of the house, and Bonnie swerved into the driveway nearly hitting the pole in the carport. Somehow she was already at the front door. She turned the knob, but it was locked.

Where are my keys?

"Ma'am? Calm down." The policeman stood next to her. "You're here now. We'll get your daughter."

Bonnie took a shuttering breath, then another. She nodded and walked to the car. It was idling, and the driver door was open. Bending inside, she turned the ignition and pulled out the keys. She grasped the handle of her purse and stepped away from the car, shutting the door as she did so.

The uniformed man knocked loudly on the front door. Bonnie surmised he did this because it was some protocol he was following.

Allow the horny teenagers to get dressed before he busts down the door.

He waited on her porch watching her. He was young—around twenty-five, she guessed. She could be his mother.

He reached forward and pressed the door bell, then knocked again. When Bonnie reached the door, she inserted the key in the lock and turned it. The policeman stepped in front of her and walked into the foyer.

"This is Officer Patton of the police department. Is anyone home?" he called. Turning his head toward Bonnie, he asked, "What's your daughter's name?" He continued walking into the living room, and she followed.

"Kayla." Bonnie said, then, "Kayla? Where are you?"

Kayla stepped into the living room from the hallway door. Bonnie noted her round eyes and startled expression. "Mom? What's wrong?"

"What are you doing home?"

"I... I didn't go to band."

Bonnie marched past the officer. "Obviously. Where is he?"

Something flashed in her eyes. "What?"

"Rex. Where is he? Still in your bedroom?" Bonnie stalked down the hall to her daughter's room. The door was

110

open. The rumpled covers on the bed drew her gaze. *Grrrr.*

"Mom! Are you kidding me? You called the police because you thought Rex was here?"

"He was here. I can smell his stench." Bonnie rounded on her daughter. "What did he do, run out the back door when he heard the siren?"

Hatred marred her face. "I can't believe you called the cops!"

"I should have him arrested for having sex with a minor!"

"You always think the worst of us. You're crazy, and I hate you!" She brushed past Bonnie and attempted to shut the door.

Bonnie stepped in the way. "I want your phone. Now." The door ricocheted off her arm and hit the wall.

"No!"

Bonnie walked in the room and looked around for the cell. There it was on the dresser. Bonnie headed toward it, but Kayla beat her to it and grabbed it.

Bonnie held out her hand. "Give it to me right now."

Kayla raised her hand and threw it, hitting Bonnie under her eye. Then the policeman was in between them, his back to Bonnie. "You're coming with me."

Bonnie touched her throbbing cheek. "You're not arresting her."

He didn't reply as he escorted Kayla out of the room.

"I hope he does. I'd rather be in jail then put up with you!" Kayla yelled from the hallway.

Bonnie bent down and picked up the cell phone. She heard a short tone, then Officer Patton's voice. "Request a 24 for teen or adult male in vicinity of 1808 Hoover's Mill Road and a possible escort from the same address after the sweep."

A voice responded. "Can you give a description?"

"37."

"10-4."

"He's not here!" Kayla shouted. "He's nowhere around here."

My God. He might actually arrest her.

Officer Patton spoke, but Bonnie couldn't make out his words, only his low tone.

"No! I won't!" Kayla said, desperation lacing her voice.

Bonnie sat down on the carpeted floor and leaned her back against the dresser. She brought her knees up and hugged her legs for a moment before letting them sprawl out in front of her.

How had they gotten to this point? What had she done wrong?

Kayla's phone dinged, and Bonnie looked at the screen.

Rex.

All clear?

Bonnie put in her override code and texted him back.

Yeah

"Come out. Come out wherever you are," she murmured.

In a moment, he texted back. *No good. 2 cop cars. 2nite?*

Yeah. Come by.

Usual time?

Fury bubbled in Bonnie. *Yep.*

It would seem she'd be spending the night in Kayla's room to await the date. Other thoughts ran rampant through her mind. Vivian's plan for Bonnie to find out how Brandt had gotten into their security system. Her picnic lunch with him. His disappearance. Then his reappearance outside of her office door as she frantically hid his tablet. His amusement when she admitted she'd tried to break into it. His proposal to her if she helped him find someone. Crazy. He made his living in covert operations. What made him think she could help him, unless he was playing games with her. Was he? And could she help him, or was it something that might get her in trouble, or worse, put her family at risk? He said it wouldn't, but she couldn't trust him, could she? He made his living lying and sneaking around. At least, it *seemed* he made his living that way.

Footsteps sounded down the hallway. Bonnie rose to

her feet shortly before Kayla and the police officer entered the room.

Kayla's stubborn expression demonstrated the policeman had not been able to elicit any remorse from her. Bonnie looked from one to the other.

"So far, the units patrolling the neighborhood have not spotted any persons of interest."

'I'm sure that's because he spotted their cars first."

"If he shows up, you may call 911. We'll be glad to come back out here."

"Thank you."

Kayla glared at the far wall.

"Would you like me to take Kayla in for assault?"

"No, of course not. She has band practice."

Officer Patton grinned. "I could take her to band practice for you."

Bonnie smiled. "That's very tempting."

"What do you say, Kayla? Want to know what it feels like to ride in the back of a cruiser?"

"No, sir."

"Do you have anything you want to say to your mother?"

"I'm sorry for hitting you with my cell phone. It was an accident, and I didn't mean to do it."

The defiant tone accompanying the words led Bonnie to believe her daughter wasn't sincere. Still. At least she had acknowledged the injury. Bonnie suppressed the urge to touch her throbbing cheek. She waited for an apology for ditching band practice and sneaking her boyfriend in the house when she knew she wasn't supposed to, but the words didn't come.

"Thank you, Officer Patton." Bonnie shook his hand. "Let's go, Kayla. If we hurry up, you can make the last forty minutes."

The girl turned around and headed down the hall.

Bonnie and Officer Patton exchanged glances before they followed her.

Kayla didn't speak during the ride to band practice.

Bonnie checked the air conditioner. The frigid air in the car had little to do with the car, she knew. When she pulled into the parking lot next to the field, Kayla opened the door.

"I'll be here when you're done," Bonnie said.

Kayla huffed but otherwise didn't respond.

Too bad, chickie. If I could trust you, I wouldn't have to waste my time babysitting you.

Her cell phone rang, caller ID stated it was a call from Bellini, Kentucky.

Well, what do you know? The cell phone company acknowledges Bellini, Kentucky. Bonnie smiled and answered.

"Hello."

"Hi. It's Brandt. Everything okay?"

"Not really, but everyone is where they are supposed to be right now, except for me."

"And where are you supposed to be?"

"Work. You're not still in my office, are you?"

"No. Although, you didn't log off your computer. I could have done all kinds of damage after you left."

"We both know you don't need me logged in to get into the system."

"I did log you off, and you're welcome."

Bonnie watched the teens on the field.

"Do you want to talk about it?"

She knew he wasn't referring to her computer. "I think my daughter's boyfriend has been sneaking in her room at night."

"Would you like me to take care of it?"

The unexpected offer took Bonnie by surprise. "What are you going to do? Make him disappear?"

"I'm a ninja. Not the Mafia. I can watch your house, and if he shows up, I can make sure he doesn't get in."

"By doing what? Hurting him a little? Or a lot." Even as Bonnie said it, she wasn't so sure she was joking.

"He's a minor, right?"

"Just barely."

"Do you trust me to keep him away from your

daughter?"

"You wouldn't really hurt him, would you?"

"I'm a professional. Physical confrontation means I've exhausted all other options."

Bonnie sighed. "I'm just so tired of having to keep watch every moment, you know?"

He was silent for a moment. "I'll keep watch tonight."

At a few minutes past midnight, a text came across on Bonnie's cell phone.

Bellini, Kentucky, again.

Situation under control. Sleep well.

Chapter Ten

The next morning, Kayla's attitude hadn't improved. She didn't speak, didn't eat breakfast, and went and sat in Bonnie's car fifteen minutes before they usually left for school.

Andy stood at the kitchen door and looked out of the window at the car parked in the carport. "How come she's just sitting there?"

"She's waiting for all of us to get in the car and go to school."

He bit his Pop-Tart as he watched her. "You can forget me ever getting a girlfriend if they make you want to go to school," Andy declared.

Curtis came over and stood next to his brother. He waved to his sister.

Andy laughed and turned to Bonnie. "She just put the sun cover on the windshield."

"Boys, get away from the window and finish getting ready." Bonnie knew the ride was going to be tense enough without Kayla's brothers irritating her more than she was already.

When they settled in the car, Bonnie removed the sun shield without comment. She drove to the elementary school to drop the boys off. A light mist of rain began to fall.

"Bye, Mom," Andrew said as he climbed out of the car.

"Put your hood on, honey. It's raining. Love you, Andy. Have a good day."

Curtis unclicked his seatbelt but didn't move. Bonnie watched him in her rearview mirror. His gaze rested on the back of his sister's head.

"Hope you have a good day, Kayla," he said.

She didn't answer.

Bonnie turned in her seat. "That's sweet, Curtis. I'm sure Kayla appreciates it. Go on and get inside, okay?"

His head dropped a little. "Okay, Mom."

"I love you. Have a good day. See you tonight."

He slide across the seat. "Love you, too, Mom. Love you, Kayla."

No response from his sister. He closed the door and walked toward the building dragging his backpack along the walkway. Bonnie resisted the urge to roll the window down and tell him to put it on before it got wet. A teacher who stood near the door motioned to him and spoke. She must have said what Bonnie had been thinking because Curtis picked up the backpack.

Bonnie shifted the car into drive, checked over her shoulder, and pulled into traffic. "You know, Kayla. I know you're angry and upset, but I wish you would not take it out on your brothers. They don't have anything to do with this."

"Yeah? *They* didn't have you sleeping in their room on the floor."

"I just wanted to be sure you were okay."

"I'm not okay. I need privacy. Why can't you give me my space?"

"Because you're not making good choices right now."

"Why don't you call the cops again. Have me arrested."

"I could have had you arrested yesterday, but I didn't."

"What do you want? A medal? I'll nominate you for mother of the year for taking away my phone, not letting me see my boyfriend, and invading my privacy."

"You're having sex with him, aren't you?"

"That's none of your business!"

"Yes, it is. I'm your mother, and you are too young to be dating Rex, and you're definitely too young to be having sex. Is he using condoms, at least?"

"Quit trying to act like you know what's going on, Mom. Things aren't like they were when you were my age."

"Yeah, back when I was your age, it was a disgrace to get pregnant in your teens. People actually got married before they had kids. What a horrible practice."

"I'm not pregnant! But the way you talk, you want me to be."

"I don't want you to be. Girls who have babies in their teens have—"

"Would you spare me the lecture just once? I heard it all yesterday from the cop." Her voice had softened. If she were still yelling, Bonnie wouldn't have felt so uneasy as she pulled the car into the driveway of the high school. "Maybe I should start riding the bus."

Bonnie didn't reply, although several comebacks flew through her mind. All of them adding pressure and heat to the simmering volcano between mother and daughter.

Bonnie drove the path toward the entrance. Her foot pressed the brake when the car arrived at the portico.

"I hope you have a good day. I love you, Kayla."

Her daughter left the car without a word.

Bonnie arrived at work, her thoughts still swirling with what to do about Kayla. This wasn't going to end well, and no matter what, Bonnie seemed powerless to stop it.

When she walked by Charles Brewer's office, he called her inside. He leaned back against his desk with his arms crossed.

"What's wrong?" She asked.

"Field assignment." He picked up a folder and handed it to her. "Vivian says there's a car waiting for you at the east entrance."

"A car? Why can't I drive myself?"

He shrugged.

"How long will I be gone? I've got kids to pick up at five. Maybe sooner."

He shrugged again.

Bonnie opened the folder.

Benjamin and Associates, Bellini, Kentucky. "Okay.

Thanks, Mr. Brewer."

Bonnie turned and walked out of his office, taking her cell phone and calling the number that Brandt had called and texted her from yesterday.

"Good morning. How's Mama doing today?"

Brandt's question caused Bonnie's skin to tingle. For the first time since she awoke, the burden of motherhood lightened. "Apparently, I'm going to be nominated for mother of the year, but I think she was being sarcastic when she said it."

"Teenagers do sarcasm well, don't they?"

"Masters of it. You know why I'm calling, right?"

"Tell me."

"Vivian is sending me to Bellini, Kentucky, today. At your request, I'm sure."

"I'm sure, although you're handling the assignment better than I anticipated."

"You kept that hoodlum out of my house last night. I owe you. I need to be back by four o'clock. Can you make sure that happens?"

"We'll have to cross state lines."

"You said it was in Kentucky."

"Yeah, but the closest airport is in Ohio. Flying is the fastest way there and back. If you agree to fly, I can have you back by four."

Bonnie had been walking to elevator. She paused midstride.

"Bonnie?" Brandt asked.

"Yes?"

"Will you trust me to make sure the mother of your children arrives back safely today at the appointed time?"

Don't do it. A voice cautioned her. *He's shown himself to be a liar.*

But my daughter slept in her bedroom last night without anyone bothering her except me.

"Okay."

****

"Ready?"

Brandt sat back on a leather seat in the back of a small, but plush airplane. Bonnie had plowed him with questions about whose it was. *Not his.* How he was able to borrow it and a pilot at a moment's notice. *Favor from a friend.* If he had planned for them to fly all along. *Yes, but plan B had been to drive the Spyder if she wasn't willing to cross the ten miles into Ohio.*

Bonnie felt the vibrations of the plane's engine through the seat. The plane taxied down the runway and was soon in the air. Bonnie watched out the window at the overcast sky and the rain hitting the port window. She craned her head, looking down for the Ohio River or any other landmark, but the clouds occluded everything.

"You're very clever. Now I have no way of knowing if we are still in Kentucky or where Bellini is."

Brandt smiled. "It's all about keeping to your timeline. Ninja swear." He held up his hand in what might have been a pledge.

"What happened last night?" Bonnie had wondered since his text to her shortly after midnight.

"A boy approached the house. I discouraged him from entering, and he left."

"Discouraged how?"

"Well, the thing about ninja work is you want to intercede without being detected. If it appeared to this kid that the bushes underneath your daughter's window tripped him and he got tangled up in their branches, then that's what happened. If then, on his second attempt, he thought a neighborhood dog might have come by and threatened him so that he ran away, then got picked up by a police cruiser, well, that was fortunate timing."

Bonnie pumped her fist in celebration. "Yes! Now, there's a police report of him in the vicinity. That's wonderful."

Brandt nodded. "They didn't keep him, but they did make a report, and he didn't attempt it again."

"Did you watch the house all night?"

"I told you I would keep watch last night. I stayed until

dawn, the end of my shift."

"You've been up all night?"

"Comes with the territory. Ninjas tend to function best at night. Darkness is our ally."

"I stayed in her room all night. I didn't hear anything."

"Not even a seventeen-year-old whimpering at the growls of a canine?"

Bonnie laughed. "I could kiss you."

Brandt's head crooked as he studied her, his eyes darkened a shade. "All right."

The unexpected comment caused her heart to skitter. He was kidding, right? She shook her head, and his hand reached over toward hers. With one finger, he trailed a line from her fingertip of her middle finger to her wrist. Then he nudged her hand over his and held it. In a fluid movement, he slid from the chair beside her and knelt in front of her.

"I didn't mean that I would...ummm," Bonnie whispered, then lost what she was about to say when he brought her fingers to his lips and kissed the end of each one.

"So you mean that you wouldn't?"

"I don't know."

"Could you, would you on a plane? In the air, In the rain?" His eyes were mesmerizing. Bonnie closed her own attempting to break the spell. She pulled her hand away.

"You're not serious." Finding some sanity, she opened her eyes and glared at him. "What is this? You're trying to seduce me with Dr. Seuss?"

"You're a mom. I'm trying to appeal to you on a level you can relate to."

Bonnie gave him her best Mom-means-business look.

"All right, how about this?" He pursed his lips and began to whistle a tune.

My Bonnie Lies Over the Ocean.

In spite of herself, she smiled, but the exasperation hadn't left her. "Clever, but it's not going to work."

"I have never known a woman to play so hard to get."

"I'm not playing at all. Don't you know that yet?"

"So, I keep hearing." He sat back on his haunches.

"I'm too old for this, Brandt."

"You're not too old. You're just afraid."

"Maybe so." She looked out the window. "I've got responsibilities. Kids."

"A mortgage."

"Yes. I live in the real world. I have to be a grown up."

"What if for a couple of hours you just…not be a grown up. Play a little bit. Have a little bit of fun."

"With you."

"Yes, with me."

She crossed her arms over her chest. "I've never been good at being whimsical. You'll have your fun, make me fall in love with you, then stomp all over my heart, and disappear into the night. I want someone who wants to settle down with me. Be a dad to my kids. Will help me clean up the kitchen and cuddle with me at night." She looked down at him. "Isn't that disgusting?"

"Yes. Really disgusting." He reached forward and ran his fingers along her legs, tucking his fingers under knees. "It will be hard to be a dad to your kids when you haven't let me meet them." He tugged.

"Have you even been around kids? What are you doing?" she asked suspiciously.

"I'm going to pull you on my lap, so you can disgust me some more with your domestic fantasies."

"I'm not having sex with you, and I don't want to be part of the Mile High Club."

Brandt laughed. "Who said anything about the Mile High Club? You offered to kiss me in gratitude for my night watch, and I accepted."

"Fine." She slid forward, settling her legs on either side of him, and saw the tactical mistake immediately. He was all muscle in his perfectly fitted suit, his scent nudging at her senses, dosing her with his ninja Zen. She wavered for a moment, considering his lips curving in a relaxed smile, strong jaw, and the sparkle in his eyes, before shoring up her resolve.

"Lay one on me. Worthy of a night of no sleep."

Bonnie tilted forward and pecked his cheek. Then leaned back and smiled at him. "How's that?"

"Lips."

"No."

"Come on. Reach back into that Mommy brain of yours and find your whimsy. I know it's in there."

She shook her head. "Not there." She was lying. The urge to be playful unfurled, nipped at her like a puppy. She focused on his short hair, and reached her fingers up, feeling it against his scalp. "How'd you get your hair to grow out so quick after pilfering through my trash?"

"That's my fake bald cap. Impressed?"

"Yeah."

"When it's daytime, I have to work harder to hide."

"You didn't do it very well. I noticed you immediatcly."

Something sparked in his eyes. "That's what I like about you. You see me. You're the only person who has ever found me. You're the only person who has noticed me when I've been working. I thought I was losing my touch, but it's not me. It's you."

"It wasn't that hard," she insisted. Her fingers ran along his hairline behind his ears and to the nape of his neck.

"Would you kiss me now?"

"Not now or later. Not here or there. I would not kiss you anywhere."

"You do not kiss ninjas in the rain or in a plane?"

"Or on your knees or if you say pl—"

Brandt moved his hands from her legs and wrapped his arms around her, pulling her closer to him, and sealing his lips against her mouth. The swift movement wasn't entirely unexpected, but what shocked her was how gentle the kiss was, as if he were unsure this was a good idea after all. The tentative feel of him appealed to Bonnie. She thought he'd plunder her mouth, force his tongue through her lips, but he didn't. He brushed his lips back and forth over hers, then he drew back a fraction, the tips of his lips a hairsbreadth from hers.

"See me," he whispered. "Kiss me."

Bonnie closed her eyes. "No," she breathed.

I can resist him.

But the whimsy was so tempting. She snaked her other hand under his suit jacket, and he chuckled and flinched away for a second then nuzzled her neck.

"You're ticklish?" she said.

"Extremely. You won't tell, will you?" He rained kisses along her neck and nipped the skin under her ear.

"Leverage." She sighed and dropped her head back.

He planted a wet kiss where her neck and shoulder met then withdrew, moving his hands back to her legs, running them up and down the sides of her thighs. He grinned at her.

"Are we done?" she asked.

"Define done."

"With…" She gestured with her hand to him then her.

"I was thinking this was a start, but you won't kiss me, and you said you didn't want to join the Mile High Club. Still. This is only about a thirty-minute flight anyway."

Bonnie slid back toward the chair, and Brandt lifted her up to the cushion. He gazed at her as if he'd won this battle of kiss or no kiss. "How whimsical do you want to be? I could ask the pilot to keep going, change our flight plan."

"See? This is what I was talking about. You're just playing with me. Let's see how I can manipulate the put-upon mother of three with a mortgage. Give her a little excitement."

"Close your eyes for a minute."

"Why?"

"Because I'm going to get up off the floor, and I don't want you to watch me. My legs are asleep."

"Oh, for heaven's sake. Who cares?"

"I'm trying to be suave here."

"Make jokes. You're good at that."

Brandt hit his leg a couple of times and with some effort put his foot underneath him and stood unsteadily before he collapsed on his own chair. "I know you don't believe this, Bonnie, but you are the most exciting woman I've met in a really long time."

"Well, that's just sad."

"I know. Isn't it? The lonely life of a ninja. Do you feel sorry for me?"

"Sorry isn't the word I'd use, no."

"You could kiss me, but let's stay in the chair."

Bonnie sighed. "I almost believed you were serious, that there was something deep you knew I had seen."

"Well, yeah, but then you started tickling me."

"Why are you bringing me on this trip? So you can show me your manufactured consulting company in a made-up town that probably isn't even in Kentucky? Your kiss was probably one more smoke screen."

"A very pleasurable smoke screen. I am bringing you to Bellini so you can see it's a real place because I want you to help me."

"Help you how?

"Remember I asked you about finding someone?"

"The person that you only have the birth certificate for?"

"Yes."

"I just can't believe with the people you work with, what they were able to do in a government office building, and you breaking into the computer, that you can't find this guy yourself. Who is he?"

"He's my brother."

"Your brother?"

"Yes. As far as I know, the only family I have, so any help you can give me would be appreciated."

Chapter Eleven

Brandt eyed her steadily, waiting for her answer.

Bonnie shrugged. "I don't think I can do more than what you've probably already done, but sure, I'll try."

The magnificent grin that lit up his face struck Bonnie so much she forgot to breathe.

"Now, I could kiss *you*."

She inhaled and held up a warning hand. "Don't. I need to temper my whimsy. Do you have any information about your brother I could look at?"

Brandt bent over and retrieved the leather satchel he'd brought with him. Withdrawing a folder, he handed it to her. "There's a tabletop you can pull up from the side of the chair," he said.

Bonnie put on her glasses and adjusted the table over her chair. She opened the folder and read the first paper there: a copy of a birth certificate for Marshall Lee Sherrod. "He's a year younger than you. How'd you get the birth certificate?"

"I took it with me the night police took us. I thought if I had his birth certificate with me, they wouldn't be able to separate us."

"The police took you from your parents?"

"My mother."

"How old were you?"

"Seven."

"What happened next?"

Brandt sighed. "It's all so fuzzy. I remember Marshall and me huddled together when the cops came. I remember them pulling us apart, and I was fighting them so I could stay with Marshall, and then I remember being in the back of the police car...I don't know. It must have been bad because I can't remember anything else about that night. I never saw him again."

"What about your mother?"

"I never saw her again either. She died."

"She died because of what happened that night?"

"No. It was later."

"When did she die?"

Brandt named a date. "My case worker came and visited me on my eighth birthday. He brought me her death notice from the newspaper."

Bonnie shook her head and sighed. "Happy birthday, and, oh, by the way, your mom died."

"Meh. It was a long time ago. And anyway, he brought me some video games and a system to play them on. I don't remember being upset about my mom. I do remember how excited I was to have the games."

Bonnie looked through the file but didn't see the death notice. Even though he was only eight when he received it, the fact he no longer had it, but still had his brother's birth certificate from a year earlier, seemed significant. "Do you mind if I write on these papers?"

"No."

Bonnie made some notes and leafed through the other papers—lists of organizations Brandt had contacted looking for Marshall without any luck.

"It's like he disappeared that night."

"Where were you living when the police took you from your mom?"

"Right here in Carlton Heights, Kentucky."

"Why did the police come?"

"Mom's boyfriend was a dealer. He was beating on her—nothing new there, and then the police stormed in."

"My God, Brandt. That must have been terrible."

"Ah, yes, and losing Marshall was the worst and going from foster home to foster home until I came to live with Delores. She was so wonderful. Saved my life, that woman did. And she made the best coconut cake. She got to where she'd make one once a month because she knew how much I loved it."

The fact Brandt seemed to have no feelings whatsoever about his mother's death struck Bonnie. No anger. No sadness. Nothing. She stored the piece of information in her mind and continued.

"You said you don't remember anything after you were in the police car. What about before? Do you remember being outside walking to the police car? Was it hot or cold?"

"It was...cool. Nippy."

"Do you remember what Marshall was wearing? Or what clothes you had on?"

Brandt didn't answer. Bonnie looked from the paper to him. He shook his head.

"Did you all have a Christmas tree up?"

"There wasn't Christmas back then."

"How about the neighbors? Did you notice any Christmas lights or Halloween decorations as you went to the police car?"

Brandt rubbed his forehead, as if attempting to massage the memory into existence. Bonnie knew this couldn't be easy for him, so she gave him time to think, to remember. She continued to read. Brandt had attempted to search the foster care database, but hadn't found anyone with his brother's name. If he had possessed his brother's birth certificate, was it possible they didn't know Marshall's real name?

"There was a jack-o'-lantern on the stoop next door. I remember because it seemed to be laughing at us for being arrested."

"Except you weren't being arrested. The police were just taking you away from a dangerous situation."

Brandt leaned forward, rested his elbows on his knees, and a look of dejection flashed across his face, then it was gone, but Bonnie had seen it. "I was just a stupid kid. What did I know?"

Bonnie adjusted her glasses and suppressed the urge to

crawl into his lap, gather him to her and hold him, tell him it would be all right, that she couldn't erase the pain of so long ago, but she'd do her best to help him find his brother.

"I'm glad that jack-o'-lantern was sneering at you. That means we know about what time of year this happened." She could scour the newspaper and police reports for the incident. Before the plane landed, Bonnie had gotten a few more details of the night Brandt and his brother had been separated, including the name of the street where they'd lived and the name of his mother's dealer boyfriend. Going back almost forty years to search for a six-year-old wasn't an easy thing to do—like looking for a needle in a haystack—but it was possible. The needle was definitely there. It would just take time. Bonnie may not be good at whimsy, but she loved playing hide-and-seek—if she could be the one seeking.

When they touched down at a small airstrip, Bonnie saw only a train track and trees. A car was waiting for them, and Brandt invited her to ride in the front. She recognized the woman driving—Sheri Stillthorpe. She looked a lot less frumpy than she had the day she'd been impersonating a secretary in the *vice president's* office.

"Do you remember Sheri?" Brandt asked from the backseat.

Sheri cast her a dismissive glance.

"She's mad because she doesn't think I should bring women to work."

"Did Batman ever bring Mary Jane to the bat cave? No, he did not."

"Of course, he didn't. Mary Jane was Spiderman's girlfriend. Batman would have brought Vicki Vale to the bat cave, if you're talking movies. If you want to be authentic and decide from the comic books who his girlfriend was, then the closest he had to a significant other might be Selina Kyle, AKA Catwoman."

"Marry me, Bonnie," Brandt crooned.

Bonnie turned and looked at Brandt over her shoulder. "You would propose marriage because I know who

Batman's girlfriend was? How have you managed to stay single for forty years?"

"He hasn't stayed still long enough to get caught," Sheri groused then shot Bonnie a meaningful look. "Until now."

"Good thing I'm not fishing."

"She means you've already caught me by finding me. This is the first time any of us have ever been detected."

"Perhaps, but I found you because of a personal matter. It wasn't business."

"It was your business."

Bonnie shrugged. "My job is looking for beneficiaries. It took me months to track you down."

"You shouldn't have been able to track him at all."

Bonnie looked out the side window instead of snapping at the other woman who was, in effect, criticizing Brandt for going to his foster mother's funeral. Brandt was a big boy and Bonnie was sure he could defend himself if need be.

"She's very good at what she does, Sheri. You know what they call her at her office?"

"The Bloodhound. Yeah, I know."

"How do you know that?" Bonnie asked.

Sheri rolled her eyes and pointed her thumb at Brandt. "He brags."

Sheri drove a circuitous route to an old house on what appeared to be a horse farm. When she paused at a closed gate, they slowly opened. Bonnie looked at the black painted borders fencing in the trees in the large yard. "How come you took Highway 14? It looked like Rural Route 4738 intersects it, and it ends right there. That would have been a more direct way to get here. I've already told Brandt I have to be back by four."

Sheri's mouth tightened.

"See what I mean?" Brandt said.

Sheri didn't respond as she drove through the opening and followed a dirt drive around the house to the back where a new four-car garage opened one of its doors; Sheri maneuvered the car inside. Two other cars resided in the other spaces, and one vacant.

"Does someone live here?" Bonnie asked.

Sheri turned off the engine and left the car.

Brandt and Bonnie exited on the other side and stood next to each other. He placed his hands in his pockets and grinned. "This is a big step for all of us, having you here. You understand if we don't answer too many questions."

"'Cause then you'll have to kill me?"

"No. That's a cliché, and therefore predictable." He walked toward the door Sheri had just gone through then slammed shut. "And I did promise to get you back safely."

"She's angry."

"She'll get over it." He held the door open for Bonnie and ushered her into a spacious room with several desks spaced throughout, and large screens on one wall. One screen must have been someone's computer monitor; the other was an aerial view of the outside of the house that switched to another view as Bonnie watched it.

"There are no windows in this room. How can that be? As big as this room is, it must be most of the first story of the house, and the outside of the house showed windows."

"Oh, my God, would you stop with the interrogation?" Sheri yelled from somewhere.

Brandt laughed.

"Where is she?"

Brandt pointed upward, and Bonnie followed his finger. A spiral staircase led to a balcony that lined two of the walls. Sheri disappeared into one of the second story doorways.

"This is really amazing."

Someone cleared his throat, and Bonnie turned.

David Bentley stood next to Brandt.

"You!" Bonnie exclaimed at the man who had impersonated the vice president of security. He wore blue jeans and a T-shirt, but it was definitely the same man.

He nodded his head with a twinkle in his eye and offered his hand in greeting. Bonnie hesitated a second before she shook it.

"Hello, I'm David Bentley."

"Really? That's really your name?"

"Yeah. We try to lie as little as possible. Easier to keep track that way."

"And you have children?"

"Why do you ask?" Brandt asked.

"While he was squatting in my office building, he told me he had kids. I'm curious how being a ninja fits family into his life." Bonnie turned to David. "You are also a ninja, aren't you?"

A sound of frustration reached Bonnie from upstairs. Sheri appeared at the balcony. "No more questions."

"They're her kids, too," Brandt whispered.

Bonnie nodded and looked at each person in turn. "So. You brought me here. I assume because Vivian Walker agreed to this, I have a specific assignment."

"Yes. We are going to advise you on information security for the Retirement Systems. We've prepared a portfolio of weaknesses, possible threats, and recommendations, which we will go over with you, then you can take it back to Vivian and report to her."

Bonnie shook her head. "I don't think so. I work in benefits. I'm not involved with these kinds of issues." She took out her cell phone. "I'll have to call Ms. Walker and verify this."

"That won't work here."

Bonnie paused her dialing. "No service?"

"No."

"You don't have service out here? That must be inconvenient."

"We have service, but you don't." Brandt handed her his cell phone and led her over to a table and pulled out a chair for her. "We'll give you a few minutes to talk to her. Can I get you something to drink? Coffee, water, cola, tea"—he glanced up toward the balcony—"Kool-Aid."

"Screw you, Brandt," Sheri said.

Bonnie called Vivian and received her confirmation

concerning information security. "I don't know what you did, Bonnie, but whatever it is, keep it up. Brandt Sherrod offered to do this consulting if you were willing to be the liaison on it."

"A liaison? What does that entail?"

"Two weeks on the project then one day a week after that until the consulting is done."

"I can't stay in Bellini, Kentucky, two weeks. He said he'd bring me back this afternoon."

"He covers all transportation costs, and you and he work out the arrangements. But I would think most of your time will be here since this is where the security issues are."

"I wish I had known this before Mr. Brewer handed me the folder you gave him and I boarded that plane. I've got open cases that are time sensitive."

"Brandt appears to be flexible with his time. Tie up the loose ends if you need to, but I'd really like to make this a priority."

"Has it occurred to you that the security they breached and the office set up was just a stunt to get the Commonwealth's business?"

"The consulting is pro bono."

Bonnie stood up and walked the perimeter of the room, scrutinizing where the windows should have been. "Yeah? Well, what about whatever recommendations they make? Contract it out to partners or take a percentage from the security and computer companies we engage with because of their recommendations."

Vivian didn't respond right away, so Bonnie continued.

"You've agreed to give this guy days, weeks of my time on a promise that he's going to disclose to you security breaches that he probably created. You've put me in a very vulnerable position. I don't even know where I am. He said we're in Kentucky, but when I found the company phone number on the rented furniture bill of lading, it was a Virginia area code."

"Do you know who Sun-Tzu is?"

"What?"

"He was a Chinese general."

Bonnie raised her hand and ran it along the wall, looking for a crevice. She scanned the room making sure Brandt and his crew hadn't entered.

"He said to keep your friends close and your enemies closer. You're doing great. See what he comes up with and keep me posted."

Bonnie ended the phone call and walked over to the desk where she noticed Brandt had set his satchel. She sat down and attempted to login using the code that was on his phone.

"What are you doing?" Brandt said.

Bonnie turned toward his voice. He stood at the table with a glass of ice and a can of diet Coke.

"Trying to use your computer." The login didn't work. "What's your password?"

"Go ahead, Batman, tell Catwoman what your password is," Sheri said as she walked down the spiral staircase though if Bonnie hadn't been looking at her, she wouldn't have known she was descending. The staircase appeared to be wrought iron, but it couldn't be. Sheri's footsteps made no sound.

"Catwoman?" David asked.

Bonnie could have sworn he hadn't been in the room a second ago. "Can you all put on bells or something? All of this silent movement is disconcerting."

"Wait until you meet their kids."

"She is *not* meeting our kids," Sheri snapped.

"How old are your boys, Bonnie?" Brandt asked.

"Five and eight."

Brandt bounced on his heels and grinned at Sheri who glared in return. "Let's sit down at the table and get this over with," she said. Pulling a remote from her jacket pocket, she pushed a button and the light dimmed in the room. One of the large wall monitors changed from the computer logon into the Commonwealth of Kentucky state seal.

And the presentation began.

About ten minutes into it, a chime sounded in the room. The room lightened.

David, Brandt, and Sheri exchanged looks.

"What's that sound?" Bonnie asked.

"Bonnie." Brandt stood and took her hand. "I'm sorry. Would you come with me?" He pulled her to her feet and escorted her upstairs to a small sitting room with a window. He gave her a look of apology before he closed the door behind him. It all happened so quickly she didn't have time to react until she was alone. Bonnie strode over to the door to see if he'd locked her in. She turned the knob and moved the door. No, she wasn't locked in, at least. The tension in her chest loosened at bit, and she examined the room—a loveseat, matching chair, and coffee table. She walked over to another door and opened it. Interesting. An empty closet with a recessed wall. False back? Bonnie looked for a handle or anything that would open it but gave up after a few minutes. She went to the window and looked out into a flat field behind the house. It seemed if it was a horse farm with the requisite fences, it would have... Something caught Bonnie's attention. A helicopter flew low on the horizon, and to Bonnie's surprise, landed close to the house, yet there was no sound. What was it about this house that everything was so quiet? As close as the helicopter was, she should be able to hear the engine and the propellers. What kind of window was this, anyway? Bonnie reached up and knocked on the glass and discovered it wasn't regular glass. It was much thicker, and made a dull thud when she tapped it. She knocked a little harder. Nothing. Experimentally, she tried harder, finally with her fist, and there was no give whatsoever.

The door opened, and Brandt strode in. "I'm sorry," he said. "I've got to go."

"What? Where?" Bonnie's heart began to beat heavily in her chest.

"Assignment. But don't worry, Sheri and David will take care of you. I wanted to take you to a nice lunch. Will you give me a rain check?"

Don't leave me here, please! "But... Brandt... I don't...."

"I trust Dave and Sheri with my life. I *have* trusted them with my life. They'll get you back home, I promise. I'll call you." He left, leaving the door ajar. Instead of following him out of the room, Bonnie turned back to the window. Sure enough, in a moment, he appeared outside carrying a black duffel, entered the helicopter, and it lifted off.

"Bonnie?" Sheri stood at the door.

Bonnie didn't look behind her. Instead she watched the helicopter become smaller and smaller. Uneasiness settled around her. When she couldn't see it anymore, she finally turned and gazed at Sheri.

Sheri's attention focused on the window for a few seconds. "Come on," she said with a tone of resignation. "We'll show you what we have, then I'll drive you back to the airstrip."

"Is he doing something dangerous?" Bonnie asked.

Sheri's pinched lips relaxed. She tipped her head, considering Bonnie's question. "He'll be okay."

Bonnie didn't like the other woman's response because she, in effect, hadn't answered Bonnie.

David took the lead with the rest of the security demonstration, pointing out several risks which Brandt had already mentioned to her—the schedule of the security guards and the cleaning crew, the practice of employees not logging off their computers, and outdated security features. In addition to those issues, David proposed software that automatically logged off after four minutes of inactivity, prompts for password changes, encrypted email with appropriate blocks, and a secure cloud.

"All of this is common sense kind of stuff," David said. "And something you all should have been doing years ago."

"In addition, we think the building should have an alarm system and IT ought to have a person on staff whose only job is information security," Sheri commented.

"And he...or she...should be high-tier-level so that

decisions administratively are made with that person's input or guidance."

"Great. That's all the Commonwealth needs. Another chief in the penthouse."

"The security there is vulnerable. Unless something changes, it's just a matter of time before a hacker comes in and has all of your benefits routed to an offshore account, and too bad for the Kentucky teachers," Sheri said.

David slid a stack of glossy folders toward her. "This is our report in duplicate. You can give it to Vivian Walker and anyone else you think should see it."

Bonnie opened the top folder and thumbed through the ten-page document.

Impressive.

"Do you have any questions?" Sheri asked.

"You mean I can ask questions now?"

She smiled—the first time today. "About the report, yes."

"Will the telephone number work if I call it?"

"For as long as we are consulting for you, yes."

"How dangerous is the mission Brandt's on?"

"That is not a question about the report," Sheri said.

"How long should I wait for him to call me before I start to worry?"

Sheri and David looked at each other. Sheri shook her head. David maintained eye contact with Sheri as he spoke. "Finding his brother is very important to Brandt. I'm sure he will be in touch with you soon to learn if you've made any progress."

"How soon? By tonight? Or a couple of days? A week?"

"I'm sorry. We can't give you a timeline," David said.

"If something were to happen to him, would you let me know?"

"Nothing is going to happen to him. He's very good at his job," Sheri said.

"Bonnie, I think Brandt was hoping you and he could get started on your research to find Marshall. He set up a log-in for you, but if you want to go back now, we can drive you to the plane and you can go on back home."

The discomfort Bonnie had felt since Brandt left, eased a bit. "Really?"

Sheri arched an eyebrow. "Brandt said we'd take care of you, so we're going to take care of you." She looked across the table at David. "Isn't that right, David? We're going to take care of Bonnie?"

"Is taking care of me a figure of speech for," Bonnie placed her fingers up and gestured with air quotes, "Taking care of me?"

Sheri's mouth turned up in a smile that looked more sinister than amused.

Chapter Twelve

Bonnie did arrive back in Carlton Heights safely and before lunch. She delivered the information to Vivian Walker's office though she wasn't there to receive it. Bonnie tied up some loose ends on her own work before surfing the web looking for anything on the night Brandt and his brother were separated, or his mother's death. She didn't find anything, so she headed over to the library to look up archived newspapers. Surely, there would be something in the newspaper about the incident. She put her phone on vibrate in case Brandt called or texted her, but nothing came through.

A week went by, and she still hadn't heard from Brandt.

One morning, she stood in the bathroom putting on her make-up when an argument from the breakfast table between the boys caught her attention.

"They do not!" Andy said hotly.

"Yeah, they do," Curtis responded.

"Shut up."

"Hey." Bonnie stepped into the kitchen. "Andy, you know you're not allowed to say that."

"Mom, Curtis said angels are boys."

"Right."

"Nuh-uh. All the angels I've seen are girls."

"Andy, I'm sure angels are both boys and girls, but Gabriel was a boy. He was the one who told Mary she was going to have a baby. He might be the most famous angel."

"What about Lucifer?" Kayla strolled into the room and reached for a can of cola. "He's pretty popular."

Bonnie snagged the drink from her daughter's hand and replaced it with a glass and gestured to the milk on the table. "No Coke for breakfast. You need calcium."

"Who's Lucifer?" Curtis asked.

"I don't like milk," Kayla said.

"Have chocolate milk."

"It's still milk, and I'm not a kid."

"Who's Lucifer?" Curtis repeated.

"He's the devil," Kayla said, batting her eyes at her mother.

"The devil!" Andy exclaimed. "I thought his name was Satin."

"Satan, you little twerp." Kayla went to the sink and poured water in her glass.

"At least eat some yogurt, and no name calling or educating the boys on demonology."

"What's demology?" Curtis asked.

"Fine. You have to control every single thing. Who I see. What I wear. What I eat. What I say." She opened the refrigerator and grabbed a yogurt.

Bonnie turned and inspected her daughter for any frays in her jeans that were too provocative or whether her shirt was long enough to cover her midriff.

Kayla rolled her eyes and retrieved a spoon. "I'm eating this in my room."

"At the table, please, and shut the silverware drawer." Bonnie walked back in the bathroom before an argument could begin.

Andy appeared at the doorway. "Mom, angels don't smoke, do they?"

"I seriously doubt it."

"Curtis said our guardian angel smokes."

"Honey, I really don't think angels smoke." Suspicion niggled at Bonnie. Did Rex smoke? Was he coming to the house at night after everyone was in bed? Bonnie made a mental note to look outside Kayla's window for cigarette butts. "Smoking is bad for you. Why would angels do it?"

"They do," Curtis called.

"Well, they shouldn't," Bonnie called back.

She took the children to school and went on to work. Sitting at her desk, she fingered a petal from the arrangement Brandt had sent. The flowers looked as fresh as the day they had been delivered—no sign of wilting anywhere. She'd have to remember to use this florist the next time she ordered flowers.

Her work on Brandt's case had yet to turn up anything. She'd called in a favor from Ted, Alicia's husband who worked on the police force. She'd told him the story Brandt had shared with her and asked if he knew how to get a hold of police records from over thirty-five years ago. He'd promised to look into it and get back to her.

****

Bonnie dreamed she was in her grandparents' house, the box fans whirred as she walked on the tiled floor the living room, noting *Hee Haw* on the console television in the corner as she walked to the front and peered through the screen door. The squeak of the chain from the porch swing alerted her someone was outside.

She grinned at the hole in the screen, about the size of her brother Mackey's foot when he'd kicked a little too well at a fly on the other side. It had never been repaired. She pushed the door open and stepped through the threshold.

The loud chorus of the cicadas greeted her. The sweet aroma of pipe tobacco wafted on the breeze, and Bonnie turned and saw Grandpa and Grandma settled next to each other on the bench seat swaying back and forth with the nudge of Grandpa's boots.

"Hi, honey," Grandma said.

Bonnie walked across the porch and sat on the stoop, leaning back on the post to face them as she'd done hundreds of times as a child.

"Where's Bubba?" She asked, referring to Mackey by his nickname.

Grandpa puffed on his pipe, and Bonnie inhaled the scent.

"He's not here. I imagine he's out by the creek

catching crawdads. Why don't you go fetch him, then we'll have some coconut cake?" Grandma said.

Bonnie couldn't recall the rest of the dream when she awoke. But the sense of peace she felt stayed with her. She had thought about Brandt often since he'd flown away on the helicopter, but after her dream, the anxiety she felt for his safety dissipated, though Bonnie didn't understand why.

She spent her lunch hour each day in the library looking through newspaper archives. She'd been through the whole month of October of the year Brandt had told her he thought the incident had occurred. She then began to look though the files for September. Still nothing.

Saturday morning, she took the boys to the library and decided to look at October of the previous year and found an article of police being called to a domestic disturbance on the street Brandt had told her he had lived. There were no further details of the case, but it was October twenty-fifth. It was likely that a jack-o'-lantern would be on the neighbor's porch. Bonnie would have to ask Brandt if it was possible it had happened when he was six and not seven. She called Ted and followed up on old cases, and he referred her to Donald Murriel, the public information officer, from the nearest precinct. She called him the following Monday, and he advised her to come to the precinct to fill out a request for the case file which she did on her lunch break.

She decided to give it a week before she called Donald again to ask if he'd had any luck locating the file.

****

"Bonnie."

Brandt's soft voice awoke her. She blinked, wondering if she had dreamed it. Him.

The clock said it was just before one in the morning.

"Are you awake?"

She hadn't dreamed it. He was here in her bedroom. Bonnie looked around. At least she thought he was. She sat up, drawing the covers to her. A shadow separated itself from the darkness, and Brandt stood next to her closed bedroom door.

"What are you doing in my house?"

"I tried to text you. You didn't answer."

"You cannot come in my—"

"Your daughter, Kayla, isn't it? She just snuck out."

"What?" Bonnie threw back the comforter she had previously used to shield herself and dashed to her dresser. "Why didn't you follow her?" She wrenched off her nightgown and grabbed a shirt putting it on quickly, then pulled on a pair of jeans.

"I wasn't sure you'd want me to."

"Of course, I want you to. How are we going to find her?" Finding some shoes in the closet, she shoved her feet in them.

"I put a tag on her."

"What?"

"A GPS device."

"How'd you do that?"

"I just got close enough to her and put it on her pants, but if she takes her pants off, and goes somewhere else, we're out of luck."

"Oh, shoot. I can't leave the boys."

She picked up her cell, noted two texts Brandt had sent, then called Veda who picked up on the first ring. "Veda, I'm sorry to call you in the middle of the night, but Kayla snuck out of the house, and I need to go find her. Is there any way I can bring the boys over?"

"Don't be silly. I'll just come over there."

In five minutes, Veda knocked on the door. Brandt had already gone outside. His black clothes would be difficult to spot in the dark. Bonnie figured he'd left so she wouldn't have to answer questions about him. Bonnie would marvel at how he could just vanish except it was often more irritating than amazing, and at this moment, rage and worry over Kayla wrestled in Bonnie's gut. She looked around quickly from the door to the car, and saw he was already in the passenger seat.

She didn't bother asking him how he got in when it

was locked.

"Where to?" she asked as she cranked the engine.

He looked at his cell phone. "She was on Adams Street. She's on the move."

"Is she in a car?"

"Yes, but she must have just gotten in. She's headed north on Oakview." He paused. "Huh."

"What?"

"They're crossing the Elam Avenue Bridge into Ohio."

"Oh, my God. Where is he taking her?"

"Don't worry. We'll find her."

"Why can't he just leave her alone?"

"Because he's a teenage boy, and he likes her. Don't you have a tracker on her phone?"

"Yes, I do, but I took her phone away. I'm going to lock her in her room until she's thirty."

"Now, why would you punish yourself that way? Listen, let's make a plan for how you want this to go. If she is in this boy's house, do you want to call the house, alert his parents? That might be a better idea than just going up to the door and beating on it."

"I don't think they're going to his house. He doesn't live in Ohio."

"Are you sure?"

Bonnie thought about it. Actually, she wasn't sure. She turned at a traffic light, and they drove on the bridge. "Not really, no. But I assume he lives in Kentucky because they go to school together." She hit the steering wheel with her hand. "I should know these things. What kind of mother am I?"

"You're a mother who trusted her daughter until she gave you a reason not to."

"If something happens to her, I'll kill him."

Brandt reached over and grasped one of her hands. "Can you drive one-handed?"

"Yes."

He guided her hand to rest between them, intertwining their hands. "Breathe."

"I am breathing."

"There's a Buddhist saying that each person is allotted only so many breaths in their lifetime."

"You're Buddhist?"

"Listen to the wisdom. Not the theology. You only have so many breaths in your lifetime. That's motivation to slow your breathing down. You'll live longer. Deep, steadying breaths." His tone of voice was calm and soothing. "Breathe in through your nose and out through your mouth. In and out. Breathe with me. In and out." He demonstrated the breaths, and Bonnie followed his lead. "Good. Slow and deep. Turn left here."

Bonnie followed his directions.

"We're going where she's going. She has a tag on. We aren't going to lose her." His fingers squeezed her hand briefly. "Okay?"

A calm settled over Bonnie. She continued to breathe the slow breaths. "Okay."

Bonnie drove to a neighborhood on the East side of Hampton. When Bonnie pulled up in front of the house in a cul-de-sac, she paused. Cars were everywhere, and every light was on in the house.

"It's a party," Bonnie said.

"Okay, so, calling his parents in the house is probably not going to work. We could call the police."

"No! What if they arrest her?"

Brandt didn't respond. Bonnie looked at him in the darkened interior of the car. His meaningful look elicited a protest from Bonnie.

"She's fifteen. I don't want her to have an arrest record."

"They won't arrest her, just bring her in, and call you. It might scare her enough not to do this again."

Bonnie parked the car and shut off the engine. She removed the key from the ignition and palmed her key ring. "I just want to go get her and bring her home."

"Okay. You go in, and I'll be your back-up."

"You'll be my back-up?"

He nodded. "I've got your back. You need me, I'll be right there."

"But people will see you."

"Not unless I need to intervene. It will be all right. I've done things like this lots of times. But a lot trickier. This will be easy."

"I wish I'd worn a bra." Realization struck Bonnie, and she covered her face with her hands. "Oh, my gosh. You saw me naked."

"Nah. It was too dark."

"You said you could see really well in the dark because of your pupils."

"Acknowledged. But you weren't completely naked. You had on your panties."

"I'm such an idiot. Just kill me. Kill me right now."

"Let's go get Kayla. You can apologize later for taking your clothes off in front of me without any apparent interest in my presence whatsoever."

Bonnie sighed. She lowered her hands and shook her head in disbelief. "Damn that Rex. This is his fault."

Brandt laughed.

Bonnie exited the car and straightened her spine. *I will be calm. I will not freak out and scream. No matter what I find.*

She walked to the front of the house and pushed the already ajar door open. Rock music met her, overwhelming her hearing and giving her an instant headache. *All these kids are going to go deaf.* Walking into the foyer, two teens shot her startled glances as they left. A large group of people congregated in the living room, and Bonnie nearly growled when she saw a keg placed prominently in the back. She scanned faces for Kayla but didn't see her.

A big screen television showed two people engaged in graphic sex. Bonnie walked in front of it, found the power button, and punched it. She turned and glared at several of the people who protested her action.

"Would your mother want you watching that trash?" she snapped to one vocal young man.

"His mother was the one in the G-string," someone

said.

"Shut up, Randal. She is not."

Bonnie walked into the kitchen and found them. Kayla held a Solo cup, and Rex had his arm around her. A few other people milled around in the kitchen, but when they noticed her, they made a quick exit.

Kayla's eyes grew round. "Mom? What are you doing here?"

Rex kept his arm around Kayla's shoulders. His bold stare held no remorse. Only defiance.

"Come on," Bonnie said. "We're going home."

"I'll bring her home after a while," Rex returned, moving a little closer to Kayla.

"No. She's going home with me now." Bonnie reached to take the cup out of Kayla's hand, and Rex blocked her. The cup fell to the floor, and the smell of beer filled the room.

"You're drinking?"

"It's just beer, Mom."

"You're underage. Both of you are."

"Why don't you mind your own business?" Rex pushed Kayla behind him, and crossed his arms over his chest. He was a big boy, at least six feet tall, and Bonnie had to tilt her head to look at him.

"Kayla *is* my business." Bonnie attempted to reach around him, but he grabbed her arm, his fingers biting into her skin.

"Rex, stop," Kayla said. "That's my mom."

The pressure increased, and Bonnie tried to pull her arm away, but he wrenched her downward, and she fell to her knees. Then in horror, she watched Rex turn to Kayla, with hatred in his eyes. "What did you say to me?" He raised his other hand to her.

"No!" Bonnie said, attempting to move in between them as a shield before he hit her daughter. But she never got the chance, and Rex never got his chance either.

Brandt appeared, and Bonnie was free of Rex's grip. She stumbled backward, and watched in amazement as

Brandt stood in between Kayla and Rex. Rex grabbed Brandt by the throat, and in an instant, Rex was on his knees with Brandt behind him, holding the boy's hands in what appeared to be a painful stance.

"Oww. Oww," Rex bellowed.

Brandt stepped forward and leaned into him until Rex lay down on his belly.

Something pushed into Bonnie's side, and when she looked, Kayla was at her side as tears streamed down her face.

"Mom. Mom."

Bonnie put her arm around her daughter and guided her out of the room, out of the house, and to the car. She put Kayla, who was still crying, beside her in the front seat.

"How could he do that? How could he knock you down like that?"

"Because he didn't care if he hurt me. I was getting in the way of what he wanted." Bonnie looked in the console and found a travel pack of tissues. She pulled one out and tucked it into her daughter's hands.

Was Brandt coming? Bonnie wasn't sure. She turned and looked through the window at the house.

"Who was that guy?"

"What guy?" Bonnie asked.

"That guy that jumped in between Rex and us."

"Oh. Did you get a good look at him? He was one of your friends maybe?"

"I didn't know anybody there. Rex said it was a college party."

Kayla, why did you go with him?

Bonnie resisted asking for now.

"Do you think he hurt Rex?"

I hope so. "Kayla, has Rex hit you?"

She didn't answer immediately. *Oh, my God, have mercy.*

"He gets mad sometimes. He's never hit me."

Bonnie puzzled over the response. *He gets mad, and he's never hit her. But he's done something else.*

"What has he done when he's gotten mad at you?"

"Mom, please. I don't want you to freak out about this."

Breathe. Breathe. "Okay. I will try not to freak out."

"A couple of times he's grabbed me, like, when I didn't want to go somewhere. But he gets over it quick. I think it's because he plays football. You know, he's used to being physical and acting on impulse."

Fury brewed in Bonnie's chest. Breathe. Breathe in. Breathe out. *I only have so many breaths.* Bonnie turned on the interior light in the car. She reached over and pushed up Kayla's sleeve and saw bruises on her upper arm.

Bonnie sighed. She turned out the light.

"You're not going to freak out, are you?"

"Honey, it's not okay for him to hurt you."

"He didn't mean to."

"They always say that, and they're always sorry afterward. If he loves you, he wouldn't hurt you. He wouldn't grab you or make you go where you didn't want to go."

"I can't believe he knocked you down. My own mom."

"What are you going to do about it?"

"I guess I'm not going to do anything. You're probably going to restrict me for the rest of my life and start sleeping in my room."

"Sweetie, there's a more serious issue here, and me restricting you isn't going to fix it. If you stay with him, he's going to keep hurting you."

Kayla reached up and wiped the tears falling from her eyes. "He's nice most of the time."

"Until you do something he doesn't like."

"Mom, I'm *somebody* when I'm with him. No other tenth-grader is dating a senior."

"Maybe there's a reason he dates tenth-graders. Maybe the twelfth grade girls got tired of him grabbing them and pushing them around."

"You just don't understand."

"I'm trying to. I really am."

The back door opened. Bonnie glanced back and saw

Brandt sit behind Kayla. He nodded to Bonnie, and she headed for home amid Kayla's tearful words.

"I can't believe he knocked you down like that," Kayla said.

"Let's just go home, and we can talk about it later."

But what could Bonnie say to her to convince her Rex was an abuser? It seemed the more things Bonnie did to keep them apart made Kayla that much more determined to be with him.

Chapter Thirteen

"I guess I'm in trouble," Kayla said looking at her mother once the car had pulled into the carport. She opened the door but didn't leave the car.

Brandt didn't move. He waited to hear what Bonnie would say.

"This has been a difficult night, and it's late. Why don't you go on to bed and try to get some sleep. Tomorrow we'll sort it out."

The girl sighed. "Are you going to sleep in my room?"

"Do I need to?"

"No."

"Okay."

Kayla swung her legs out and stood. She looked remarkably like her mother except her hair was a darker shade of red and longer. She shut the door and walked to the house.

Bonnie looked back at him. "She didn't even know you were in the car."

"She's upset. People who are upset aren't observant."

"Can you stay a little while?"

Brandt wanted to reach forward and touch her, comfort her. "Sure."

"Would you wait here until Veda leaves?"

Brandt nodded though he exited the car when Bonnie did. She walked into the house, and Brandt stood at the corner of the house out of the illumination of the light until he saw Bonnie's neighbor walk across the yard to her own house across the street. He slipped into the house, listening for movement. Bonnie wasn't in the living room or kitchen, so he waited a couple of minutes, stepped to the hallway, and heard shower sounds coming from the bathroom.

Bonnie's bedroom door was open. He paused at the threshold and saw she was inside sitting on the edge of the bed. She looked up when he entered.

"May I come in?" he murmured.

She nodded and stood, closing the door behind him. The room was dim, the only light coming from a lamp on the bedside table. She stood inside the door and crossed her arms over her chest, rubbing her hands up and down her arms.

"I don't know what to do. I don't know what to do." The expression on her face was at once desperate and hopeless. "He's got some control over her, and I can't protect her."

The need to soothe her tore at Brandt, but he didn't approach her. He waited for a signal from her. "Tonight, she's safe. You made sure of that."

"What if you hadn't been there? What could I have done? He would have hurt her, and I was powerless to do anything." She sat down on the bed, looking at him with tears in her eyes. "When she goes to school Monday, it's going to start again."

Brandt knelt in front of her. "You've got the weekend to figure something out."

"Maybe I should keep her home from school."

"No. She should go. He won't bother her."

Bonnie took his hand that had been resting on his thigh. "Come sit here with me before your legs go to sleep." As he moved to join her, she asked, "How do you know he won't bother her? I've made it worse by going in and taking her from the party."

"I had a little talk with him after I invited him to lie down on the floor."

"What did you say?"

Brandt shrugged, not wanting to tell her he'd scared the shit out of the asshole, threatening him within an inch of his life if he said or did anything to hurt Kayla again. Brandt was specific when he talked to the guy because he didn't want to leave the dumbass any loopholes or leeway.

During his speech, Brandt had moved Rex's arm so far behind his back the boy had begun to whimper in pain. And just for an added bonus, he growled in his ear while he had him pinned to the floor.

He thought with such strict stipulations, Rex would probably break up with Kayla, but Brandt hadn't told him to do so because those kinds of decrees made the relationship sweeter to pursue—like a Romeo and Juliet kind of deal, and Brandt had seen enough tragedy without being the cause of one.

"I said, 'Be nice.'"

Bonnie exhaled a breath of surprise. "Do you think he'll do it?"

Their clasped hands rested between them on her unmade bed. "I think so. I gave him the ninja nudge. It's an effective method of persuasion."

Her fingers tightened on his. "Thank you, Brandt."

"You're welcome."

Her gaze dropped to his lips. He thought she wanted to kiss him, but she didn't move. Was she afraid he didn't want her to or that he did? He reached up and caressed her cheek and she moved her face into his hand. Then she leaned forward and touched her mouth to his. Immediately, the kiss became desperate and searching. Brandt figured all the tension and anxiety feeding her adrenaline now enflamed the passion in the kiss. He tempered her emotions, slowing her hurried pace by cherishing each touch and taste.

"I think," he whispered against her skin, "you are so beautiful."

She stopped and drew back, gazing at him intensely. "I wish I knew you were real," she whispered back.

"I'm trying to show you I am." He moved her hand under his shirt, to rest on his chest over his heart. Her fingers pressed against his skin, and her thumb moved to graze his nipple, making him shudder.

She kissed him again, but a sound from the hallway

stopped him. "Your daughter," he said.

Bonnie's eyes widened. She pushed him to the far side of the bed. "Get on the floor," she hissed at him.

There was a knock on the door. "Mom?"

Brandt scooted across the mattress, looking behind him at Bonnie who stood and scrambled to the doorway. Placing his feet on the floor, he crouched down on the floor and was in the process of getting below the level of the bed when he spotted a little boy lying down next to the bed. He gazed at Brandt solemnly, and in shock Brandt returned his stare.

This had to be Bonnie's younger son, the five-year-old.

The door opened. "What is it, honey?" Bonnie asked.

"Can I lay down with you?" Kayla asked.

"Let's go to your room," Bonnie suggested. They moved down the hall.

Brandt sat up, and so did the boy. He wore pajamas, and his light brown hair stuck up in several places. His eyes were the same color as Bonnie's. He blinked at Brandt like a wise owl.

"Smoking's bad for you," the youngster said.

****

He'd disappeared again.

When Bonnie came back to her bedroom after Kayla had fallen asleep, she'd found her bedroom empty.

No note or anything.

He'd texted her the next day and said he'd come by the Commonwealth offices at two on Monday afternoon if that suited her. She'd texted him back and accepted.

At two on the dot, Tammy had called Bonnie and told her Brandt was in the lobby. When Bonnie stepped out of the elevator, she didn't see Brandt in front of Tammy's desk where she expected him to be. Then she heard a familiar whistled version of *My Bonnie Lies Over the Ocean.*

Joy filled Bonnie's chest, and she turned and saw him leaning against a pillar on the far side of the room. Dressed in the same black he had on Friday night with sunglasses shielding his eyes, he looked sophisticated and a little mysterious.

My bonnie lies over the ocean. My bonnie lies over the sea.

Bonnie walked toward him, realizing she felt relief he had kept his word. He said he'd be here at two, and he had done just as he said.

He'd ceased the song as she approached and stood as if made of the marble he leaned against. She stopped a respectable distance from him.

What should she say? *Hi, Brandt. Thank you, Brandt. Why did you leave without saying goodbye? Will you kiss me again?*

He pursed his lips.

My bonnie lies over the ocean. Oh, bring back my bonnie to me.

Bonnie laughed.

"Come on," she said, indicating he should follow her with a crook of her head and began to walk toward the elevator. "Before security asks you to leave for incessant whistling."

Joy. Relief. Now, Bonnie felt nervous as they rode up in the elevator.

"How is Kayla?" he asked.

"She was very quiet all weekend, but she engaged with me and the boys. She came to the table without me having to harass her, and last night she watched television with us. I think she was nervous about going to school today, but she didn't fuss about it. I think she knows she's walking on thin ice after sneaking out Friday night. She's a little afraid to push me too much."

The elevator doors opened, and Brandt fell into step beside Bonnie heading toward her office. She closed the door after they entered, and when she turned around Brandt had already sat down in front of her desk and was in the process of taking off his sunglasses.

Indecision ran through her. She wouldn't have minded a hello kiss, but maybe they weren't to that point. Or, would they ever reach it?

She walked around to her desk and sat down. Folding her hands in front of her, she leveled a calm stare at him. "I want to start off by saying how much I appreciate what you did last night. But I want you to be truthful with me."

He didn't reply, just watched her.

"You're sneaking in here and replacing these flowers."

He didn't break eye contact, though the flower arrangement he'd given her was on the far corner of her desk.

"Well?" she asked.

"I'm waiting for your question."

"I rewrapped the wire on the stem of one of the roses, and it's different this morning. I want to know how many times you've broken in here to change the flowers."

He hooked his elbow over the back of the chair. "Four, but this will be the last time I do it. From now on, I'll let the florist deliver them."

Bonnie sighed in frustration—both because he'd admitted to breaking in here four times and by his confession and his offer not to do it again, he'd robbed her of her righteous indignation.

"Another question. And I want you to be truthful about this one, too."

Brandt nodded.

"Are we dating, or is this a collaboration to find your brother?"

A chuckle escaped him. "I like your direct approach."

Irritation prickled at Bonnie. "I don't like the way you avoided the question. It makes me think it's a collaboration with benefits."

Brandt straightened and lifted his hands in surrender. "Bonnie, I'm in uncharted territory here. I've not been involved with someone like you before."

"Someone like me." She nodded. "A boring forty-one-year-old mother of three, you mean."

"No, yes, yes."

"What?"

"Not boring, no. You'd think you'd be boring, but you keep surprising me. I don't like that because I can usually predict people's moves, but the unpredictability intrigues me, and I keep thinking about you."

"Oh."

"Do you think it's time for me to meet your kids?"

Talk about unpredictability. Bonnie sure didn't see that question coming. "Just because you helped out with Kayla, which I really appreciate, doesn't mean I'm ready for them to meet you. I don't even understand this...this whatever it is. What am I going to tell them about you?"

"Curtis thinks I'm an angel."

"What?"

"He was in your room the other night. On the floor on the other side of your bed."

"Oh, no. Oh, my gosh." They had been kissing. What had Curtis seen? What if they had gone beyond kissing?

"So, you and I...whatever this is...you probably need to figure out what you're going to tell him, and the other two if he tells them there was an angel in Mom's room last night."

"An angel? Where did he get that?"

"He saw me outside of the house. He thought I was a guardian angel. I told him I was just a regular person, but he didn't think a regular person would be able to get in his mom's bedroom in the middle of the night."

Bonnie raised her hands to her face in disbelief. "He was there when... Wait a minute. He and Andy were talking about angels smoking. But that was days ago."

"Yeah. I got back Tuesday and came by for a few hours to keep watch, but then I got called out again for a consulting job."

"A ninja job."

He shrugged and nodded.

"You've been watching the house?"

"It seemed something that was needed. However, I think you need to look into a security system. It will alert you if any doors or windows are opened when the system is on. That way, you can tell if Kayla sneaks out or if someone else sneaks in."

"Including you."

"Well, depending on which system it is, I can bypass it.

Some are easier than others to get around. I can give you some recommendations for the most secure, if you like, so that not even I could get in without you being aware of it. And anyway, with Curtis knowing about me and with what's going on with Kayla, I promise not to come in the house anymore unless it's by invitation and with their knowledge, if they're in the house. I don't want to cause any problems with your kids, Bonnie."

Her heart flip-flopped at his words. If she could believe what he said, he was putting her children's welfare above his own wants.

A definite turn-on if ever there was one.

"Thank you for saying so. Yes, I would like to know what security systems not even a ninja could fool."

Brandt smiled. He stood up and indicated the chair. "May I?"

Bonnie nodded and he lifted the chair and settled it next to hers behind the desk. "You okay with me using your mouse and keyboard?"

She moved them across the desk in front of him, aware of the fluttery feeling in her chest because he was close enough she could see a shadow of a beard beginning.

"What time did you go to sleep?"

He shook his head as his fingers flew across the keyboard. A website for a security system appeared on the monitor.

"You haven't been to sleep yet?"

"No. When I'm working, I usually sleep in the mornings, but something came up earlier, so I took care of that instead."

"You must be really tired."

"I'll sleep later." He dismissed her concern, but winked at her to soften the blow. "This company is local. They are a little more expensive, but the service is worth it."

"Can you bypass this one?"

Brandt shifted his gaze to her; a sly grin creased his face. "Yes, but Rex won't be able to."

He walked her through several systems from different

companies.

"I can see why you can get by with calling yourself a consultant. You're knowledgeable, about security companies, at least."

"We're sort of on the other side of security, so the more we know, the better."

"Maybe you could become legitimate and start working in security."

"Who says we're *not* legitimate?" He slid her keyboard back toward her.

Bonnie arched an eyebrow at him. Maybe he did pay taxes, and maybe he had taken her to his office—wherever it was—but she still wasn't sure what he did was legal. He'd given up sleep to watch over her house, he'd gone with her to get Kayla, and he'd given her advice about keeping her kids and house safe. He hadn't brought up the subject of his brother, but Bonnie was sure he wanted to know if she'd done any searching. She opened a drawer and withdrew a folder and placed it on the desktop.

"I've been looking for Marshall."

"Marshall?" He blinked at her, as if he couldn't believe her words.

"I don't know much, but I found something." She opened the folder and slid it toward him. He picked up the paper and began to read. "There was an incident in October, but it was a year earlier than you said. Is it possible you were six when you and Marshall were taken away from your mother?"

"No. I had to be seven. That was when I went to my first foster."

"Well." Bonnie shrugged. "I looked through every newspaper for the months of September through November of that year, and I didn't see anything that fit. However, the previous year, I did find something and I researched it. Are you sure you weren't six?"

Brandt ran his fingers through his hair. "I always thought I was seven. The Myers were my first foster, and I came from the system to them."

"I requested the police file for what I think is when it happened. I'm not saying you're wrong, but this is pretty compelling. Look at this." Bonnie reached over and turned over a page. "Child Protective Services was called in because of two children at the residence. Both boys. One child was placed in temporary foster custody, and the other one was taken to the hospital. You say you don't remember anything after you and your brother were separated. It seems one of you went to the hospital. I've met with CPS, but unfortunately, their files were destroyed when the basement flooded about fifteen years ago. But if you were the one who went to the hospital, you can go in and request your hospital records. You've got the date, so it shouldn't be too hard to get if they still have them."

"But which hospital? There are four in this area alone."

"Yes, but only Community and St. Joseph's were around back then. But I'm betting it's St. Joseph. They have the children's wing of the hospital, so if a child was in distress, it's likely they would go there, especially if CPS was involved because St. Joe deals with indigent and charity cases since they're not-for-profit. If you were injured that night, it might make sense why you don't remember anything."

"Because of HIPAA, only you can access your own records legally." Bonnie cast him a meaningful look. "If it was your brother who went to the hospital, you'll probably have to have a court order to obtain the record, even though as his closest living relative, they may let you have it. I don't know."

"I saw from the notes you gave me you had talked to a case worker about several of your foster families and didn't come up with anything. Another option is to look at mental health or group care facilities. If there was no foster care available—and if the facilities had room—a child could be placed there until other arrangements were made. Even if one of you went to a medical hospital first, after discharge, you guys should have been put together. But who knows what the system was like forty years ago?"

Brandt studied the papers carefully, took off the reading glasses he had been wearing and placed them on top of the open folder, then he turned to Bonnie. He gazed at her for a long moment. Finally, he reached forward, gathered her in his arms and kissed her. All of it was so unexpected, she laughed against his mouth. She felt his own lips turn up in a smile. He broke the kiss.

"I knew you could do it. I knew you were the right woman for the job when I heard about you."

The hope emanating from his eyes made Bonnie uneasy. She straightened her glasses, which had been knocked askew in the kiss. "Now, wait a minute. I haven't done much, and we haven't found him."

"You're going to, though."

"Maybe so. Maybe not, Brandt. I've got a whole drawer in the filing cabinet over there of people I haven't been able to find, and most of their cases are a lot newer than yours."

"In two weeks, you've found out more than I have in five years."

"I just built on what you'd started. But this isn't going to be easy."

Brandt leaned forward and kissed her one more time. "The Bloodhound."

"I don't want you to get your hopes up because we may not find him."

"Too late. Listen, I'm going out of town tomorrow, but I'll be back Saturday morning. Can I take you out for breakfast?"

She could go out for breakfast without worrying about the children since they'd be at Guy's this weekend. "I suppose so, or you could come to the house, and I could cook."

"You'd let me come for breakfast?"

"Sure. The kids will be at their dad's."

Brandt's smile fell.

Bonnie got it. He wanted to meet her kids officially. "Don't pout. We haven't even had a first date yet."

"I flew you to Bellini."

"Yeah, and you gave me a rain check for lunch and left me in the clutches of Sheri, who doesn't seem to like me very much. I've never had a...male friend, so I want to be cautious about this, especially where my kids are concerned."

"I'll take you to lunch right now."

"Lunch was about three hours ago, and I have to get back to work." Bonnie stood up.

Brandt raised his face, grinning at her devilishly. "You're really bad for my ego."

Bonnie ignored the tingles his sexy smile sent through her body. She motioned for him to stand and pointed to the door. "Go on. You may call me later."

He pushed away from the chair and meandered toward the door. "You playing hard to get just makes you more enticing, you know."

Bonnie finished out her workday and picked Kayla up from band practice. When her daughter entered the car, Bonnie noticed her set expression.

Uh-oh.

Kayla put on her seatbelt and sat back.

Curiosity got the better of Bonnie. "How bad was it?" she asked.

"It wasn't that bad. Rex was acting really weird. I thought he would be mad, but he wasn't. He said he was sorry for everything."

Of course, he was. Bonnie bit her lip to keep from commenting.

"Catherine Towns is in study hall with me. She and Rex used to go out, and I asked her about it. She...umm...she said she got tired of him controlling her. The night she broke up with him she had worn a shirt he told her he didn't want her to wear because she looked like a slut in it, and he grabbed the shirt and ripped it. Her parents heard them fighting and told him if he got near her again, they were going to have him arrested."

Bonnie drove the car through the parking lot and

headed toward home.

"He tells me what to wear, too. I liked it at first because I thought he was paying attention to what I looked pretty in, but, you know, I think he just didn't like other guys looking at me. But...I should be able to wear what I want, and I don't own any slutty clothes because you won't buy them for me anyway."

"That's true."

Bonnie drove the route and waited for Kayla to say more.

"He doesn't like my friends either, but I think it's just that he wants all my time. He told me he'd break up with me if I went to Hannah's party. Not like I could go now anyway since I'm restricted."

"When did he tell you that?"

"Friday night. We were actually having a fight about it when you got there. Today he barely spoke to me other than to apologize. I think he was embarrassed because that man took him down. Rex plays left tackle, so he's not used to someone jumping him. He's used to being the one to jump someone else. I wonder who that guy was."

"Someone who knew we needed help." Bonnie wanted to ask Kayla if she was done with Rex, but figured she wouldn't push it.

"I'm sorry for sneaking out. I guess you'll never trust me again."

"You'll have to earn back my trust. When is Hannah's party?"

"Friday night. I guess you'll tell Dad what happened so he'll know I can't go."

Bonnie didn't answer. Usually those kinds of conversations ended up with Guy criticizing Bonnie's parenting skills. Like Guy was parent of the year. He'd given Kayla a case of Mountain Dew for her birthday.

After arriving home, Bonnie began preparing supper and sent Kayla over to get the boys. As Bonnie suspected he would, Curtis came in the kitchen to help.

"Hey, buddy," she said. "How was your day?" She

retrieved a vegetable peeler from the drawer and the potatoes she had rinsed.

"Good." He opened the dishwasher and reached for the silverware.

"Wash hands," she reminded him.

He did so without complaint, pushing a chair to the sink to stand on it.

"So," Bonnie cleared her throat. "I heard you met my friend Brandt the other night."

Curtis soaped up his hands. "Yeah."

Bonnie sat at the table and began to peel off the skins. "What did you think of him?"

"He's nice."

"What did he say?"

Curtis rinsed his hands and turned off the faucet. He shook the water from his hands and jumped off the chair. "He said he's trying to quit smoking, but it's hard."

"Oh." Did Brandt smoke something other than a pipe?

"If he's not our guardian angel, how come he watches over us?"

"He was…doing a favor for me."

"Because of Kayla and Rex."

"Is there anything around here you don't know about?"

"Nope."

Chapter Fourteen

Rita and Bonnie sat across from each other in the cafeteria. Both had brought their lunches today. Sheila had told them she'd be a few minutes late meeting them, and Alicia was buying today, so she hadn't joined them yet.

Rita pulled out a sandwich encased in plastic from her bag and began to unwrap it. "Hey, let's get the girls together Saturday night. Your kids are at Guy's, right?"

Bonnie considered how she could break it to her friend that she was hoping to be with Brandt Saturday night. If she could make him breakfast Saturday morning, she could suggest he provide the evening meal. That was only fair, wasn't it?

Rita's eyes narrowed. "What?"

Bonnie shrugged and looked away, trying to play it down. "Nothing."

"Do you have a date Saturday night? Oh, my gosh, you do, don't you? With Brandt. Bonnie, that's wonderful!"

"I don't exactly have a date with him Saturday night. He's coming over for breakfast, and I'm hoping we can eat supper together, too."

"He's coming over to your house Saturday morning, and your kids are going to be gone?" Rita's eyes grew wide.

"Stop. He invited me out, but I love cooking breakfast, and he probably doesn't get a lot of home-cooked meals."

Sheila sat down next to Bonnie. "Hi. Who are we talking about?" she asked.

"Bonnie's fixing breakfast for Brandt at her house tomorrow."

Sheila grinned. "Is he spending the night tonight?"

"No. He's been working all week. He's not getting

back until late tonight."

"So he could come over tonight," Sheila pressed.

"But he's not. He asked me to help him find his brother. We'll eat breakfast then probably go to the library when it opens." Of course, Rita and Sheila didn't know Bonnie had flown with him in a private plane to a town he swore was Bellini, attempting to seduce her probably somewhere over Frankfort. Then he had hopped a helicopter, leaving her to fly home alone.

Sheila's grin faded. Disappointment dimmed her gaze. "Oh. I guess you're taking it slow. I suppose I don't blame you. Do the kids know about him?"

"Curtis does. He was…Curtis, that is…was sleeping on the other side of the bed, and I didn't know it. Brandt came in, and…well…."

"Well, what?" Rita asked.

"Kayla came to the door, and I told Brandt to hide, and his hiding spot was the other side of the bed with Curtis. They had a brief conversation about smoking and guardian angels, and that was it. Brandt wants to meet the kids—officially, as it were—but I don't know. He's got this job that seems shady, and he's just not who I picture as being a good fit with me and the kids. You know?"

"And yet, he was in your bedroom. Were you and he…?"

"Not exactly."

Rita leaned forward. "Not exactly? Really? You're not going to tell us?"

Bonnie huffed. "We were mostly talking about Kayla. She snuck out that night, and I wouldn't have known it except for Brandt."

Sheila pursed her lips. "Mostly, huh? Were you mostly undressed at the time?"

"Sheila!" Rita gasped. "Bonnie wouldn't do that." Rita's eyes cut to Bonnie, a look of uncertainty in them. "Would you?"

Bonnie decided not to share that she'd stripped in front of Brandt since nothing had come of it, except as a joke between them. "We were both dressed, and he was sitting next to me on the bed. On top of the covers. Nothing illicit." Just a heart-pounding kiss. "I was pretty on edge about Kayla and this boy who makes me cringe every time I think about him getting near her, but Brandt was really helpful that night. I owe him a lot."

"It would be okay if you settled up with him this weekend, you know. It would be good for you." Sheila patted her friend's hand as an extra encouragement to have sex with Brandt.

Alicia walked to the table and set her tray down next to Rita. Peering at Bonnie, Alicia asked, "What would be good for you, Bonnie?"

****

Bonnie's cell phone rang, waking her up. She picked it up, and squinted at the lit screen. Brandt was calling her.

At five in the morning.

She touched the screen and brought the phone to her ear. "Hello."

"I apologize for waking you up."

Bonnie sat up and yawned. "Apology accepted."

"I caught an earlier flight in. How much trouble would it be to come three hours sooner than we planned?"

"Where are you, the airport?"

"I'm in your driveway, and I want it noted that I am in your driveway and not your house."

Bonnie threw the covers back and slid out of bed. "Then how'd you know I was sleeping?"

"Because it's five on Saturday morning, and your lights are out. Should I drive around for a few hours?"

"Give me a minute. I'll meet you at the back door." Bonnie went to her closet and took her flannel robe off the hook where she kept it. She put her arms in the sleeves, shrugged into it, and tied the belt. Then she yawned and stumbled her way across the house to the back door.

So much for fixing her hair and make-up before he got here. Maybe she could beg off after she fixed him some coffee and jump in the shower.

In the kitchen, she turned on the carport light, illuminating a figure dressed all in black.

His ninja garb, she was sure.

The hinges squeaked when she opened the door, and he stood there giving her a sexy apologetic smile. A shot of adrenaline ricocheted through Bonnie. He had a couple days' beard growth, and it made him look mysterious and appealing. His dark gaze caressed her.

"Good morning," he said, all gravelly, as if he, too, had just awoken.

Bonnie swallowed and tightened her belt, in case it had slipped open without her noticing. All of his...appeal was happening much too early in the morning without enough caffeine.

"Come in. I'll make us some coffee." She hit the light switch, and the kitchen became bright. Walking over to the coffee maker, she retrieved the pot and filled it with water then emptied it in the maker and placed the grounds in next. As she made the coffee, Bonnie caught sight of Brandt from her peripheral vision. He crossed the threshold and shut the door, the hinges making no noise this time.

How did he do that?

"How was work?" she asked for lack of anything better to say.

"It was fine." He leaned his hip on the counter and crossed his arms.

"Why don't you sit down at the table?" His hovering was making her nervous.

He bent forward with his elbows on the counter and stared through the glass-domed cover at the cake she'd made last night. "What is this?"

Pride filled Bonnie, but she attempted to act nonchalant. "Coconut cake."

He straightened. "Really? I love coconut cake."

Yes, Bonnie remembered he had said how much he liked the coconut cakes Delores used to make. Bonnie walked to the refrigerator and retrieved eggs and bacon. "I was going to make biscuits, but they'll take too long."

"I can wait." He looked at her with a hopeful expression with one hand on the raised cake base. Bonnie suppressed the giggle threatening to escape. "Someone having a birthday? This cake hasn't even been cut."

"No. No one's birthday. I just was in a baking mood last night. You can have a piece if you like." She put a plate next to him on the counter and opened the silverware drawer, gesturing for him to take what he needed.

"Are you sure? You made it for your kids, right?"

"I made it for you. You said you liked it. I had a recipe for it, and like I said, I was in a baking mood last night." She cut small squares of butter then measured flour and the other dry ingredients into a bowl. From behind her, she heard glass scraping against ceramic, and a slight ping as the cake cover was removed. The telltale sound of the knife dragging across the plate signaled the cake had been cut.

Haha. No ninja silence when there was coconut cake to be had. Finally, she'd figured out his weakness.

"How much can I eat without you losing respect for me?" he said, obviously with a mouthful of cake.

Bonnie smiled; she turned to him and saw the look of pleasure on his face as he ate from the generous piece he had placed on the plate he held.

"It's yours. Eat as much as you want. But if you're going to fill up on cake, it doesn't make sense for me to cook us breakfast."

He nodded and placed another forkful of cake in his mouth. "I'll save room for breakfast."

"How is it?"

"Delicious." He licked the icing off the tines of the fork. "It's so good. I could put my whole face in that cake and die happy."

"Death by cake." Bonnie snickered. She pressed the butter into the flour mixture, listening to his lip-smacking with amusement. Adding buttermilk to the bowl, she stirred, then turned the dough onto a floured cutting board.

She noticed he cut himself a second piece. She wanted

to ask him if it was as good as Delores's, but resisted. Delores had provided him a home and love for the first time in his life. Even if her coconut cake wasn't as good as Bonnie's, the affection and loyalty he had for the woman would have made it perfect.

"You're amazing, Bonnie Moore."

"Want some coffee?"

"I'll get it. Where are your cups?"

She pointed to a cabinet with a floury finger. He took out two mugs and poured coffee in them. Pouring a generous dollop of cream in one cup, he placed it next to her on the counter. It didn't surprise her he had prepared her coffee how she liked it, but she did wonder how he knew.

They sat down to a breakfast of eggs, bacon, and biscuits with more coffee. Bonnie nursed her cup as she watched him eat a third piece of cake afterward.

The cake may not be as good as Delores's, but obviously it was good enough.

He set down his fork and wiped his mouth with the napkin. Balling it up, he placed it next to his plate and sat back with a satisfied smile and looked at Bonnie.

"I want to sleep with you," he said.

Bonnie set down her mug. "I want to set a good example for my daughter."

Brandt stood up and gathered their dishes and walked over to the sink. He ran water over them.

"You don't have to do that," she said.

"I know." He threw away the used napkins.

"So, anyway, what I was saying was if Kayla finds out I'm sleeping with you, then what message is that going to send to her? That I'm a hypocrite. I just don't need that added stress. Not to mention that you and I don't really know each other that well, and what you're talking about is a big step."

Brandt turned off the water and wiped his hands on a towel then approached her. He held out his hand, and Bonnie took it. He tugged her to her feet and guided her out of the kitchen, across the den and toward her bedroom.

"Brandt, are you listening to me?"

"Every word."

"Then why are we going to my room?"

He led her through the doorway and turned toward her. His thumb ran over her knuckles, and his dark gaze assessed her. "Do you ever fantasize?"

"No."

"Would you like to hear my fantasy?"

"I swear, if you pull out a pair of handcuffs and a whip, I'm calling the police."

Brandt burst out laughing. He extricated his fingers from hers and smoothed a strand of hair away from her face. "I think you'll like this fantasy. In it, we've been married for a while."

He must think she was so boring. She rolled her eyes. "Yeah, and to bring back the excitement, I'm a cheerleader, and you're the quarterback. Give me a break."

He shook his head and laughed again, "Where do you get this stuff?"

She raised her hand in an *I-don't-know* gesture.

"How long have you been divorced?"

"Four years."

"That's not long enough. Let's say we've been married ten years."

She hardened her heart against the way his mesmerizing gaze attempted to lure her into his reality. "This isn't going to change my mind."

"It's my fantasy. Can't you just humor me?"

"I am humoring you. You're standing in my bedroom, aren't you?" He looked so good all in black with a three day growth of beard, saying no to him wasn't easy.

"Please?"

"Fine. We've been married ten years."

"That's not a bad fantasy, is it?"

Bonnie shrugged. Where was he going with this?

"And I've been on assignment all week, and I call you just like I did this morning, and I apologize for waking you up, and you say 'apology accepted.' And your voice is all soft and sexy because I did wake you up. And I picture you here in bed. Your hair spilled over the pillow, and you're wearing a gown. May I?" He reached for the belt of her robe. Bonnie looked down and watched his hands undo the knot. The lapels of the robe fell open revealing her gown. "This one, as a matter of fact."

The gown was certainly not anything she would have put on if she'd known they were going to play fantasy marriage. It was probably ten years old. Haha. Maybe it was a wedding gift, but it looked more like a granny gown than something for her trousseau.

"If we're married, then why would you call me, and wake me up?"

"Because we have a routine. I come home from working all night and we eat breakfast together." He tucked his hands under her robe on top of her shoulders and inched the robe down her shoulders. He watched the slow progress as the robe slid lower and lower, and oh, my goodness, it brought goose bumps on Bonnie's skin, more so than the cool air on her arms.

Do not fall for this.

Bonnie thanked the practical voice whispering in her head. "I'm not taking off my gown."

"Of course not." He walked over to her closet and hung up the robe on the hook where she always hung it.

"I don't like that you know where my robe goes."

He turned to her. "We've been married ten years. Don't you think I should know that by now?"

Bonnie sighed. "I hate to break this to you, but people who have been married ten years don't have sex that often."

Brandt smiled at her. "Then why are you so nervous?"

"Because I know a seduction scene when I'm in one. I may be rusty on all of this, but I'm not stupid. And I'm also aware that we're alone in the house. I don't want to be coerced."

The smile slid from his face. "No coercion. I swear.

I'm about forty-two hours now with no sleep. When I say I want to sleep with you, sleep is what I mean." He sat on the edge of her bed and took off his shoes and socks, tucked his socks in the shoes and then slid them under the bed. Then he took off his outer shirt, leaving on a tight black T-shirt that hugged his chest and shoulders. He slid backward across the mattress. "That's your side, right?" He laid the shirt on the far bedside table.

"You really meant sleep."

He yawned. "Truly."

Bonnie turned off the light switch and sat on the bed and watched him settle under the covers. Maybe he really did mean to sleep. "I guess I could lie down for a few minutes."

"As any good wife would." He plumped the pillow and lay down with a contented sigh.

Bonnie reclined on the bed and watched him. His eyes were already closed. His arm shot out, wrapped around her, and pulled her to him.

"Hey!" she said.

"We're sleeping, right?" He settled his face on her shoulder, and a little too close to her breast for comfort. "Sweet dreams, my bonny wife," he murmured in a Scottish accent. His hold on her loosened within about thirty seconds, and to Bonnie's amazement, she realized he certainly was asleep.

Bonnie listened to him breathe, aware of the odd sensation of a man's body pressed against hers. She closed her eyes thinking there was no way she could actually fall asleep. When she shifted to her side and Brandt spooned her, she awoke with a start.

What?

Oh, that's right.

Brandt had wanted to sleep with her, and she had acquiesced.

And he was really close, the weight of his arm over her waist and his hand tucked under her hip.

The ninja was a cuddler.

Bonnie smiled at the thought.

She slowly worked her way out from his grasp, and he sighed and turned on his back. Bonnie gazed at him, so handsome and dangerous, in her bed. She left the bedroom and went down the hall to the bathroom. She locked the door before taking a shower just in case he awoke and wanted to continue his little marriage fantasy and enter the bathroom while she was naked.

He slept until nearly noon, and then he appeared in the kitchen where she was folding laundry. A tuft of his short hair stuck up near his forehead hampering his dangerous scruffy persona.

"May I borrow a toothbrush?"

Bonnie's attention caught on his under shirt and how it outlined his pectoral muscles and shoulders. The shirt had ridden up displaying part of his stomach, and his pants rode low on his hips. Bonnie studied the thin trail of hair south of his naval until it disappeared at his waistband. What had he asked her? Bonnie focused on the towel in her hands. Fold in half. Fold in half again. Tri-fold and put on the stack. Oh, right. Toothbrush. Did she have any extra toothbrushes? No. She'd meant to buy some last week when she'd taken the kids to the dentist.

"You can use mine," she offered.

He grimaced. "Eww." Then his face relaxed and he smiled. "All right." She realized he was teasing her.

"It's in my bathroom."

"Thanks." He turned around and walked out of the room.

Hopefully, he'd pull his shirt down before he came back. Bonnie didn't need that kind of distraction in the house.

In a few minutes he was back and, yes, with his shirt tucked in his pants. Shoes on, too, she noticed.

"Thank you for letting me sleep here for a few hours."

Warmth spread through Bonnie when she remembered lying next to him and when he'd treated her like his teddy bear.

"Sure. Are you hungry? I could fix us some lunch."

Brandt's gaze strayed to the cake on the counter. Bonnie bit her lip to suppress the smile. That boy liked coconut cake. She stood up and walked across the kitchen.

"You don't have to wait on me."

Bonnie opened the cabinet and retrieved a plate. "Oh. Did you fantasy divorce me already, or was that just so you'd have a warm body next to you when you napped?" She laid it on the counter and opened the silverware drawer, pulling out a knife and fork. She pulled off the cover and cut a piece of cake. "I must be getting worse. Guy put up with me for eleven years. Of course, he was...."

Brandt pressed against her back, wrapping his arms around her body and pulling her back flush against him. The knife clattered against the platter and fell on the countertop. "I wish you wouldn't sneak up on me like that."

He nuzzled her neck. "In my fantasy or in real life, I don't expect you to serve me."

Bonnie shivered as the breath of his lips caressed her skin as he spoke. Bonnie gripped the counter, its edge biting into her hip. An image of them making love on the counter flashed through her mind. Plate. Butter knife. Fork. Cake. Raisin bread. Honey wheat bread. Hot dog buns. She examined the objects on the counter's surface in an attempt to rein in her imagination.

I'm a responsible, mature woman. I don't make love on the kitchen counter.

Right?

Your kids are gone.

You could make love on the kitchen counter.

Brandt's thumb razed across her stomach. Her bare stomach. His hand was inside her shirt!

"What are you doing?"

"Touching your skin." His voice dropped to a rumble. "So soft." He shifted, and his pelvis moved against her butt.

Bonnie closed her eyes. *Oh, my gosh. I cannot have sex on my kitchen counter. My kids make peanut butter and jelly sandwiches on this counter.*

He sucked the patch of skin where her neck met her shoulder.

"Brandt," she breathed. She realized she had leaned back against him. "Don't you dare give me a hickey on my neck."

His low laughter nearly undid her. "Where would you like it?" His fingers slid under the waistband of her pants. In the quiet of the moment, she heard the elastic of her panties pop against his hand.

"Not there."

His finger traced the flesh above her pubic bone. "How about here?"

"No."

His hand moved north, and relief and regret wrestled within Bonnie.

"You know what I'd like?" He reached forward and swiped the icing off the piece of cake she'd cut which was still resting on the cake platter.

"If you start talking about smearing me with coconut cake, you're going to lose ground."

His finger hovered at her mouth, then disappeared, and she heard him suck the frosting off. "Mmmm." His hand appeared again, and Bonnie watched him pick up the fork and spear the cake on the tines. His body shifted once again, Bonnie thought, to give him better access to the dessert, but his other arm still encircled her. He ate the cake from the fork, then reached for more. The sound of him chewing so close to her ear sent tingles all through her body. "Want a bite?"

"Of cake?"

He gifted her with that sexy laugh again. "I like how you don't leave me any loopholes." He held the fork in front of her face. Reaching up, she guided the fork in her mouth with her hand. The sweetness of coconut and moist cake melted on her tongue.

"That *is* good." *This recipe was definitely a keeper.*

"Yes, it is." The next bite was his.

"Here's an idea. Why don't we sit at the table and eat it."

"You're not enjoying this?"

Bonnie pushed against Brandt, then straightened and stepped out of his embrace. She turned around, probably not a smart move because Brandt was temptingly, dangerously close. Bonnie tilted her face to meet Brandt's gaze. "It just seems with cake…or other things…you shouldn't have to compete. You know?"

Brandt moved and leaned a hip against the counter, reaching the fork for the cake again. "You mean, you want to eat the cake and enjoy it without getting distracted with anything else." He placed the utensil in his mouth and chewed. Then cut a small portion of the cake and offered it to her. She reached for the fork, but he moved it out of her reach. "Why don't you trust me?"

"Because I can feed myself."

"Of course, you can. Come on. Trust me."

Bonnie arched an eyebrow at him.

"Here comes the airplane. Open up the hangar so it can land." He mimicked an engine sound, and made the fork fly through the air.

Bonnie smiled at his silliness. "You think I'm going to fall for that?"

The engine sound continued, and he moved the fork back across her line of vision. He sputtered. "Oh, no. The plane is running out of fuel."

"Silly." She opened her mouth, and he placed the fork inside, brushing her lip and leaving some frosting there. "You see why I want to feed myself? Because you—"

Brandt swooped down and covered her mouth with his, and then nothing else existed but this cake-flavored kiss and Brandt holding her close. Her body began to thrum with desire, and Bonnie opened her mouth and tasted Brandt right back. She reached up and put her hand over his shoulder, feeling his muscles beneath the soft material of his shirt.

She heard and felt his breath mingle with hers, his inhalation, and Bonnie, also, breathed in, and smelled the sweetness of cake. Brandt lifted her against him, and Bonnie gasped in pleasure when he grasped her backside and ground into her.

I was wrong. I do like cake and lovemaking together.

Brandt lifted his head. "Bonnie." He gave her cheek a lingering kiss. "You're right. You're distracting me from the cake."

Bonnie moved her hands to grip the front of his shirt. She leaned her forehead against his chest and felt him place her on her feet fully again.

"You're distracting me too." It was a little scary, but for the first time, Bonnie felt the excitement of it as well.

"What do you want to do?"

The question was so unexpected that Bonnie looked up at Brandt. Was he asking if she wanted to make love? His dark gaze watched her, waiting.

She shook her head. She didn't know.

He stepped away, but grasped her hands. "I'd like to take you out tonight. A nice dinner, dancing."

"Dancing?"

"Sure, or whatever you want."

"I don't know about dancing. I haven't danced in years."

"Movie? Movie seems rather lame."

"I'm sure for a ninja it is."

"You want to go see a movie?"

"Well, I haven't been out to see a movie in a long time. It might be nice."

"Okay. Pick one. We'll go see it."

"Any movie?"

Brandt's eyes twinkled. He bent down and kissed her, making Bonnie forget their thread of conversation. "Can we make out in the back row?"

"With the thirteen year olds? Ugh."

Brandt drew back; his brilliant smile made her toes

curl. "I don't want to leave, but I need to go."

Disappointment filled Bonnie's chest. "Oh."

"Debriefing. I could pick you up at seven. Is that too late to get something to eat then go to a movie?"

Bonnie shook her head.

Brandt lifted her hands and kissed her knuckles. "Dinner and a movie. Ladies choice on both."

"Anywhere?"

"Yes. Anywhere you want. I want to impress you, so fast food probably should be out. Unless you really, really want fast food."

"I think I can think of a few slow food places."

He kissed her again, a gentle, lingering kiss that made her wish he didn't have anywhere to go right now.

I'm in so much trouble.

Chapter Fifteen

Brandt drove the Spyder through town, enjoying the potential of its power at his hands and feet, the low purr of the engine, the sleekness of the design, and Bonnie sitting beside him. He'd taken her to dinner. She'd chosen a chain eatery because she said they had a great salad bar and her kids didn't like to go there. The dining room had a high-end feel to it, with tall-backed cushioned seats in the booths, real tablecloths, and low lighting. The movie was an action-adventure flick.

When they'd stood outside of the theater, and she'd named the movie, he'd been surprised.

"It's rated R for violence and sex," he said. "You sure you don't want to see *First Date*?" He would have bet his life that would be her choice.

A look of distaste crossed her face. "It's a chick flick."

Brandt lifted his hand in a gesture of agreement.

"If I want to see a chick flick, I'll go with my girlfriends. They love those kinds of movies."

"And you don't?"

"You said it was my choice. I see kid movies with my kids. I see girly movies with my friends, and now I'm seeing a shoot 'em up movie with…whatever you are."

Brandt smiled. She was so cute. "Whatever I am."

"Yeah, so come on. I don't want to miss the previews." They'd yet to touch up to that point, so when he sat down next to her in the theater, he had taken her hand and placed it on the armrest between them. He'd expected she'd pull her hand away when the sex scene played on the big screen, but she hadn't, and Brandt resisted the urge to caress her palm while the two characters in front of them made love.

Well, if you could call the gratuitous maneuvering in front of them lovemaking.

Brandt pulled the car into her driveway and parked behind her SUV. He shifted into park and killed the engine. Going around to the passenger side, he opened her door and watched to see if she hesitated before moving her feet to the ground. She didn't, so he didn't take her hand to help her out.

He had already decided he was going to walk her to the door and kiss her goodnight without any comments about going inside unless she invited him. But oh, did he want to. Wanted to go inside the house. Wanted to go in her bedroom. Wanted to engage in some gratuitous lovemaking of their own.

But Bonnie didn't seem to be that kind of gal.

Brandt hadn't believed women like her even existed. No one—no woman—had *ever* played hard to get with him.

Maybe it explained why he was so attracted to her, why he wanted her, why he couldn't stop thinking about her. Her approach was ingenious, really. Just act as if you're not interested, then watch the men beg you for any scrap of attention.

Brandt knew all of this, and he wanted her anyway. Would beg if he thought it would do any good whatsoever.

She walked past her car to the porch, the light illuminated the auburn highlights of her soft copper hair. He was sure when she was younger it was probably a dark Irish red, as her daughter's hair was. As light-complected as Bonnie's skin was, the brilliant red would have complimented the ivory tone. She pulled her key ring out of her purse and unlocked the door. With a loud creak, the door opened.

She glanced back at him. "Do you want to come in?"

And the night continued. All kinds of licentious ideas of what he wanted to do with Bonnie inside her house played in Brandt's head. *Play it cool, Sherrod, or you'll crash and burn.* He worked to keep the lustful expression from his face when he answered her question. "Yes."

She nodded and walked inside. He followed her. The kitchen light came on, and she set her purse down on the counter. Brandt closed the door behind him and waited.

"Want some coffee?"

"No, thank you."

Something flickered across her face. Nervousness, he thought.

"Anything to drink?"

He shook his head. *Only you.* But Brandt didn't say it. The next move was going to be hers, if it killed him. Instead he said, "How's Kayla doing?"

"Oh." He saw the tension leave her body, and she began to walk into the living room, turning on a lamp in the corner as she did so.

He sat on the couch, and she sat near him, but not next to him, he noticed.

"I think she's starting to get mad about how Rex treated her." Bonnie slipped her shoes off and folded her legs under her on the cushion. The posture was so natural and relaxed, Brandt felt his desire heighten. She had no *idea* how sexy she was.

"They haven't broken up?"

"Not that she's told me, but she talked to one of his ex-girlfriends, and I think Kayla is seeing now the kind of person he is."

"You must be relieved."

"I'm not celebrating yet, and I'm certainly not letting her see how happy I am about how all of this seems to be turning out. Otherwise, she'll probably get back together with him just to spite me."

"She wouldn't do that, would she?"

Bonnie smiled, as if he'd made a joke. "Of course, she would. You don't have kids so you don't know…" Her smile fell a bit. "You don't have kids, right?"

"No, I don't have any kids."

"Would you know if you did?"

Her question should have bothered him, but it didn't.

As much of an enigma as she was to him, he was one to her as well. They were two alien creatures attempting to figure each other out. "You still don't think much of me, do you?"

"It seems with all of the traveling that you probably do, and being in your forties and never having been married... You haven't ever married before, right?"

Brandt chuckled. "This is beginning to feel like an interrogation."

"You didn't answer the question."

"Do I get a reward for full disclosure?"

"You know all about me. Why can't I know about you?"

"You know a lot about me that even Sheri and David don't know. I know nothing about your childhood."

"Yes, but you only told me those things so I could help you find your brother. That's why I still wonder if this is just a collaboration with benefits."

"What benefits, Bonnie?" Not that he minded too much right now. This anticipation was agonizingly enjoyable.

She arched an eyebrow at him. "You like to flirt."

He shook his head. "Most people never notice me, so I rarely get the chance."

"In your work, perhaps, but I don't believe you don't..." Her eyes fell.

Make love when I want to. Come on, Bonnie, just say it. "I don't what?"

Her gaze lifted to his, and she gave him the Mom-means-business look. "That you don't have sex when you get the urge with whomever is available at the time."

The white wall appeared in his mind. Brandt laid his arm across the back of the couch and reached his fingers to a strand of Bonnie's hair.

"Brandt?"

Silk. "Yes?"

"What did you think of the love scene in the movie?"

He twisted the strand around his fingers and watched

the curl unwind. "The actress is probably not going to win an Oscar for it."

"It wasn't that great, right?"

He gathered more hair in his hand. "She sure wanted everyone to think it was great."

"But it wasn't real, even if they were actually having sex, though it looked like it. They were beautiful people— their body parts, but what we saw in the movie isn't real."

Brandt moved closer to her and combed his fingers through the strands.

"Brandt, look at me."

Frustration bumped into the white wall. "I am looking at you."

Bonnie turned her body to him. She took his hand from the back of her head and gripped his fingers between hers. "Sex is easy. Lots of people do it, and it's not that big of a deal. But it's not real, and I don't do fake. I want to make love, and to do that you have to let me in. You have to make love to me with your heart."

Brandt pulled his hand away and stood. He looked down at her. Her blue gaze cut into him, and a hairline crack appeared in the white wall. *I have to get out of here.* "I don't know what you're talking about."

"Yes, you do, but I understand this is scary."

Another crack. *She's not going to make me run away.* "I'm not the son of a bitch you've decided I am. You think I pick up women in bars or pay for prostitutes? I don't do things like that."

Bonnie stood up, and Brandt didn't move to give her room, but it meant they were practically nose to nose.

"I believe you."

Anger brushed his control. He felt it against his wall, buckling the breadth of the barrier. "No, you don't. You think I'm a liar, that I'm a fake."

"I know you've worked hard to be fake. You lie because it's easier to blend in that way, to hide, and that's how you make your living. But it's not who you are." She put her arm around his waist.

His anger grew, and Brandt stepped backward out of reach. "You don't know me."

"I want to. I want to know you. Let me in."

"I have never lied to you. Not ever. Everything I've said to you has been the truth."

She nodded. "I know that now, and it gives me hope."

Uneasiness edged into the anger. "I don't understand what you want from me."

Bonnie bit her lip. Her eyes narrowed as if she were studying him. "Let's go eat some cake. Will you eat a piece of cake with me?" She walked around the couch and headed for the kitchen.

Warning bells sounded in his head. She was messing with him, and he didn't like that. She shouldn't be able to get to him like this. *That's it. I'm leaving.* He walked to the door and put his hand on the knob and turned it. The door opened.

The sound of the glass cover bumping against the cake base snagged his attention. The taste of sweet cake and coconut frosting filled his memory, and the face of Delores Park filled his mind's eye. Delores, his foster mom, the only woman who had loved him—really loved him, who had made him feel safe and that he was more than a piece of shit, a mistake, a problem for someone to deal with. When he'd come home from school, Delores would sit across the table from him with the coconut cake in between them.

Tell me what happened at school today, she'd say.

More sounds. The cabinet door opening. Ceramic plates moving. The sliding of silverware.

Dammit.

Brandt shut the door.

With the dread and determination of a man walking to the gallows, he pivoted and moved to the table. Bonnie placed a plate in front of him with a huge piece of her cake on it.

She sat down cattycorner to him. "I need to make sure we eat all of the cake before my kids come home in the morning. Anything we don't eat either has to leave with you

185

or it goes down the garbage disposal."

None of that cake was going down the disposal if he had anything to do with it. He resisted the urge to lean his face forward and eat it like a dog with his kibble, and picked up the fork instead.

They ate in a peaceful silence.

Brandt scraped the fork along the plate to catch the vestiges of the frosting and brought it to his lips. Then he licked the fork. Maybe Bonnie thought that was gross. At this point, Brandt didn't think it mattered much.

"I have to tell you how impressed I was when you took Rex down the night we went after Kayla."

"Yeah?" There was a dollop of frosting on Bonnie's plate. Was she saving it?

She moved the plate toward him. "Help yourself. It turns me on to see how much you enjoy my cake."

Brandt scooped up the frosting and ate it. "Sure it does. That's because I'm making love to your cake with my heart, right?"

Bonnie chuckled. "Actually, yes."

Brandt grinned at her, relaxed for the first time since her emotional probe. "And yet, you won't allow me to smear you with coconut icing."

"I have the recipe, so I can make the cake whenever I want to."

What was she saying? That at some future time he could eat cake off her naked body? He liked that idea.

But the way she looked at him wasn't a promise of one day eating cake naked. It was the Bloodhound look. She was about to probe some more. Brandt's guard went up.

"So, anyway, about the other night. Can you show me how you did that?"

"Did what?"

The hunger on Bonnie's face surprised him. "How did you bring him down? He was choking you, and all of the sudden, you had him bent over in pain with his arm behind his back. He's as big as a refrigerator. I can't believe how easy you made it look. Can you show me that move?"

It was an advanced martial arts move. Brandt shook his head.

"Please." The look in her eyes pricked his craw. It occurred to him then that somebody had threatened her, maybe more.

Bile rose in his throat and his teeth clinched in anger. The son of a bitch. Who was it? "Bonnie, has somebody hurt you?"

Her lids lowered. When she met his gaze again, the hunger was replaced by determination. "I'd like to learn how to do that, how to take someone down like that." She pushed her chair back, pulled him to his feet, and guided him to the middle of the kitchen. She dropped his hand and walked backward. "Right now. Will you show me?"

She approached him with her arms outstretched. "So, I'm choking you. What do you do?"

Brandt allowed her to place her hands around his neck. "Really do it," he suggested.

She hesitated.

"Trust me…Hurt me."

Her fingers tightened, but not much.

"You can do better than that," he murmured.

More pressure, but he could breathe and speak easily.

He shook his head and chuckled. "You're weak. I gave you more credit—" That was as much as he could get out before she leaned into him with her eyes flashing fire.

Air caught in his throat. Instinct rose, but Brandt kept control. He leaned into her, and in a slow and deliberate motion, he rose and placed his elbows into the crooks of her arms. With firm, but gentle pressure, he pressed down, down until she had no choice but to let go of him. Grasping her right hand, he pivoted on his foot and twisted her arm slowly moving her body around so that she now faced away from him.

"Okay?" he asked.

"Yes." She was bent at the waist away from him, an automatic response to the arc of the arm. Brandt noticed the graceful line of her neck and back. Her ass close to his own body. He wanted to—

"Can I try it?"

Brandt released her. Immediately she faced him, moving from one foot to the other, her hands gesturing to her neck. "Take me, Brandt. Grab me."

Heat emanated in the vicinity of his groin. *No.*

"Be a man," she urged.

"I am a man. A man doesn't use force." If he knew anything, he knew that. No matter what.

"Show me. Trust me." Bonnie fingertips forged trails down the skin of her neck, then back up.

Trust. They'd thrown the word back and forth with each other. Brandt decided at a later time he'd press her to disclose a little of *her* history, like she wanted him to do with her. But not now. Now she wanted a mini course in self-defense, and he wanted to help her.

Brandt licked his lips and blew a breath out. *I can do this. I'm helping her. She wants to protect herself.* He placed his fingers loosely on her soft skin. Even though the pose was manufactured, uneasiness engulfed him.

Bonnie raised her arms.

"No," he counseled. "You go inside, up through my arms. Lots more leverage that way."

She did so, bringing her elbows down on his, pushing with more force than necessary. "Like this?"

"Yes, now you've got to be quick because you've only got a second before he'll try to hurt you again. Grab my thumb. Twist it, and move my arm down." As he instructed, they moved into the positions until Bonnie held his arm, and his back was to her. "Now when you've got me like this, you move my arm back up. It's not supposed to bend that way, so the natural inclination is for your opponent to bend forward. See? Good."

"Now what?"

"Break my thumb or my arm, or both. Well, not really, but you know what I mean."

She didn't move.

Brandt looked over his shoulder at her. "You have to

be very quick. Your speed is what will save you. If you're too slow, he'll be able to get control back. You don't want that."

She pushed his arm a little more, and Brandt breathed into the discomfort. She was too timid, and was going to get hurt worse if she tried this on anyone. Brandt dropped to his knees, whipped around, grabbed her around the waist with his arm and locked her legs with one of his, falling down to his back bringing her down on top of him.

She had time to give a quick yelp, but that was about it.

Brandt grinned up at her. "Gotta be quick."

Her eyes blinked at him. "I need to work on that, obviously, but it seems a bad move on your part. I mean, I'm on top. You're at a disadvantage."

For a few seconds, she didn't move. Brandt reveled in the feel of her body against his, and how horizontal they were. She moved a bit as if to get up.

Mmmmm. That was even better.

"Let me go."

"But you've got the advantage. Please, take advantage of me while you can."

Bonnie moved against him again, a look of irritation settling on her face. "Really funny. Let me up, Brandt."

He relaxed his arms and legs and lay spread eagle. She climbed off him with a glare. "You enjoyed that a little too much."

Chapter Sixteen

He raised his hand to her. "How about some help?"

She grudgingly took it and tugged. "You don't need my help."

He did, he admitted to himself, if he was going to learn how to make love to her with his heart. But, that, too, would have to be a conversation for another time.

"Want to try it again?" he asked.

"You're not going to flip me on the floor again, are you?"

"Gotta be quick. Quicker than me. And don't worry about hurting me. I'll be okay. Give me what you got, and let's see how good a student you are. Ready?" he stepped toward her and waited for a signal.

She took a deep breath and nodded. Brandt reached for her neck and she moved her hands as he had shown her, then she was behind him forcing his arm up.

"That's great, Bonnie. You did it."

She let go with a laugh, and he turned toward her.

"You weren't faking that, were you?" she asked. Her skin was flushed, probably because of the excitement of being able to overpower him.

"Nope. You did it."

She laughed again. "I can't believe it." Stepping back, she clapped her hands together. "One more time, just so I know I have it."

He went toward her again, and she slammed his arms and twisted his arm behind him.

Damn. She was a good student.

"Okay. Let me go before you break a bone."

"Do you promise you're not just pretending to let me

win?"

"Well, I wouldn't really try to choke you, but yes, you've got me helpless when you have my arm like that. Just for a second or two, but that's all you need."

Bonnie stepped toward him and hugged him in celebration. "Thank you, Brandt. I'm so excited!" The second her body pressed against his, Brandt felt her tense, then pause. He wrapped his arms around her, and gazed into her eyes.

"Nice work, Ms. Moore," he said, then lowered his head and placed his lips on hers. Her mouth was instantly pliant, and to Brandt's surprise, Bonnie slipped her tongue across his lip. He opened his mouth, allowing her to taste him and take what she wanted. He followed her lead, and reveled in her boldness when her hand untucked his shirt and moved across his bare back.

Oh, yes.

He liked where this was going. He'd attempted a few caresses on her bare skin in the past, but she'd shot him down. Guess all he needed was to let her rough him up a bit as a foreplay to the foreplay.

Brandt could handle that.

She was unbuttoning his shirt now, and she kissed the skin she uncovered. Her lips grazed his chest, making him shiver. She stopped and looked up at him, her fingers gripping the sleeves of his shirt.

"I don't want you to leave, but there can only be sleeping tonight. Can you handle that?"

"Where will the sleeping be? You'll be in your bed, I suppose."

"Can you sleep with me again—and only sleep?"

"I suppose. I did well enough this morning, but I was tired, and I don't think you stayed with me very long."

"This is a big step for me. Sharing the night. Spending the night."

It was a big step for him, too. Sharing a bed without sex was definitely not something he'd ever done with another woman, but he wasn't about to tell Bonnie that.

She already seemed to think the worst of him without him disclosing this fact to her.

"We can play fantasy marriage again. You said married people rarely make love." He wasn't sure he believed it. He'd walked in once on Dave and Sherri, and they'd been married almost fifteen years. After that, Brandt made sure he knocked when he went in their living quarters, especially when their kids were at school.

"You'll have to leave early. My kids get home at ten in the morning. Sometimes Guy drops them off earlier."

She was nervous. Brandt took her hands in his. "Bonnie, what do you want?"

Her luminous eyes held his. "I think I like you, but I don't want to because liking you complicates my life. I have to consider what's best for my kids. I'm not sure you being here is what's best for them even if they don't know about you." She shook her head.

Brandt cradled her face in his hands. He leaned down and kissed her briefly. "You can kick me out early in the morning. Or later tonight if you're too nervous with me being here. All right?"

She nodded and went to the kitchen door, turning the lock.

"Before you do that, let me get my bag out of the car."

Her eyebrow rose at him. "You brought an overnight bag?"

"I've been on assignment."

"You had it with you this morning? You could have used your own toothbrush."

"Well, yeah. I suppose so. When I came in your house this morning, I...."

"You what?"

Brandt resisted the urge to shrug and say something cute. But Bonnie wanted him to open up to her. "I just wanted to see you. I wasn't thinking about anything else. And I suppose I could have gone out and gotten my bag, but..." The image of the white wall appeared in his mind. He took a deep breath and focused on the woman in front of him. Stepping forward, he put his hands on her arms. "I just wanted to stay inside. I didn't even want to walk to the car until I had to."

Her gaze searched his. If she'd shown any pity or sympathy, it would have bothered him. He didn't want that from her. He just wanted her to accept him, give him a chance to be someone she'd like to be with. He liked thinking he could be a regular guy with a woman like her.

Bonnie nodded and put her arms around him. "All right."

Brandt retrieved his bag, and when he came back inside Bonnie was no longer in the kitchen. He turned off the lights, locked the door, and then walked into the living room, which was also vacant.

Had she gone to bed already?

Brandt walked through the house, stepped to the threshold of her bedroom, and saw her private bathroom door shut. The shower was running, he noticed. So, she's getting ready for bed.

I'm going to sleep with Bonnie.

Could he convince her in the dark of night to make love? Maybe. Or maybe he wouldn't need to. Maybe she would change her mind and turn to him. She would move her hand under his shirt, run her fingers over his skin, lean over and kiss him, the ends of her hair tickling his face.

He took his duffel in the hall bathroom and engaged in his own nighttime routine before returning to the bedroom. The bathroom door was still shut, but the shower was no longer on. Instead he heard a hair dryer. Brandt sat on the edge of Bonnie's bed and took off his socks and shoes. His heart thumped in excitement, as if he were seventeen again, and he was getting ready for a date with Amanda Coleman. He'd really liked her, and to his surprise, she'd agreed to go out with him to the prom. They'd gone out a few months until....

The bathroom door opened, and a flowery aroma wafted into the room along with Bonnie wearing a long flowing gown with lace on the sleeves and neck.

Her beauty took Brandt's breath for a second, and he laughed.

"What?" She reached up and ran her fingers through her damp hair.

"You're pretty."

She wrinkled her nose at him as she walked around the bed. "Flattery."

"Yes, but it's true."

She walked over to the light switch and turned it off, leaving the room illuminated in the soft light from the bedside lamp. Brandt couldn't believe she had offered to let him sleep in here.

With her.

She had picked up her pillow and was plumping it. The domesticity of her actions made his heart pump faster. He stood and moved back the covers then began to settle on the bed.

She paused in her action, hugging the pillow to her. "What are you doing?"

"Going to bed."

"With your clothes on?"

"Yes."

"Why are you keeping your clothes on? Because I'm not willing to make love?"

"No. I always sleep in my clothes."

Bonnie set the pillow down on the bed and sat on the mattress, leaning back on the heard board. "You always sleep in your clothes?" The disbelief in her tone set Brandt on alert.

"Yes."

"Since when?"

"I've always slept in my clothes."

That look came across her face. Oh, dammit. She was on a scent again. *Oh, man, I need a cigarette.*

"That's interesting. Since you were a child?"

"Yep." Brandt faked a yawn and lay down. He put his back to her.

"Gee, it didn't take you long to learn the turn-my-back-to-my-wife-so-I-won't-have-to-talk-to-her pose."

"What are you talking about? We've been married ten years."

"That's funny. It only feels like one day to me."

"Time flies when you're having fun, so they say. Goodnight, my bonny wife."

He looked at the far wall and waited for the Bloodhound to continue.

It took her about ten seconds.

"Do you ever remember a time you didn't sleep in your clothes?"

Brandt pushed his shoulder down on the bed and settled on his back. He turned his face toward Bonnie who lay on her side with her head propped on her elbow. She watched him.

"I take my clothes off for showers and sex. Since you've already had a shower, I'm guessing you changed your mind about the other."

Bonnie's mouth turned up in a smile. "What about swimming?"

"I don't swim naked."

She moved her finger across the quilt between them, tracing the pattern there. "It's very unusual for a person to sleep fully clothed. I think it means something."

The desire to jump out of bed and go outside to smoke picked at Brandt. But he was out of his pipe tobacco.

Still.

He could buy a cigarette and already have it to his mouth in less than ten minutes if he left now.

"You want me to take off my clothes?"

"I just think it's interesting that you sleep fully clothed." Her gaze followed her finger on the cover between them.

"All right. I'll take off my clothes, if you take off yours."

"I'm wearing appropriate sleepwear."

"So am I. For me."

"Why do you do it? Maybe because you think you'll

need to get up quick. You need to always feel prepared."

"Or I just sleep in my clothes. It doesn't have to mean anything."

"Why don't you try sleeping in less?"

"Just admit you want to see me naked. You think I'm hot, and you want to see me."

"It's not that."

"What do you want me to wear? What do most men sleep in? I have to admit, I don't know since I've never slept with a man."

"Well, I've only slept with one, but I think most men sleep in their underwear, or pajamas, or even sweats and a T-shirt."

"Or naked."

"You shouldn't sleep naked. At least, not with me...tonight."

"I'll make you a deal. I will sleep in my underwear, if you'll sleep in my shirt."

"Your shirt?"

"Yeah."

"Just your shirt?"

"Keep your panties on, if you want." It's not as if she were going to let him get in them. At least, he didn't think so. This exchange made him wonder. It made him anticipate.

"Gee, thanks."

"Is it a deal?"

"Lights off."

"Okay."

"And you can't touch me."

"No promises there."

"Oh, that's right."

"What's right?"

"You like to cuddle."

Brandt opened his mouth to deny it, but realized she was right. "Hurry up and decide. I'm getting sleepy."

He watched her finger move along the quilt. An image of her tracing a pattern on his chest sans shirt ran through his mind.

Bonnie reached over and turned off the lamp. In the dark, she stood up. "Give me your shirt," she said.

Yes!

****

It was three in the morning, and Bonnie's sleeping buddy was restless. His tossing and turning had awoken her several times. She reached over, sought his hand, and clasped it. His fingers curled over hers.

"What's wrong?" she asked.

"Sorry. Am I keeping you awake?" He yawned.

"Can't you sleep?"

"No."

"You haven't been to sleep at all?" The quilt rode low on his body, and though it was dark, Bonnie could see the planes and curves of his torso.

He had been on his back, but he shifted to face her. *My gosh, he had a beautiful body.* Only when she felt the skin of his shoulder and bicep did she realize her hand was exploring what her eyes admired.

"No."

"Do you want your shirt back?"

Brandt laughed that low sexy laugh he had. "Yes, I do, and I want to watch you take it off and hand it to me."

"Dream on, Mr. Ninja."

The best he was going to get was what Bonnie had already done. She'd turned her back to him when she'd slipped her gown over her head then put on his shirt.

Perching on the edge of the bed, she crouched down to pick up her gown where she'd dropped it. From behind her she heard him get up and put on his pants. The soft sounds of material against skin and the slide of his zipper made her body tingle.

The bed dipped with his weight. "It feels like we're going backward."

In a few seconds, she had her gown on and reaching behind her, she handed him his shirt.

"You probably think so, but I don't. I appreciate that

we can do this. It makes me know I can trust you." She climbed under the covers and watched him put on the shirt.

He lay back down and folded the pillow under his head. "Bonnie?"

"Yes?"

"Did your ex-husband ever abuse you?"

Bonnie sighed. "No. Guy never did, but when I was in college, I went out a few times with a man who I think would have been abusive. We were kissing, and all of the sudden he was choking me. Luckily, he stopped, but he tried to talk me into letting him do it again. He said if I didn't fight it, I could get a high from it. It was scary. He had choked me hard enough to leave bruises. I never went out with him again." Bonnie didn't speak for a moment. "When I think about my daughter and her being involved with Rex…that monster, I just want to kill him. And I want to shake her for thinking that how he's treating her is okay. I thought I'd taught her better than that."

"You have taught her better than that," he said. "I'm sure of it."

Brandt moved closer to her. He moved his fingers through her hair.

Closer still.

He bent his head and touched her lips briefly, then trailed tiny kisses across her cheek to her ear where he nibbled on her lobe.

"I want to make love to you with my heart, Bonnie, but I don't know how," he whispered, then he brushed his lips back and forth across her mouth so gently that it brought tears to her eyes. He settled next to her, folding his arms around her and sighing in contentment. His body relaxed, and in a few minutes, Bonnie noticed his breathing changed.

He'd done it again.

He'd fallen asleep.

He might not think he knew how to make love with his heart, but he sure could have fooled Bonnie tonight.

****

The following morning, Bonnie fixed breakfast, and they sat across from each other at the table.

"Listen," she said. "If you can come over for lunch tomorrow, maybe we could go to the library and look through some of the old yearbooks. If your brother was adopted, maybe his name was changed, but you might still recognize him in a picture."

"That's a good idea. How about if I do that in the morning, then take you out for a nice lunch? I still owe you one after I had to leave you in Bellini."

"It can't be too nice. I only get thirty minutes."

Brandt's dark gaze met hers over his coffee cup. "Vivian won't mind if you take a longer lunch if she knows you're with me."

"She doesn't like that you had the lieutenant governor tell her what to do. Apparently, she's a Republican."

A secretive smile passed across his face. "She doesn't have to like it."

"Yes, but she's still the boss of my boss. She can make trouble for me after you're long gone."

"Who says I'm going anywhere?"

"You're a ninja. If a ninja settles down, it makes it hard for him to hide, doesn't it? And besides, Louise Tackett said you were a rolling stone."

Brandt set his mug down on the table and folded his arms in front of him. He studied her until Bonnie dropped her gaze.

"And what do you think? Do you think I'm a rolling stone?"

Bonnie thought he wanted her to help him find Marshall. After that, Bonnie didn't think Brandt would come around anymore. She had to remind herself of that, because she was falling in love with him, and she couldn't let that happen.

He'd break her heart.

"I think," she said carefully, "that I've only known you for a little while. But I think you're a good person, and I like you."

Brandt looked away and shook his head. "What a very tactful answer, Ms. Moore." He stood up. "I better go before your children arrive. We wouldn't want them to get the wrong idea."

"I'm sorry. I didn't mean to hurt your feelings." Bonnie pushed her chair back, walked over to the counter and picked up a plastic container. "Here. This is what's left of your cake." She went to where he stood at the door and held it out to him. He didn't move to take it, so Bonnie stepped forward and kissed him briefly. "I loved having you here. It was very nice. Do you want me to meet you somewhere for lunch tomorrow, or do you want to come by work and pick me up?"

He accepted the container and laid it on the table. Then he wrapped his arms around her and gave her a kiss that made her weak in the knees. He stepped back, and Bonnie held onto one of the kitchen chairs in case her legs gave out.

Brandt's eyes glittered at her as he picked up his cake. "I'll come by and get you. Twelve noon." He opened the door and left without a backward glance.

Chapter Seventeen

The next day Bonnie sat at her desk and watched Brandt walk toward her door. Their eyes met as he approached. Bonnie had her phone to her ear, so she could only wave him in when he stood at her threshold and waited for an invitation. She pointed to the chair in front of her desk and finished up her phone call.

"Didn't we have a deal about you not sneaking in to secure locations, like my floor?"

Brandt lounged in the chair, gracing her with a lazy smile. "I thought I'd see if Vivian had put any of our security suggestions into effect. Obviously, she hasn't."

"We're state employees. Everything takes a long time to do."

"Where are we going for lunch?"

"About that lunch." Bonnie opened a drawer and picked up her purse. "I have a huge favor to ask. Dan and Frances Little were in charge of the concessions tonight at the peewee football game, but they've got the flu. How do you feel about grabbing something in the drive-thru, and going with me to get food and drinks to sell at the game tonight?"

"Sounds like fun." He followed her out of the office.

They stood in front of the elevator. "It doesn't sound like fun to me. They should have bought that stuff already. And who am I going to get to help me in the concession stand?"

"I could help you."

Bonnie turned disbelieving eyes to him. "You?"

"Sure."

"You can't help. Anybody who works the stand has to have a criminal background check."

Brandt rolled his eyes and pulled out his phone. He began to tap the screen.

"What are you doing?"

The elevator doors opened, and they entered. Bonnie pushed the button to the ground floor. She planned to remind Tammy on the way out that Brandt did not have security clearance, and she should not let him get past her.

"I'm sending you verification that I'm safe to sell hotdogs and pop to peewee football players. I'm a level four which means I can get in the White House if I wanted to."

"You're kidding."

He pushed his screen one more time and raised an eyebrow at her. "Verification sent. Where are we going to buy the junk food?"

"You can't really go in the White House, can you? I mean, you could probably sneak in—I can believe that—but…"

They arrived at the receptionist desk. Bonnie paused. "Tammy, you see this man? He isn't supposed to go upstairs unless he's accompanied by a state employee."

Tammy looked from Bonnie to Brandt then back to Bonnie. "He didn't go upstairs."

"Yes, he did. He just walked into my office."

"He couldn't have. I've been sitting here the whole time." Tammy stood up. "How'd you get upstairs? Did someone let you in a fire door?"

Brandt grinned. He took Bonnie's hand and guided her toward the door.

Bonnie went grudgingly. "If it is true that you have security to get in the White House, you still don't have clearance to get in our building, so stop it."

"Is this going to be your tactic with a disgruntled tax payer or claims person who decides to come in here with a gun? Take them to Tammy and tell her not to let them in again, then tell them not to come back? Why did Vivian even ask for help closing the security holes when she hasn't done anything about it?"

"It's only been a couple of weeks. I told you it takes time."

"Inefficiency." He led her to his car parked at the curb.

"We should take my car. We won't be able to get everything in your spy car."

"I can fit two bodies in the trunk. It's big enough."

"Of course, you're joking. You said you had a missile launcher in the trunk."

"Of course, I'm joking. Then and now."

That evening, Brandt showed up, as promised, to help with concessions. Bonnie hoped having him there hadn't been a mistake. Though Curtis was playing football, he would likely see Brandt and remember him. And because Bonnie was going to be in the stand during the game, Andy would likely be in and out the entire time. Still. Bonnie needed the help, and when Brandt arrived, wearing jeans, a T-shirt, and a baseball cap, he could have been a dad to any of the players on the field.

He blended.

Of course, he was a ninja. They were good at that.

Suppressing her anxiety, Bonnie introduced Brandt to Andy who had settled on a metal chair in the corner with his tablet, intent on playing a video game.

The boy glanced up at the man before returning to his game. "Hey."

"How's it going?" Brandt said.

"Good," he said absently.

Bonnie and Brandt's eyes met. Brandt gestured his hands. *See? No sweat.*

"You just wait. Curtis is going to remember you," she said in a low tone.

"We'll be in big trouble then." Brandt patted his pocket then pulled out a sheet of paper. "I've been meaning to give you this." He handed it to Bonnie. "It's information on a self-defense class. You and Kayla could take it together—you know, sort of a mother/daughter bonding thing, and you can learn to kick anyone's butt who's messing with you."

Bonnie looked at the sheet of paper and Brandt's small neat handwriting. This was the kind of gesture that endeared him to her. Brandt put on plastic gloves and began the preparations for the hotdogs. In between customers, their conversation turned to Brandt's search for his brother.

"So, were you able to find anything out at the hospital?" Bonnie asked.

Brandt shook his head. "No. They never had a Marshall Sherrod as a patient."

"They told you that without a court order?"

"I have a lawyer friend who walked me through it."

"What about the county hospital?"

Brandt shrugged, but the disappointment was evident in his eyes. "We checked both hospitals. We even checked the hospital in Port Helen. It's the next closest hospital. I guess the police report was wrong."

Two girls came to the counter. "What will it be, ladies?" she asked.

"Two colas, and two giant pixie sticks," one girl said.

"I want a ring pop," the other child said.

"Okay, a giant pixie stick and a ring pop."

Brandt put ice in cups and poured the drinks while Bonnie took the money and retrieved the candy. After the children left, Brandt threw the gloves away as Bonnie had instructed him to do.

"You know, there were two police officers whose names are on that report. Janet Pino and Eric Tatchocelli. Eric died fourteen years ago, but I haven't been able to track down Janet Pino. Maybe she would remember."

Brandt wore a grim expression and walked outside. Bonnie followed him. He lifted the grill lid and turned the hotdogs on the rack.

"If it was easy, you would have already found your brother," Bonnie said.

"Even if you do find her—Janet Pino—there's no way she is going to remember something that happened thirty-five years ago. That was one night on a job for her. She probably saw thousands of cases just like it."

"Well, if she doesn't remember, then we keep looking. If Child Protective Services was involved, then there had to be a case worker."

Brandt skewered the dogs and placed them in a tin, then closed the lid. He went back inside. "I've already looked. No one from CPS remembers anything. There are no records. The first family I was with don't remember anything."

"Except that you were seven when you went there."

Brandt had been putting the wieners in buns. He stopped and looked at her. "What?"

"You said you were seven when all of this happened, but you were six. That means you were somewhere else first. We need to find that first family."

"No." He shook his head. "My first foster family were the Myers. I must have been mistaken about my age."

Bonnie looked at her son. "Andy, go check on the game. If Curtis is on the bench, ask him if he wants a snack."

The boy got up from where he sat and ran out of the room. Bonnie turned to Brandt. "But you were so sure you were seven. Don't you think that's odd?"

"No, I don't."

"Do you remember going to the Myer's house? The day you arrived, I mean."

Brandt rubbed the bridge of his nose in a gesture of fatigue and frustration. "Can we stop this? I don't want to think about it right now."

"Okay." *Poor man.* This was taking a toll on him. Bonnie stepped close to him and held on to his belt loops. "I'm sorry. I know this is hard."

He put his hands on her hips and pulled her closer. "No, I'm sorry. You're trying to help me, and I'm making it more difficult. It's just… I try to remember, but it all goes blank."

Bonnie stood on her tiptoes and kissed him quickly, then stepped away. Andy would be back in a minute.

A knock sounded on the sliding window, and Bonnie opened it. "Hi. Can I help you?"

It was halftime, and Bonnie and Brandt worked steadily serving the customers. Bonnie liked working with Brandt. He was efficient and quiet, staying in the back of the kitchen with food preparation while Bonnie served customers. Kayla showed up. Guy must have brought her. He'd had to work late, but he'd told Curtis he'd come to watch him play. Since Kayla had band practice, Guy had picked her up and brought her.

"Hey, Mom," she said at the doorway. Her attention left Bonnie and went to Brandt, who was leaning on a back counter with arms folded across his chest. Anxiety stuck in Bonnie's throat. Would Kayla recognize him?

"Hi. Where's your dad?" Bonnie asked.

"He's in the bleachers with Andy. We got here about halftime." She looked at Brandt. "Whose dad are you?"

"No one's."

"Huh." Kayla turned her gaze to Bonnie.

"This is Brandt Sherrod. The Littles have the flu, so I needed some help."

"I could help," Kayla said.

"Great," Bonnie said with enthusiasm she didn't feel.

Brandt's mouth turned up at the corner as he watched Bonnie and her daughter. He pushed off the counter and walked outside. Kayla put her hands on her hips and pivoted toward Bonnie.

"What's his deal?"

"What do you mean?"

"He's here, and he doesn't even have a kid? Who is he?"

"He's *umm*. His name is Brandt Sherrod."

"Yeah, you told me his name already."

A knock sounded on the window. Guy stood on the other side of the glass. Bonnie slid the window open.

"Hey, Bonnie."

"Guy. Thanks for bringing Kayla over."

"Sure. I'll take a couple of dogs. Got any chips?"

Bonnie glanced behind her to see if Brandt had come back in. Kayla was no longer in the building. Now where did she go?

"Yes, we've got chips. Is Curtis playing?"

"Yeah. One of the kids on the other team just ran the wrong way. Scored a touchdown for our team." Guy laughed.

Irritation prickled at Bonnie. "I'm sure they won't count it."

"Well, they should. He made a touchdown."

"Yeah, but his own team isn't going to tackle him, and our team probably wouldn't either because he was running the wrong way."

"One of our kids was yelling at him to go the other way instead of tackling him—giving the other team strategy. Little idiots, but they're so cute."

"Don't call them idiots. I'm sure they're doing the best they can."

"Glad I'm not coaching."

Yeah. You and me both.

Bonnie walked to the door and saw Brandt cleaning the grill. Kayla stood outside of the door, her attention on Brandt's actions.

"Kayla, I thought you were going to help me."

The girl turned and came inside.

"Your dad wants two hotdogs. They're in that warmer there. Guy, you want something to drink?"

The game wound down with the Marlins, Curtis's team, winning by two touchdowns. Near the end of the game, Brandt washed his hands at the sink after sweeping the floor. "I'm going to leave, unless you need me to do anything else?"

"No. I think Kayla and I can handle it. Thanks for all your help."

He touched the bill of his cap as a sign of farewell. It

was such a simple and sweet gesture Bonnie's insides turned mushy.

"Who *is* that guy?" Kayla asked the moment Brandt walked out the door.

"A friend of mine."

Kayla's eyes grew big, then squinted. "Like a...boyfriend?"

"Oh, Kayla. Be serious. I'm too old to have a boyfriend." Bonnie scrubbed a stain on the counter within an inch of its life.

"Well, then what is he?"

The look of disgust on Kayla's face would have been funny except Bonnie was so uneasy about the conversation. Bonnie returned her attention to the counter.

"Basically, his foster mom died and left him some money. I located him, and he's been looking for his brother, so basically he asked me to help him. He was at work today, and he offered to help me tonight, so basically, that's who he is."

"Basically," Kayla said.

"Yeah." Bonnie moved on to another spot.

"OMG, Mom."

"I don't like that term, young lady."

"Do you basically not like the term?"

Bonnie stopped wiping the painted surface and studied her daughter, who smirked.

"Very funny."

Kayla allowed the subject to drop, but on the way home after the game, Brandt was a topic of conversation once again.

"Hey, Mom," Curtis said, "Brandt gave me a high five for winning. Wasn't it cool that he was at my game?"

"Yeah. Cool," Bonnie said. *Please let that be it.*

"How do you know him?" Kayla asked her brother.

"He's our guardian angel."

"What are you talking about?"

"He watches over us, doesn't he, Mom?" Curtis said.

"Well...."

"When did you meet him?" Kayla asked Curtis.

"Let's not—"

"He was in Mama's bedroom."

"Really?" Kayla said, a whole lot of meaning in that one word.

"Oh, boy," Bonnie muttered. She turned the radio up hoping to discourage the conversation, but all she was doing was putting off the inevitable. After all, she was the Bloodhound, and Kayla had inherited Bonnie's bloodhound tendencies.

After the boys were in bed, Kayla came into the living room and sat on the couch next to Bonnie.

"Mom." She huffed. "I am really disappointed. After all the lectures you've given me about not having sex and here you are all along doing it with that…that guy. You're such a hypocrite. And all of those times you were telling me I better not do anything and spying on me."

"What makes you think I'm having sex with Brandt?"

"Because he was in your bedroom." Kayla paused for a second. "Basically."

"*Basically*, Rex has been in your bedroom too."

Kayla's face fell. "Yeah, but…."

"But what? You're fifteen years old. You're a minor. You're not on birth control, and I'm your mother. What you do is my business. I don't want you pregnant or getting some venereal disease from Rex, who has probably had sex with and beat on half the girls at your school. I'm an adult. I'm no longer married to your dad, so if I want to have a boyfriend, then it's okay for me to have one. Just so you know, I have not had sex with Brandt Sherrod. The reason he was in my bedroom was because *he* was the one who pulled Rex off of me the night I came and got you. Brandt was helping me. He was helping both of us. If he hadn't been there, I'm scared to think what would have happened. But he was there. And if I ever decide to have intercourse with him, you can believe that it will be because we are in a committed relationship, and we will use a condom to prevent pregnancy because even though you think I'm old,

I can still get pregnant. And even when I do go through menopause, I can still get an STD, so a condom is always necessary unless you want to get pregnant or you know without a doubt your partner is completely clean. Any questions?"

Kayla stood up and glared at her mother. "I try to talk to you, and this is what I get. I don't know why you have to turn every single conversation into a lecture. Geez. You know?"

She stormed out of the room, and Bonnie heard her door slam. Bonnie placed her hands behind her head and smiled.

Okay, that wasn't quite fair. Kayla had wanted to talk about Brandt and what was fair and all of that, but honestly, Bonnie didn't want to hear it.

The very idea my fifteen-year-old daughter was going to lecture me about sex?

Give me a break.

****

Brandt didn't seem to have a set schedule. This wasn't really an issue, except their time together the previous weekend felt to Bonnie like they'd entered a new phase in their relationship. She wanted to have contact with him.

She thought about him—wondered what he was doing and whom he was with.

On Thursday, she sent him a text inviting him to lunch, but the only response she received was a five-digit number. She tried again, thinking perhaps it was an error, but the same number came through.

She waited a few more days and still didn't hear anything, so she sent an email asking if he'd made any progress in his search for Marshall. She didn't get a reply back.

Had he found Marshall? Was this why he hadn't contacted her? He'd found his brother, so he didn't need her anymore?

It hurt Bonnie to think about it. Maybe Louise Tackett was right. Maybe he was a rolling stone. But what if it wasn't that? What if he had gone on some secret mission? That could be the case. But he'd told her before when he was going to be gone. What if something had happened? He'd gotten hurt. How would Bonnie know?

She tried to put it out of her mind. He was probably fine—just on a job. One night sharing a bed and a T-shirt and a few kisses didn't give her the right to know his coming and goings, did it?

She sent another text, but his only answer was the number she'd received before. What did it mean? Was his phone messed up?

She decided to bake a coconut cake—as if that might conjure Brandt up. Soon, Andy was with her. After they had mixed the batter, Bonnie set the electric beater upright on the counter, with the metal agitators dripping over the bowl.

Andy reached a finger across one of them, swiped it, and put it in his mouth.

"Uh-uh," Bonnie said. "Don't do that. The batter has raw eggs in it."

"Aww, Mom. But it tastes so good."

"I know, but it could make you sick. Let's bake the cake first, then you can eat it."

"I want to lick the beaters."

"When we make the icing, you can lick the beaters then, all right?" Bonnie dropped a kiss on top of his head.

After supper that evening, she served up the cake for herself and the boys.

"How come we made a cake, Mom?" Andy asked before putting a rather large piece of it in his mouth.

"Who cares?" Curtis answered, obviously enjoying his share of it.

"Since Kayla's not here, can I eat her piece?"

Kayla had gone to a movie with a friend. "No. We're going to have to pick her up after a while. She'll probably eat some after she gets home."

When Kayla's text came, Bonnie put the boys in the car and drove to the theater. Kayla and her friend Hannah stood inside the lobby, waiting at the window. When Bonnie drove up, the girls entered the vehicle, their faces bright and flushed with joy.

"It must have been a good movie," Bonnie said waiting for the girls to put on their seatbelts.

"It was. I won't sleep for a week," Hannah said.

"I didn't think it was scary." The rating had been PG-13.

"It wasn't really scary, except for one part. But, ohmygosh, the suspense was awful," Kayla replied.

"I had to pee so bad, but I waited because I was afraid I was going to miss something."

"She almost peed her pants." Kayla laughed.

The boys who had been silent in the rear seat, burst into laughter at their sister's comment.

Bonnie looked at her daughter in the rearview mirror. It was so good to see her happy and doing things with her friends again.

Back home, Bonnie hustled Andy and Curtis to bed. When she came back to the living room, Kayla had settled in the corner of the couch with a plate of cake.

Bonnie joined her. "So, the movie was good?"

"Yeah. Mom, I've been thinking about something."

"All right."

"That guy—Brandt—was he really the same guy who threw Rex to the floor? How did he know you needed help that night?"

"He was with me."

Kayla took a bite of the cake. "You mean, he was here at the house with you?"

"Not exactly. He knew I was worried about you, so he said he'd come look out for anything suspicious, and when you snuck out of the house, he let me know, so we went to get you. He let me go in first. He was my backup."

"But you left him there."

Bonnie smiled at her daughter. "He was in the backseat. He rode home with us."

She shook her head. "No, he didn't."

"Yeah. He's sneaky, like that. It's the kind of work he does."

"What is he, like a narc?"

"Something like that."

"I've been thinking about what you said, and I guess it's okay with me if you have a boyfriend. I mean, you deserve to be happy."

Bonnie reached over and patted her daughter's leg. "Thanks, sweetie."

"I mean, Dad's married to Rene, and she's not too awful as a stepmom. I guess, if you hook up with Brandt, as long as he doesn't try to be my dad or paw you in front of us, it would be good for you."

"It would be good for me, huh?"

"I guess you know Rex and I broke up."

"Really?"

"Yeah. Don't be mad, but Hannah and I met a couple of boys at the theater. Well, we didn't plan it. They were watching the same movie as us. Shel is in band with me. He's pretty funny. I never really talked to him before, but he's kind of cute. He bought me some Skittles."

Hmm. Those were over three dollars a pack.

"Did you have to share?"

Kayla grinned at her. "No. He likes Mike & Ike. I'd never had them before, so he gave me a few."

Wow. Relief spread over Bonnie. *So long, Rex, you jerk.*

"What instrument does Shel play?"

"The oboe. It's a really hard instrument to play. Shel's first chair."

Hmm.

After still not hearing from Brandt, Bonnie waited three days then called the number Sheri had given her the day Bonnie had flown to Bellini.

"Hello."

"Hi." Bonnie didn't recognize the male voice. It wasn't Brandt, and she didn't think it was his associate David either. "My name is Bonnie Moore. Who is this please?"

"Who would you like to speak to?"

"Brandt Sherrod. Sheri gave me this number when I was there—at Benjamin and Associates."

"When you were here. Where were you exactly?"

"Since Brandt flew me there and Sheri drove in circles from the air field, I don't really know where Bellini is, but I've been trying to call Brandt, and I'm worried. Is he at a job? Do you know whom I'm talking about? Did I even dial the correct number?"

"Yes, I know who you're talking about. Brandt is not on a job. He's been given medical leave."

"Medical leave?" Bonnie's heart sped up. "Was he injured in the field?"

"No. He's in a mental health hospital until further notice."

"Oh." Bonnie sat back in her chair, trying to process what she'd just heard. "Thank you for the information. If you talk to him, would you tell him I called?"

"Sure. Goodbye."

Bonnie hung up the telephone.

Brandt was in a mental hospital. She'd brought him into her home. She'd lain down with him and slept. She'd introduced him to her children.

He could get in her house even when it was locked.

With shaking hands, she opened her desk drawer and took out the paper where she'd written the names of security companies and called the one that had the system Brandt had admitted was too secure even for him.

Chapter Eighteen

Brandt was in a mental hospital.

Hadn't Bonnie called him crazy early on? Dismissed him as delusional? But he'd been so convincing.

And she'd fallen for it.

She'd fallen for him.

Bonnie sighed.

What would she do when he was discharged and contacted her again? She couldn't be involved with someone with mental illness.

Could she?

Maybe it was depression. Lots of people had that.

Or maybe it had something to do with this fantasy world he seemed to live in at times. Calling himself a ninja. Working in a city that didn't exist. Claiming he could walk in the White House because of his security clearance. Inviting her to pretend they were married.

And I'd gone along with it.

Fear struck Bonnie like lightning, pinging all along her nerve endings, and she shivered. She'd come to believe him because he'd flown her to a house in the middle of nowhere and let her meet two of his friends who were just as delusional as he was.

Hadn't she known this on some level?

What would she do about helping him find his brother?

What if there wasn't a brother? What if all of that, too, was a delusion? A fantasy? A piece of a make-believe world?

But, no. She'd found the newspaper article and the police report.

Maybe if she could find Janet Pino, she could verify that one of the little boys from that night was Brandt.

And maybe she needed to find Brandt as well. Maybe if she could talk to his doctors or therapists, they could help her understand if she should continue to help him find his brother, or if her help was enabling his delusions.

Stop it, Bonnie. You don't know what his diagnosis is.

Do what you're good at—be the Bloodhound. Find him, then you will know.

Bonnie made a list of all of the mental hospitals in Kentucky and nearby Ohio. She began with the ones close to her and also included ones she thought were close to Bellini, estimating the distance because of how long the plane ride had taken them.

Then she picked up the telephone.

"Landon Mental Health Hospital."

"Hello. Do you have a patient named Brandt Sherrod?"

"Do you have a privacy code?"

"No."

"I'm sorry. You'll have to have a privacy code before I can tell you anything."

"What kind of code? Like his social security number?" Bonnie opened her drawer and drew out his folder. "I can give it to you."

"Every patient has a privacy code. You have to tell me the privacy code before I can give you any information about a patient."

"Okay. Thank you."

Bonnie hung up the telephone. She rapidly clicked the pen she was holding.

How was she supposed to find out where he was?

She called Benjamin and Associates once more hoping the man who had told her that Brandt was in the hospital could tell her which one.

But when she dialed the number, it had been disconnected.

Darn it.

Why did they have to always be so secretive?

Would she have to wait until Brandt got out and contacted her? And what would she say to him? *Sorry. I have enough on my plate without falling in love with someone with mental problems.*

What if it was something minor like anxiety? He'd acted stressed when Bonnie had pressed him about the disparity between his age of when he thought he'd seen Marshall last and when it had actually happened.

If he was in a mental hospital, it explained why he hadn't responded to her texts and emails.

Or had he?

Bonnie picked up her cell phone and looked at the screen. She scrolled to the texts she'd sent him and the numerical responses she'd received back each time.

693810

Bonnie reached over to her office phone and called Landon Mental Hospital.

"Can you check and see if you have Brandt Sherrod as a patient?"

"Do you have a privacy code?"

"Yes. 693810."

"I'm sorry. We do not have Brandt Sherrod listed as a patient here."

"Thank you."

Bonnie called New Hope Hospital and received the same response. Then she tried Breckinridge Hospital.

"Good Morning. Breckinridge Hospital. May I help you?"

"Yes. Do you have Brandt Sherrod as a patient?"

"What is the patient's privacy code please?"

"693810," Bonnie said.

"Yes. He is a patient here."

Excitement ran through her. She'd found him! And it was only a half hour from where she was. "What are your visitor hours?"

The visiting hour began at four in the afternoon, so Bonnie signed a leave slip and arrived at Breckinridge with ten minutes to spare. She had to leave her purse in a locker and receive a visitor sticker. Though the hospital appeared clean and bright, every door Bonnie went through had to be unlocked first. On the third floor, she pressed a doorbell and a man in scrubs and a staff badge answered her summons.

"I'm here to see Brandt Sherrod," she said.

"All right. Let me show you to the visitor room." Bonnie followed him down a corridor and into a room with couches, chairs, and a mounted television. Several people sat in the room, one man wore a hospital gown, another person—a woman—wore street clothes with hospital socks on her feet. Another person sat in a wheelchair with his foot braced in an air cast.

Bonnie smiled at them as she waited for the staff person to unlock the door he'd led her to. They walked in an oblong room with a conference table and several chairs. In the corner, a desk sat with a telephone. The man picked up the telephone and asked someone to tell Brandt he had a visitor.

Bonnie's nerves jangled as the minutes ticked by. She turned and looked at the door, and there was Brandt wearing blue jeans and a black T-shirt, the kind he used as an undershirt. He had on tennis shoes, but the laces were missing. The whiskers on his face testified he likely hadn't shaved since Bonnie had seen him last, and the expression in his eyes was one she hadn't seen before.

"Thanks, Jon," he said without breaking eye contact with Bonnie. He stopped in front of her, and the corner of his mouth curved upward. "I knew you'd figure out what the number meant."

Emotion closed Bonnie's throat, and she swallowed a few times. "What happened? Are you okay? What happened to your shoes? Do you need me to bring you some shoe laces?"

He shook his head. "We can't have shoe laces in here. Or belts, or anything else that someone can hang themselves with."

Oh, mercy.

"It's all right. Really." He gestured to the table. "Let's sit down."

Brandt sat on the end of the table, and Bonnie sat down across from him. A thousand questions crowded her mind, but she waited for Brandt to speak.

He glanced at the man he had called Jon. Bonnie did as well. It must be that patients were not allowed unsupervised visits.

"I checked myself in here."

"Okay."

"I thought about what you said—about the missing time in my life. You said that sometimes the system will place a child in a facility if there isn't a placement available or if he's got problems. So, I decided to visit a few, and when I walked in the lobby here, something happened to me. I started sweating. My heart started to race. This wave of nausea hit me like I had the flu. I left and went and sat in my car, and the feeling went away, and I realized that I must have been here before."

Bonnie sat back. "You were here before? Brandt, that's wonderful that you figured that out. But I don't understand. Did you have a panic attack? Is that why they committed you?"

He shook his head. "No. I told them I was suicidal."

"Oh."

"I told them that because I knew they'd probably agree to keep me here for observation, and it would give me the opportunity to look at their files to see if I had been here."

"They're not going to let you look at their files."

"Don't I know it. People watch you all the time. I haven't been able to do anything without a nurse or tech looking over my shoulder. For someone like me who prides himself on being invisible, it's humiliating."

Bonnie shook her head in derision. "Brandt, you told them you're suicidal. Of course, they're going to watch you every second. You've got to tell them the truth. They're your records. Why don't you just ask them to look?"

"I didn't think I would have to, and besides, if I tell them everything," Brandt's dark gaze dropped, "they might decide there's something really wrong with me. And then I won't be able to leave when I want to."

Bonnie's heart knocked painfully in her chest. She reached over the table and took Brandt's hands. "Let's find someone to talk to. I'll be here with you. We'll do it together."

Bonnie turned and asked Jon if anyone were available for them to talk to about Brandt's diagnosis. The young man who was sitting at the desk, picked up the receiver. "You probably should talk to Crissy Mayford. She's the director of therapeutic services. I'll see if she's available."

Within twenty minutes, Jon escorted Brandt and Bonnie to a smaller room with a table and three chairs. Sitting down at the table, a thin woman with dark hair entered the room.

"Hi," she said sitting on the vacant chair. "I'm Crissy Mayford. Tell me what's going on."

Brandt didn't speak. Bonnie looked at him. He watched the tabletop in front of him, and a drop of sweat ran down his temple. Bonnie scooted her chair closer to his and grasped his hand again. His fingers tightened on hers.

"Brandt has something he needs to tell you."

"Are you family?" Crissy asked.

"She's my wife," Brandt declared.

"Brandt, the truth. Tell her why you're here."

"I'm here because…" He sighed. Then he shut his eyes tightly. Bonnie didn't think he was going to say anything else.

"Brandt—"

"It's all right," Crissy said. "Just give him a minute."

Opening his eyes, he looked at Crissy and told her the story of the night he and his brother were separated, the many foster homes he'd lived in before coming to live with Delores. Crissy asked a few questions as Brandt talked. He sat back in his chair and crossed his arms across his chest and told another story Bonnie hadn't heard before.

"When I was a senior in high school, I was dating a young woman. I was arrested for raping her. I pled guilty."

"Did you rape her?" Crissy asked.

"No. I never would have forced her to do anything she didn't want to do. Or any woman. I don't remember a lot about my mother, but I do remember a man beating her the last night I ever saw her because she wouldn't do what he wanted. I have never treated a woman like that. Not even close." Brandt looked at Bonnie. "But this girl—she was sixteen, and her parents were unsympathetic."

Bonnie listened to Brandt's story and marveled at his role in the incident involving Kayla and Rex. Bonnie tried to remember her past comments. Did Brandt think she placed him in the same category as Rex?

"Do you blame her for what happened, for you going to jail?" Crissy asked.

"I think she was too scared to tell them what really happened. I didn't hold it against her. It is what it is, you know? But I didn't go to jail. At least, not for long. After the conviction, I had to wait for the sentencing. A man came to see me. He said he could divert my sentence if I would work for him. He was in an organization that dealt in covert operations. So, I said, okay."

"Brandt, why are you telling me all of this now?" Crissy asked.

"Because I don't want to kill myself. I just wanted to find out if I was a patient here when I was a kid."

"We didn't admit you because you were suicidal. We admitted you as a patient because you were symptomatic of PTSD."

"Really?"

"Have you been taking and swallowing your medicine?"

Brandt pinched his lips together and stared at Crissy.

"I see. Where are the pills?"

"I threw them in the trash when I could, and one I saved until supper and then I put it in my milk carton before I took my tray up."

"I should have known. You were much too compliant with your meds. Most patients who willingly take their medicine don't try to sneak out."

Brandt smiled. "Your staff are top-notch. You have no idea how good I am at leaving and entering places undetected, and I haven't been successful here once."

"Except you weren't medicating, and we were not aware." Crissy stood up. "What year was it that you think you were a patient here?"

Brandt answered her.

"All right. Jon will show you back to the visitation room." Crissy opened the door and left. Even before they crossed the threshold, Bonnie felt Brandt's distance.

"You don't have to stay," Brandt said as Jon accompanied them to the other room.

Bonnie turned and searched his face, but she couldn't read any emotion.

"Do you want me to go?"

"I appreciate your advice. You accomplished in an hour what I haven't been able to do in four days."

Disappointment and confusion swirled in Bonnie's mind. "But do you want me to go?"

The wall—or whatever it was—fell, and fear marred his face. "No. No, I don't."

Then it was gone, but Bonnie had seen it. She took a step toward him, and then they were in each other's arms. Brandt's mouth descended on hers, the bristles from his whiskers scraping against her lips and skin deliciously. Bonnie opened her lips and tasted him, giving him more than he asked, putting all of her doubt and relief in the kiss, hoping he understood what she hadn't the chance to tell him with words. Vaguely, she realized his arms encased her, and her feet weren't touching the ground.

"Sorry. Sorry, guys, you're going to have to stop." Jon was speaking, and Bonnie became aware of catcalls from the other patients. "Conjugal visits aren't allowed and especially not in the day room."

****

Before visiting hours were over, Crissy had met with Brandt and Bonnie once more. She had researched Brandt's suspicion he'd been a patient previously, and he was right. Crissy located the file in the hospital's record storage room.

"There's nothing here about your brother, but you were here for seven months—from ages six to seven. We treated you for PTSD and panic disorder. Those aren't uncommon at all for someone who experienced what you did."

"Is it strange that he has no recollection of being here?" Bonnie asked.

"Obviously, you did remember subconsciously," Crissy spoke to Brandt. "That's why you were able to be so convincing the day we admitted you. Profuse sweating. Your temperature and blood pressure were both elevated, and you exhibited signs of extreme stress." Crissy shook her head. "But it isn't uncommon for our minds to block out traumatic events in our lives. Obviously, you were able to develop some coping skills and overcome the tragedy of your past. It's exciting to meet you after knowing you were a patient here, even if you misrepresented your circumstances to get in."

"Next time, just ask," Bonnie said.

"Yes. Next time, just ask."

"So, can I go?" Brandt asked.

Crissy smirked. "No. You haven't been discharged yet. I've had a consult with the doctor, and he'd like to meet with you about what you've told me. Whether you need to be hospitalized for the symptoms you're presenting remains to be seen, especially since you have not been compliant with your medication. You could leave AMA, but the doctor is not going to discharge you today"—her attention turned to Bonnie—"and visiting hours are over."

With one last soul-wrenching kiss, Bonnie left Brandt and the unit.

"Call me," she said. "Okay?"

"I will. I promise."

Stopping by Veda's on the way home, Bonnie picked

up the boys. Bonnie was later than usual, so she had called and ordered pizza to be delivered to the house. She kept her cell phone close by in case Brandt texted her, but he didn't.

The next day, he did call.

"Hi," he said.

Bonnie's heart thumped quickly. "Hi. Are you okay?"

"The doctor wants to keep me a couple more days."

"Okay."

"I'm in a mental hospital."

"Yes."

"And they think I need to be here."

Bonnie heard the dejection in his voice.

"You just found out there is about seven months of your life you don't remember. You think the doctor doesn't want to talk to you about that?"

His sigh came through the line.

"Brandt, you have the opportunity to explore some things in your life that were very painful. Maybe you can find out why you're afraid to be naked."

"I asked about it. They call it a coping mechanism because a lot of the traumatic things that happened to me as a kid took place at night, and the doc says it's all right if I want to sleep in my clothes. Even though, he thought the exercise you and I did with letting you wear my shirt was likely beneficial."

Bonnie cringed. "You told him about me?"

"Yes. Listen, I know you've been reluctant to be involved with me from day one, and I don't blame you if you don't want to have anything else to do with me. I'll let it go, and I won't stalk you or try to contact you again. I promise you don't have to worry about me."

"What about Marshall?"

"Of course, I still want your help, but I can keep it professional."

Fear slammed into Bonnie. She didn't want to keep it professional.

Wait. What?

Oh, mercy me.

I'm in love with Brandt Sherrod, ninja.

Bonnie's mind began racing with the implications of loving someone who had a letter as part of the zip code at his job, who had no qualms breaking into the governor's office and stealing sports memorabilia, who was presently residing in a mental institution, and whose kisses made Bonnie lose her breath.

Of course, I still want your help, but I can keep it professional.

Was he saying that because he had changed his mind about her?

Or because he thought she didn't want him?

Bonnie took a fortifying breath. "Let's talk about it when you're discharged. All right?"

****

A text from Brandt showed up on Bonnie's telephone the following evening:

Sprung from the nut house Appreciate everything you've done.

Bonnie smiled. She texted him back: *Want to come over? Kids are in bed.*

Half hour?

Come to the back door, Bonnie sent back.

A soft knock alerted her that he had arrived. She went to the door and opened it. Brandt stood there in black denim jeans and a black golf shirt with his tennis shoes laced up. His whiskers were fuller, covering his face in a dark beard. Yearning to touch him, to kiss him, filled Bonnie. Instead of jumping on him and kissing him, she stepped backward and gestured to the table. "Would you like to have some cake?"

A wide smile split his beard. "You know I do."

Bonnie cut him a large piece and arranged it on a plate in front of him.

"How are you?"

"I'm okay, at least Breckinridge says I am." He meticulously divided the cake on his plate. Why wasn't he eating it? "I know you didn't know all of my history."

"You didn't know all of your history either."

225

"I'm talking about my conviction. Even though my record doesn't show I raped that girl, I admitted to it, and I took responsibility for it. So, I understand why you don't want to see me anymore." His gaze focused on the cake.

"But you didn't rape her."

"No."

"Okay, so you didn't, and it all happened a very long time ago. We all did stupid things when we were young."

"Yeah? What did Bonnie Moore ever do that was stupid?"

"I fell in love with Guy Moore and married him."

"You got three kids out of the deal."

"That's true. I'd like to think that in my forties, I'm smarter about such things. More discerning. More wise. Eat your cake. You make me think you don't like it the way you're pushing it around your plate."

"I love your cake." He shoveled a piece of it and put it in his mouth. "See? Mmmm."

"Brandt, I know that all of this with your brother and your lost time, it's a lot to process. I don't want to add to your stress."

"Since I'm crazy and everything?" He took another bite.

"Would you stop with that? I don't think you're crazy. I need to tell you something. When you were at Breckinridge, and I didn't know where you were, I started to worry about you. Were you hurt or dead? It scared me, and I wished that I hadn't…."

"Played hard to get?" He stuck the fork in his mouth and cleaned the rest of the icing off it.

"Yes."

Her one word answer made him pause. For the first time since they sat down, he met her gaze.

"Falling in love, it's not responsible," Bonnie said. "I've got my children to consider, and it's scary to think that I've given my heart away again, because I know how much it hurts to love someone who can't love me back."

Brandt laid the fork down next to the plate and stared

at her. "No."

"I don't want this to be awkward between us. I judged you when we first met, and a lot of times since then, but when you show you care about my kids, well, that just makes it that much harder for me not to love you. I didn't think I'd fall in love with someone again, but I have. I do, so if you don't want to stick around after we find Marshall, that's okay. I just want us to be discreet, so that my kids won't get too attached. All right?"

Brandt blinked at her. "You want to have an affair with me?"

A nervous laugh escaped her mouth. "A discreet one, I guess. If it turns into something more permanent, that'd be wonderful."

A little smile turned his mouth upward. "Secret affair," he sang the words of a popular song. "Hide me in your closet when your dad comes to the door. Secret affair. Brag to the boys at school that I made a weekend score."

"Shh. Shh! Would you be quiet?"

"Sorry." He scooted back his chair and picked up her hand, then tugged. "Come sit here and tell me about this discreet affair we're going to have."

Bonnie allowed him to maneuver her onto his lap. "I don't think this is it. If one of the kids walks in, me being on your lap is going to look suspicious."

Brandt grinned at her and planted a wet kiss on her palm. Bonnie's body tingled all over as if that spot on her hand connected with every other part of her.

"We still have our clothes on." But a wicked light had entered his eyes. His other hand slid under her shirt. His thumb slid across her bra.

"Brandt." She was about to tell him to stop, when he leaned forward and kissed her.

Yearning battled with uneasiness. He was nibbling her neck now, and she was pretty sure he'd unhooked her bra.

"Brandt." Bonnie shook her head to clear away the lusty haze. "We have to stop."

He palmed her breast. "I don't want to stop," he said

against her lips.

She held onto his forearm. "Neither do I, but I don't want to do this in the kitchen."

Brandt slid his fingers down to her waist. His intense gaze held her, and he began to stroke her hip.

"What has gotten into you? All of the sudden, you're acting...."

"What?" He caressed the material above her pubic bone, sliding her panties back and forth. Bonnie's body began to hum.

She stood up and crossed her arms over her chest. "I said we need to stop. I don't want to carry on like this when my children could wake up and come in here."

Brandt watched her, a nearly dangerous look in his eyes. "Maybe I should just go."

"If you can't control yourself, maybe you should."

They stared at each other for a long, horrible moment. Bonnie tried to decipher his expression, but she couldn't. It was as if Brandt Sherrod had disappeared, and this stranger had taken his place.

"Yes. Yes, I think you should go."

His head moved forward in a nod, but he never broke eye contact with her. Standing up, he strolled to the door. "I'll see you around, Bonnie."

And he was gone.

What had just happened?

Bonnie had never seen this side of Brandt before. Why was he acting this way?

She ran through their conversation in her mind.

He'd brought up his past and said he understood why she didn't want to see him anymore. That was weird. Why would he think that? It seemed early on when she didn't want anything to do with him, it hadn't occurred to him to leave her alone. Now it was as if...he was setting her up to dump him.

She'd told him she had fallen in love with him, and he'd pushed her away.

Why?

To test her?

Was that what this was, a test to see if she really did love him?

Oh, no, you don't.

Bonnie opened the door and ran into the night. His car was pulling out of her driveway. Could she get his attention?

"Brandt, Brandt!" She kept running right out to the street and stopped in front of his car.

His narrowed eyes studied her. He rolled down the window. "What do you want?"

She put her hands on her hips. "I'm not finished with you."

A car turned the corner and approached them on the street.

"Can you pull back into the driveway?" Bonnie asked.

He shook his head "I better go."

"Please, Brandt. This won't take long." Or maybe it would. She didn't know what this was or how long it would take. She just knew he couldn't leave yet.

He looked at the rearview mirror then back at her. She stepped on the curb and waited. Finally, he turned the steering wheel and the car rolled from blacktop to pavement.

Yes!

Bonnie walked up to the car. "Engine off."

"What did you want to tell me?"

"It's a secret. You like secrets, don't you?"

He arched an eyebrow. Killing the motor, he stepped out of the car, shut the door, and leaned against it. "What?"

"Yeah, what?" She held out her hand for his keys.

The corner of his mouth turned up, and he shook his head.

"Why not?"

"What are you going to do, throw them?"

"I'm much too sensible to do that." She gestured for them, and to her surprise, he placed them on her palm. "Thank you," she said.

He resumed his stance against the car. "Now what?"

She swung the key ring around her finger a couple of times. "You're good at your job. Being a ninja."

"And you're good at your job. Being a bloodhound."

"Yes, but I missed a scent back there in my kitchen, and I'm sorry about that."

Brandt folded his arms across his chest.

"I know it took a lot for you to come here tonight after being at Breckinridge, knowing that I knew what you were accused of, knowing some of your history you just found out about. As a ninja, you're used to hiding and not being detected. I imagine just coming by tonight was uncomfortable after so much disclosure. Maybe it was unfair of me to tell you I've fallen in love with you. I should have played hard to get a little longer until you got used to me knowing you, seeing…really seeing you."

Brandt looked away.

"What are you thinking?"

He shook his head and shoulders as if he were trying to loosen up his muscles. "I'm thinking of a joke."

Bonnie sure hadn't been expecting him to be thinking about jokes, but maybe all of this was too intense. Maybe he needed a reprieve, and this was his way of taking one. She decided to practice patience and acceptance.

"All right. I like jokes. Let me hear it."

"A three-legged dog walks into a bar, sits down, and says 'I'm looking for the man who shot my paw.'"

Bonnie smiled.

"Corny, huh?"

"Yeah. Want to come to dinner tomorrow night?"

"Where will your kids be?"

"Here. You can tell the joke to Andrew and Curtis. They won't think it's corny."

"Me eating dinner here with your kids doesn't sound like a discreet affair."

"It's just dinner. If you like, we can meet you somewhere, act like we just happened to run into each other."

"Kayla will never buy it."

"No. So, just come over to the house." She tossed his keys to him, and he caught them. "We'll eat at six. See you tomorrow." Bonnie turned and began to walk back to the house.

Brandt appeared in front of her. Then she was in his arms, and he was kissing her as if his life depended on it.

"My Bonnie. Oh, my Bonnie," he whispered as he kissed a trail from her mouth to her ear. "I don't know what the hell I'm doing with you, but I think it's loving you with my whole heart. It scares me to death."

"Where's your ninja whimsy you were telling me about? Come on and play with me, Brandt. Falling in love can be a lot of fun."

His hands ran up and down her back. "You don't want someone who can't love you back. You told me that inside."

Bonnie drew away from him so she could gaze into his eyes. "You already do love me, I think. That's why you're scared. It's all right. We'll figure it out together."

The next morning, Bonnie hummed happily as she settled into her desk at work. Brandt had accepted her dinner invitation after a few more soul touching kisses under her carport. She'd led him under the darkened interior for fear the neighbors would see Bonnie's response to his confession. This morning when she'd told the children Brandt was coming for supper, they'd seemed happy about it. Bonnie logged onto her computer and checked email. One new message waiting in her inbox caught her attention. She clicked it open:

Dear Bonnie,

I received your message via Facebook inquiring if I used to serve on the police force in Carlton Heights, Kentucky. Yes, I did for eight years. Pino was my maiden name. I am now Janet Thorn. I live in Oma, West Virginia. My telephone number follows.

Bonnie immediately picked up the telephone and dialed the number at the bottom of the message. Janet picked up on the first ring, and Bonnie identified herself.

"I'm calling to ask if you remember a case you worked about thirty-five years ago. The incident was a domestic disturbance in which a woman was beat up by her boyfriend. The woman had two sons who were at the house that night."

"That describes about half the calls I had while I was a police officer. I'm not sure I'll be able to help you."

"Can I tell you a little more about it to see if it might trigger your memory?"

"What business are you in?"

"I work for the Commonwealth of Kentucky locating beneficiaries."

"Oh. Okay."

"The man I'm trying to locate is one of the little boys. The woman's name was Susan Sherrod. Her sons were Brandt and Marshall Sherrod. They were five and six years old. According to the police report, one boy went to the hospital and the other one was taken into custody by Child Protective Services."

"Actually, yes, I do remember the Sherrod boys. I was new to the force, and it was the first time I ever had to deal with something like that."

"Can you tell me what happened?"

"The assailant beat up Susan and one of her sons. When we arrived on scene, Marshall was cradling his little brother. We had to pull them apart so that Brandt could go to the hospital."

"Wait. Marshall was the younger child."

"I don't think so. Marshall was the older boy—dark hair and eyes. Brandt was the tow headed one. He looked like a little doll. Marshall kept screaming for Brandt who was unresponsive at the scene. I can still hear that boy screaming his brother's name. They transported Brandt to St. Joseph's hospital where he died a few hours later.

"Are you telling me Brandt Sherrod died that night?"
"Yes."

Chapter Nineteen

Bonnie changed the phone from one ear to the other.

Janet continued. "A CPS worker took Marshall, who I heard was taken to a mental health facility in a catatonic state. Oh, my gosh, it was one of the saddest things I've ever witnessed. I had to go to therapy to deal with it."

"Are you sure?" Bonnie asked. "Are you sure Brandt was the little boy who died?"

"All I can tell you is that his brother kept screaming his name. I can still hear it in my head. 'Brandt! Brandt!' It took three people to get that boy away from his brother."

"And the boy who kept calling his name was the dark-haired boy. He was the one who had to go to the mental hospital?"

"Yes. Marshall Sherrod. Like the school. That's how I remember his name."

Bonnie massaged her head as she listened to Janet's story. All of this was unbelievable.

"So, you're trying to locate Marshall Sherrod?" Janet asked.

"Well," Bonnie sighed, "I thought I was. Do you think you could meet me today? I know the boy you're speaking of. He'd like to meet you so you can fill in some of the missing pieces of his life."

****

Bonnie met Brandt at her front door. "Are you sure you're up to this?"

This was dinner at her house with her children.

She still wore her work blouse and skirt, but she had a tea towel thrown over her shoulder and an apron at her waist. He took note of her troubled expression and wringing hands, but it was the red toenail polish on her bare feet that captured his attention.

The caveman in him grunted enthusiastically. "Please tell me I'm going to see you barefoot in the kitchen tonight. Every man's fantasy."

She shot him *the look*, and he pulled her to him and dropped a kiss on that no-nonsense mouth.

Bonnie pushed him away. "Don't do that. I don't want them freaking out before we've had a chance to ease them into our relationship."

So, the discreet affair had morphed into a relationship. Interesting, what a heart-to-heart talk in the driveway and a serious necking session in her carport could accomplish.

"If you don't want me getting all frisky, you need to keep the shoes on," he said.

Bonnie motioned for him to come inside the house. Brandt strolled inside, and she shut the door behind him.

Brushing by him, she walked toward the back of the house. He'd used the front door as a formality, but it seemed her kids hadn't noticed. "Yeah? And what was your excuse last night?" she threw over her shoulder.

"Apparently, I was trying to offend you enough to kick me out, and it would have worked, too, if it wasn't for your pesky bloodhound tendencies making you chase me down the street." Brandt followed her.

He should be reeling from his meeting with Janet Thorn. Well, he was, actually, but Bonnie had gone with him. She'd sat next to him when Janet had recounted her memories of that terrible night when he was six. Bonnie had held his hand on the way back as he processed the truth of adopting his brother's name as his own, of blocking out the memories of what had happened to Marshall…or Brandt. She'd suggested options for finding where Brandt had been buried.

He should be sad, but he wasn't. There was nothing but relief in finally knowing, finally having all the pieces of a very old puzzle, knowing who he was and who his brother was.

And having someone to share the burden and the celebration with.

It felt so damn good.

He watched her hips sway in front of him and wondered what time her kids went to bed. She raised her arm and pointed as they passed the living room. Brandt looked in the direction she indicated. Her sons stood inside the doorway. They returned his curious stare.

"Mom says we have to play a board game with you," Curtis said.

"Kayla has to play, too." Andrew smiled.

Kayla lounged on the corner of the couch. She held her cell phone in her hand, but she watched him as well.

"We're playing Uno," she informed him. "And every time you draw a card from the deck, you have to answer a question from us."

Brandt glanced behind him and saw the last of Bonnie as she swished into the kitchen.

The traitor.

He followed the boys in the room.

Andrew pointed to a rocking chair placed next to the coffee table. "You sit there."

Brandt did so. He looked at each person in the room. "I shuffle the cards before we start," he announced and then laughed when three faces fell.

"You can't shuffle the cards," Curtis said.

"Yeah. We already shuffled them," Andrew added.

Kayla grinned wickedly.

Brandt picked up the large deck of cards. "You guys wouldn't be cheating just so you can ask me a bunch of questions, would you?"

****

Brandt, Bonnie, Kayla, Andy, and Curtis stood at a grave next to the fence line in Carlton Heights Memorial Cemetery. After Janet's news, Brandt had searched and found the death certificate for his brother and hospital records showing the Catholic Sisters at St. Joseph's hospital paid to have the child buried with a small gravestone to mark the grave.

Andy put a small flag with a picture of his favorite video game symbol on it. Curtis laid a football next to the flag. Each child had decided to bring an item for the trip to see Brandt's brother's grave.

"It's weird to see your name on a tombstone." Kayla placed a bouquet of red roses on the grave and stood.

"It's even weirder to see *my* name on a tombstone," Brandt replied.

"That's what I meant."

"I know. I was trying to be funny."

"It's not really funny that he's your brother, and that he died," Andy said. "I would cry if Curtis died, and they put my name on his rock."

"Tombstone," Kayla corrected.

"It's a rock," Andy said.

"Technically, Brandt was his name, but the state got mixed up, and I didn't know it. I always remember my name as being Brandt."

"It's kind of neat, I guess," Kayla said. "A way that you keep your brother with you. Like he's part of you, and you're part of him."

"And when you die, you can just be buried here since you already got your name here," Andy said.

"Andy," Bonnie admonished. "Don't be so morbid."

"What's morbid mean?" Curtis began climbing the fence.

"Don't climb that fence."

"Morbid means don't climb the fence?" Andy asked.

"It means creepy," Kayla said. "But Mom doesn't want the creeper climbing the fence."

"I guess the memorial service is over," Brandt said.

Bonnie squeezed his hand. "You said they could come. What did you expect? That they'd be reverent?"

Brandt's lips lifted in a small smile. "I guess Marshall would like kids here since he was a kid when he died. I mean, Brandt."

"He's been Marshall to you a long time. I think you

can still call him that, if you like."

Brandt bent down and touched the headstone. Bonnie dropped his hand and moved her fingers to his shoulder.

The headstone read, *Brandt Sherrod, Child of God* with the dates of his birth and death.

"How does it feel, finally knowing what happened?"

"I'm not sad, and that surprises me. I'm thankful that I finally know, and I guess I'm thankful he didn't suffer any more after that night." Brandt straightened. He tugged Bonnie into his arms. "I'm especially thankful that the Bloodhound tracked me down. Without you, I would have never found my brother."

"Will you guys not hang all over each other in front of us?" Kayla said. She took Curtis's hand. "The boys and I are going to walk around. Okay, Mom?"

"All right." Bonnie moved to Brandt's side. "What do you want to do now?"

"Go home with you. I've got to fly out tonight at eleven on a job. If you're agreeable, we can order in pizza."

"I like that idea."

THE END

Dear Reader,

Thank you for reading Brandt and Bonnie's story. Brandt is my kind of hero, a little broken, but a lot of integrity.

I have a goal for 2017. To release a book each month.

Want to see my other stories, find me at:

http://booksbyjenniferjohnson.com

www.facebook.com/jenniferjohnson.author

Here is an excerpt from my recent release *Tomorrow's Child.*

What do you say to a man to get him to open his vein and give you his blood?

Tamara crossed her legs in the elegant but impersonal waiting room and contemplated that question.

Hello. I'm Tamara Wallace. Would you mind undergoing a medical procedure for someone you've never met before?

Tamara had Googled Nicolaus Pack. What she read didn't give her much hope that he was going to help her. But Tamara had to try. Her entire future rested on her ability to elicit compassion in a man who made his living putting his feelings aside in the name of justice.

Oh, Nicolaus Pack. Please help me. Please help my baby.

"Tamara Wallace."

Tamara stood up and walked in front of the secretary's desk. "It's pronounced Tah-mara. The emphasis is on the second syllable. It sounds like *Tomorrow.* Tamara Wallace." She wouldn't make such a big deal about it except she'd explained it when she first came in two hours ago.

The woman's eyebrow arched. Tamara looked at her

nameplate. Jessica Adams. Not too many ways one could mispronounce *that* name. "I'm sorry. Mr. Pack is not going to be able to meet with you today."

"I have an appointment, and I've been waiting two hours." Tamara was proud of herself for not whining about the horrible way Nicolaus Pack was behaving, as if her time didn't matter. Well, certainly, it didn't matter to him. That was obvious.

"If you could just tell me what this is about."

Nope. Tamara wasn't sure what she'd say to Nicolaus if she were even able to speak to him. Trying to communicate through his secretary was not the way to go. "It's a personal matter."

Her eyebrow lifted. "This is Mr. Pack's place of business. He doesn't conduct personal matters here."

"If I could reach him at home, I would."

"I'm sorry, Ms. Wallace." The woman stared at her.

"I can hire him as my lawyer. I will pay him for his time, if that's the issue. Then it will be business."

She shook her head. "No."

Who does she think I am? An ex-girlfriend? Hardly. She had never seen the man, but Tamara was guessing by the set-up of his office, he liked young leggy blondes, not forty-something overworked doctors. Yes, she was judging the man. But his present action of not giving her the time of day, while robbing several hours of hers wasn't sitting well.

"This is my name and number," Tamara said taking a piece of paper from her purse and writing on it. "Would you give this to him? He can call or text me."

The secretary accepted the card and placed it on her desk without looking at it. "I will put it in his inbox, yes."

Tamara wondered if that was code for throwing it in the trash after she left the room. Nodding, Tamara placed her purse strap on her shoulder. "Thank you." She walked toward the door and opened it, exiting the offices of Pack, Bryan, and Levine.

I've got to see him, but how?

Tamara had tried calling, but hadn't even been able to

reach his personal secretary. She thought if she made an appointment with him, she'd at least have the chance to speak to him face to face. Her mistake had been that she'd said it was personal and not business.

She walked toward the elevator and pressed the down button. The lit number on the panel indicated it was on the ground floor. A nearby window provided a view of downtown, and Tamara stepped over to it, studying the overcast day. She didn't like being in the city. It was a violent place, stabbings and shootings on the news every night. Why would he have his office here anyway?

A slight twinge in her eye caused her to blink. Stupid contacts. She hated wearing them. Tamara lifted her hand and pinched her eyelid hoping to readjust the contact, then blinked again. Her eye teared. Great. She'd have raccoon eyes thanks to the mascara.

A door opened down the corridor, and Tamara heard purposeful footsteps approaching—two sets. She wiped the skin beneath her eye and noticed the black smudge on the end of her finger. She wiped again with another finger.

"Call Springer and see if we can reschedule for four o'clock Tuesday, and I want you to go to the courthouse and go to the records division. Look for anything from April for Fitzpatrick at the address we have."

Two men appeared and stood in front of the elevator. Both in business suits, the younger one frantically pushed on the screen of an electronic pad while the older man spoke. He glanced at her before turning his attention to the elevator buttons, and Tamara's heart thumped hard in her chest.

He had the same color eyes as her daughter.

Butterflies fluttered in her stomach, and she took a steadying breath. It could be the situation making her nervous. Certainly meeting her daughter's grandfather could cause a physiological reaction. Or asking him to go through a medical procedure so the granddaughter he didn't know he had could live. Anyone would react with an elevated heartbeat. Probably elevated blood pressure, too, if the warmth in her face was any indication.

This had to be Nicolaus Pack.

Wow. He was younger than she expected. Probably close to her own age. He must have had Reginald when he was in his late teens or early twenties, whereas Tamara was forty when Miranda was born.

Tamara closed the distance between them. "Hello."

"Hello," he returned, not looking at her again.

The younger man nodded at her.

"Are you Nicolaus Pack?"

His mouth tightened in a grim line.

"I had an appointment with you."

"I'm sorry." His finger pushed the down button. "Something came up, and it's very important." His voice was deep, almost melodic. Yes, she could imagine him in a courtroom. That timbre of voice would command respect, attention.

"Your son Reginald—"

"Is dead. I'm sorry if he owed you money. I don't pay his debts."

"Yes, I know. About his death, I mean. I'm sorry for your loss."

He pushed the elevator button again.

"He doesn't owe me money. It's nothing like that. He... Reginald is...was the father of my daughter."

He laughed and shook his head, not even bothering to look at her. "Nice try, but I don't think so."

Tamara didn't take it personally. Reginald had been nineteen years old when he had made the donation. At twenty, he had become a father, though he hadn't known it. Tamara wasn't cougar material. She'd gained thirty pounds when she was pregnant, and hadn't lost it though Miranda was four.

"He was a sperm donor at a bank. I never met him."

Nicolaus didn't have the decency to glance her way. "You're delusional, lady, and you're also barking up the wrong family tree."

The elevator door opened, and he stepped inside.

"Please take the next elevator. I'm very busy, and I don't have time to play Kardashians with you." The younger man followed him in and turned around to face the front, blocking Tamara's view of Nicolaus Pack. The other man shot an apologetic look at Tamara.

"She has leukemia. Please if you would just—"

The door closed.

Dammit.

You can find *Tomorrow's Child* at many digital stores and in print on Amazon and at Consigned Books in Ironton, OH.

JENNIFER JOHNSON BOOKS